TOO CLOSE FOR COMFORT

Climbing out of the Chevy with an armload of groceries, Philip heard the shot and saw a man running from the house. The door into the kitchen stood open, and Hull burst through it, screaming her name.

Mary Rose was slumped against the living room wall, staring at a bullet hole in the wallpaper, a foot away from her. Hull grabbed Mary Rose and pulled her to him, oblivious to the bread knife in her hand. His arms were shaking. "Oh, Jesus, I'm sorry," he said into her hair. "I never should have left that sword out. I should have known they'd think—Are you all right?"

Mary Rose nodded, her face against his chest. He didn't let go of her, and she didn't move. "They took it," she said. Her voice was tight with anger. "Damn them, they took it."

THE MOONSHINE BLADE

by Amanda Cockrell

BANTAM BOOKS

TORONTO • NEW YORK • LONDON • SYDNEY • AUCKLAND

THE MOONSHINE BLADE

A Bantam Book / August 1988

*Grateful acknowledgment is made for permission to reprint
an excerpt from Rudyard Kipling's VERSE, Doubleday. Lyrics
on pp. 167–69 are reprinted by permission of Dover Publications
and are from AMERICAN FOLK TALES AND SONGS by
Richard Chase, © 1956, 1971.*

ISBN 0-553-27341-8

Published simultaneously in the United States and Canada

*Bantam Books are published by Bantam Books, a division of
Bantam Doubleday Dell Publishing Group, Inc. Its trademark,
consisting of the words ''Bantam Books'' and the portrayal
of a rooster, is Registered in U.S. Patent and Trademark
Office and in other countries. Marca Registrada. Bantam
Books, 666 Fifth Avenue, New York, New York 10103.*

PRINTED IN THE UNITED STATES OF AMERICA

KR   0 9 8 7 6 5 4 3 2 1

This book is for my father,
Francis M. Cockrell.

For their kind assistance in technical matters and a couple of good stories, I am indebted to Richard Meyers, DEA, formerly with the Fresno County (California) Sheriff's Department narcotics division, and to Russell Wright, special agent with the Virginia Department of Alcoholic Beverage Control in Roanoke, Virginia. Further information on the production of illegal liquor came from *Moonshine*, a study of North Carolina bootlegging by Alec Wilkinson.

1.
Funeral in March

The gray Buick slid with a sickening rush down the icy road. With an awful, eternal clarity, Steven Cullen saw the trees looming up ahead. The narrow road gleamed, opalescent with ice, as it twisted under the car, and the wind howled and battered wetly at the windows. He tried to lift his hands to turn the wheel, but they didn't move. As the Buick slithered sideways and plowed over the embankment, a piece of paper fluttered up from the passenger seat. Vaguely he saw his own name and signature on it. He slumped unmoving behind the wheel as the trees rushed toward him. *Why?* The thought fought through the haze in his mind. *Why me . . . my God, WHY?*

"Most merciful Father, who hast been pleased to take unto thyself the soul of this thy servant, grant to us who are still in our pilgrimage . . ."

Mary Rose Cullen stared at her husband's grave in Sarum's small, old cemetery, the knuckles of one black glove pressed against her mouth. The last unseasonable ice storm of the year had blown itself out, and the frozen drops that coated the budding branches of the trees dripped steadily into the grass. The newly turned earth was forlorn and muddy.

The minister patted her shoulder in a friendly, comfort-

1

ing fashion, and Mary Rose gave him an uncertain half
smile. She wasn't a regular churchgoer, and neither of
them really knew what to say to the other. Behind her she
could hear her fellow professors gathering themselves together in a rustle of umbrellas and distressed murmurs.
They didn't know what to say either, she thought. None of
them had known Steven for more than two months. He
had come to Sarum College at the start of the second
semester to take an assistant professorship in the Humanities Department. Two weeks ago, to the audible surprise
of the rest of the faculty, Mary Rose had married him.
Now he was gone. She looked numbly at his grave. How
did you mourn someone you were just getting to know?
Mary Rose wiped her gloved hand across her eyes, wondering with a dreadful sadness if she was mourning the
loss of the electricity that Steven had put into her otherwise ordinary life, more than Steven himself. It wasn't
fair.

Anne Ogilvie, the dean's wife, brisk and competent in a
black wool coat, put an arm around her. "Come along,
child. We're going to have to feed these people, you
know. I have it all set up at my house, so you can leave
when you want to and not have them underfoot all day.
People do tend to *stay*."

Mary Rose nodded gratefully and turned with Anne
toward the cars, the faculty of Sarum College following, a
little line of black coats and umbrellas.

At Anne's house she settled into a wing chair by the
fire. Peter Ogilvie, the dean, firmly put a glass of bourbon
and water in her hand. Mary Rose took a gulp of it, and
tried to say the right thing to the people coming up to
condole with her. She caught a glimpse of her face in the
gilt mirror on the far wall. She always looked so dreadful
in black. Her face floated in a disembodied fashion between her dress and her dark hair, and there were dark
smudges under her eyes. She wriggled her toes inside her
black kid shoes. Sarum was an agricultural college and
Mary Rose spent most of her time in the field. High heels
always made her feet hurt. She drank more of the bourbon and leaned her head back in the wing chair, closing

her eyes. She opened them again to murmur something suitable as Lee Bowling, the president, patted her shoulder in ineffectual comfort. Why did people always want to pat you? It seemed to be a universal impulse.

Having offered their condolences, the guests retreated gratefully to the food and drink, and Mary Rose closed her eyes again. Around her she could hear snatches of conversation. Mingled with the usual shoptalk of research and publication and faculty infighting was a low-voiced current of interested sympathy and speculation.

"Poor Mary Rose, only two weeks . . ."

"And none of us *knew* anything about him."

"His credentials were excellent."

"But just to up and marry some man from California that she met in Williamsburg, of all places, and dragged back here to apply for a post . . ."

"Well, I for one was glad she did." That was Bill McGinnis, chairman of English and the Humanities, which at Sarum were lumped into one department, feebly struggling to instill at least a modicum of the liberal arts into its agricultural and animal husbandry students. Bill sniffed. "It isn't as if Sarum paid Harvard wages, or even Tech's, and in my poor stepchild of a department, I was glad to have him." He sipped his drink moodily, the thought that now he was going to have to find a replacement obvious but unspoken.

"I thought at the time she was being hasty." Louise Evans of Biochemistry shook her head as if confirming her diagnosis. "And look what came of it."

"For God's sake, Louise, he didn't wreck his car on purpose."

"It wasn't his car—he rented it. . . ."

"And then drove off into an ice storm like a damn fool . . ."

There was a general, subdued tut-tutting at this. The Virginia Blue Ridge Mountains which surrounded Sarum were crisscrossed with narrow county roads that were sheer hell in bad weather. If there was ice, anyone with any sense stayed put.

"They don't have ice storms in California," Bill McGinnis

said. "They don't have weather, to speak of. He wouldn't know."

"Yes, he would," Harold Robley of Veterinary Science said decisively. "I rode down to town with him a couple of times. He was a damn good driver."

"Well, what did he go clear to Roanoke and rent a car for?"

"You all are goin' to upset Mary Rose." Anne Ogilvie wove her way through the crowd and shooed them gently toward the table. "Go and have some of my nice cheese puffs."

They were probably still at it, Mary Rose thought as she put her purse and gloves down on the hall table in her own house at the end of Faculty Row. She didn't blame them. What *had* Steven been doing with that car? He had a perfectly good car of his own. She had come back from class to find him gone, and an hour later a subdued trooper of the State Police had appeared on her doorstep. She looked dully around the living room. What did it matter now? She picked up the framed photograph of their wedding. It was the only picture she had of him. There she was, in a blue taffeta dress, a rakish-looking dress, bought in the same unaccustomed mood in which she had married Steven. And there was Steven, tall, thin, blond, with a delicate, fine-boned face. He had his arm around her and she was grinning like an idiot. But there wasn't any life in the picture now, nothing of the feeling that had been Steven—an aura of intensity; almost, oddly, of danger, which had contrasted so strongly with her placid, orderly life that Mary Rose had fallen in love with it. With it, or with Steven? It wasn't fair to wonder that now. Nothing was fair.

She put the picture down and went into the kitchen to find something to eat. At Anne's she hadn't wanted to eat badly enough to leave the refuge of her chair. She pulled an apple and a cold pork chop from the refrigerator, put them on a plate, and sat down at the table, wondering for the first time why Steven had married *her*.

"You're a very restful woman." She could almost hear

Steven saying that now; almost, not quite, see him sprawled in his bathrobe on the sofa, while she pottered in the kitchen with bacon and eggs. Except for her own student years, Mary Rose had spent all her life growing up in the town of Sarum and then teaching at the college. Her work in genetics was beginning to be highly thought of, which was professionally satisfying and not much else. Never in all her life had she ever done anything out of the ordinary until she met Steven in Williamsburg, prowling about the restored Colonial armory there.

He had been looking at the long flintlocks, standing in neat bundles like corn shocks, and she had asked him if he knew why they stacked them like that. The tour guide's voice was drowned out in the screaming of an overtired child who'd had his fill of museums.

"This is a field stack," he said. "They're always stacked in the same place in every camp, so each man knows where to find his musket in the dark." His present-tense explanation made him sound like he knew what he was talking about, like a man who would know where to find his own musket in the dark.

Mary Rose looked at him with interest. She had to tip her head back to do it. He was taller than she by almost a foot, slender, with blond hair that drooped in a curl over one eye. It was a face that should have looked placid, but it didn't. There was something that moved, alert, just below the surface.

"I'm Mary Rose McCaskey," she had said. "Is this your first trip to Williamsburg?"

"Yes." He had looked around him, as if drinking in the museum stillness that lay beneath the buzz of swarming tourists. "It's interesting, being somewhere where things have quit happening. Like being in suspended animation. I wonder if it's healing." He smiled at her suddenly and held out his hand. "I'm Steven Cullen. Would you like to go have dinner somewhere?"

After dinner he had taken her to hear a concert of Colonial tavern songs and kissed her under the lantern outside the Capitol Building. When he said that he had once been a teacher and was, as he put it, "at a loose end just now," she had brought him back to Bill McGinnis.

All the same, when he had taken the job and stayed, she had been mildly surprised. She suspected it surprised the rest of the college too; there was something about Steven that made him stand out from the rest of the faculty, as if a zebra had taken up residence in the horse barn. His interests were scholarly and far-ranging, from John Donne to all things Oriental, but beyond that there was that feeling of intensity, of something bright and dangerous. Maybe he had found his balance in her very ordinariness, Mary Rose thought. Whatever it was, he found something in her he wanted to hold on to. For her, his presence had painted her world in deeper colors. Now that he was dead, they all seemed to have faded to gray again, and Mary Rose, trying to hold on, found nothing to grasp.

She put her head down on the table. *Tomorrow I'll sort out his things*, she thought listlessly. It wouldn't take long. Besides his car, there were only clothes, a few books, some knives and swords about which Mary Rose knew nothing except that they were Japanese and had been Steven's hobby, and his shaving things in the bathroom. It didn't seem right that there should be so little left of him.

The reference librarian at California State University, Fresno, kept one eye, expressive of mingled disapproval and suspicion, on the man squatting on the floor among the reference stacks and pulling books from the bottom shelf. She sniffed. It wasn't as if this were still the 1960s, when one *expected* the students to look like rag and bone men.

Philip Hull felt the eye boring into the back of his dilapidated fatigue jacket and grinned. She probably thought he was going to make off with a first edition, but he had a perfectly valid student-body card. The night karate class he took to keep his hand in was sufficient to rate that.

He dumped another book down on the growing pile on the floor and scowled at it. He knew it was here somewhere. He had seen it, but it must have been a year ago.

You always saw things before you knew you needed them, he thought, aggravated. He pulled the next book out and concentrated on the title page. *Aha.* He turned the pages feverishly, with a glance at his watch. If this wasn't it, he'd have to come back tomorrow.

The paragraph he was looking for leapt out at him, and Hull sat down suddenly on the linoleum. Christ, there it was—a photograph of a long, graceful blade. You could even see the temper line, like moonlight on water. He ran a hand through his unkempt brown hair and stared at the page with excitement and greed. He and Steven had hit the winning ticket. He began stuffing books back into the shelves. This ought to get Steven back from whatever the hell it was he was doing at that cow college in Virginia, and give him a little breathing space. It would also buy a lot of beer. A lot of choices. A lot of anything. Hull stood up, resisting the temptation to dance a jig in the sanctified stacks of the reference library. He picked up his hat, a broad-brimmed western felt as battered as his jacket and jeans, and set it jauntily on the back of his head. Then he strolled out, giving the wary librarian a wink and a raised eyebrow.

"You're late, man." Lopez peered at Hull through the murky gloom of the Café Azteca. His skin was pallid and the hand holding his beer shook just enough to notice. There was a dispirited plastic rose in a glass on the table, and Lopez's left hand picked at it nervously.

You've been using your own stuff, my friend, Hull thought. He edged in behind the grubby table. That was going to make Lopez unpredictable. "I've been taking care of business." He patted the pocket of his jeans suggestively.

"You got it?" Lopez swiveled his head owl fashion to look behind him. Hull wondered what Lopez's name really was. In California there were as many Lopezes as Smiths. He shrugged. Maybe his name really was Lopez. Unless Hull was particularly unlucky, he was going to find out.

"Yeah, I got it." He poked a finger at Lopez's glass. "You gonna finish that beer? I haven't got all day, man."

Lopez clutched the glass and drained it. Hull stood up. "Where you goin'?"

"Outta here."

"You don't trust me, man?"

"No." Hull flicked an eye around the Azteca, which looked much too plainly Lopez's own turf. He walked to the door, and after a moment Lopez followed.

Outside, Hull slid behind the wheel of a dented blue Lincoln. Lopez blinked in the sudden sunlight and balked. "I got wheels, man. We'll take mine."

"Like hell we will. I got better connections than you. You don't wanta deal, get lost." Hull carefully unclenched his hands from around the wheel and glared at Lopez. He hated getting in a dealer's car. He hoped like hell he wasn't going to have to. He turned the key in the ignition and tried to project mental images of vanishing cash at Lopez. The Lincoln crept forward. Lopez dived at the door.

"We go where *I* say, understand?"

Hull shrugged. "Sure."

Lopez looked over his shoulder again. "That way. Toward the park."

Hull swung the Lincoln out into the traffic, past a secondhand plumbing supply with a yard full of bathtubs, and a used car lot hopefully labeled Fred's Fine Cars. Hull looked in the rearview mirror. The knot in his stomach loosened a little. If Lopez wanted to go to the park, this would be a piece of cake. Roeding Park on a Saturday was full of picnicking families taking their kids to the zoo, and lowriders with hydraulic lifts hopping their cars up and down like toads. Not a likely place to double-cross on a drug deal by shooting the buyer. He whistled a little between his teeth as the light changed at First Street.

The cars ahead of him began to slow down, and Hull squinted through the windshield at the afternoon sun. Up ahead the railroad crossing bar swung down across the tracks.

"What are you doin', man?"

"Stopping for the train," Hull said with elaborate patience as the black snout of a diesel nosed its way at a snail's pace along the tracks. Oh Christ, four engines. That meant about a mile of boxcars.

"I don't like this." Lopez's voice developed an edgy whine.

"Whatta you want me to do? This isn't a helicopter." Cars were jammed solidly beside and behind them. "You don't like it, go yell at the bastards who gave 'em a fifty-year lease on track across the middle of town," Hull muttered. The Southern Pacific trains were a sore point with anyone who had to drive east-west through the city. There was a freeway, but it only went north-south. Lopez fidgeted in the passenger seat and Hull flicked an eye at the rearview mirror again. Lopez caught him at it.

"What're you lookin' at?" Lopez peered into the mirror, then over his shoulder.

"Nothing. The traffic."

"What're you *looking* at? Get us outta here!" Lopez's face was sweating, his voice rising.

"It's a fucking *train*, man. I can't move a train."

"You're a fucking narc, man!" Lopez was panicked, yelling, clawing at the inside of his jacket.

"You're paranoid. Loony, *estupido*!" Hull swung around, yelling back. "I don't run the goddamn trains!"

"You're a *narc*!" Lopez screamed. His hand came out of his jacket with a knife in it.

Hull wrenched his door open. He slammed the heel of his hand into Lopez's face and backed out the door, diving for the holster in his boot. Lopez came after him, sending him sprawling on the asphalt, half over the yellow line. The bars across the tracks came up and a car swerved past them, from the opposite direction, honking furiously. Hull kneed Lopez in the belly and grabbed his knife hand.

Lopez's black eyes glittered at him as he stuck his other hand in Hull's face and wrenched the hand with the knife free. "I'm gonna *kill* you!"

Honking cars swooped around them and the thud of running feet came down the asphalt. Hull brought his fist up into Lopez's face and rolled out from under him, nearly under the wheels of a truck.

"Freeze! Police officers!"

Lopez looked up at the two plainclothesmen running toward them. Hull dived for him, sending him sprawling. He grabbed the knife out of Lopez's hand and threw it under the car. He jerked Lopez up by the collar and pinned him forcefully against the hood of the Lincoln. "He's holding," he informed the backup, "but I didn't make the buy."

"Yeah, we know," one of them said sarcastically. The body wire Hull was wearing had broadcast the fiasco plainly to the backup car. "The captain isn't gonna like this."

"You have the right to remain silent," the backup's partner was informing Lopez. A cacophony of horns was blaring from the traffic stacked up behind them.

Hull slumped against the Lincoln, letting his adrenaline die down to a level where he didn't want to pound Lopez's head through the pavement. "Tell the captain to write a letter to Southern Pacific," he muttered.

The backup stuffed Lopez into their car and headed downtown through the snarled traffic, with Hull following, glaring at their brake lights through the Lincoln's windshield. They'd been trying to nail Lopez for six months, and now they weren't going to be able to charge him with anything but possession. Possession of one hell of a lot of crank, but they wanted him for dealing. Hull slammed his fist into the steering wheel in disgust. The son of a bitch had been making stuff that was ending up in the high schools, and three months ago there had been three dead kids. Nice kids, new users, two boys and a girl, fifteen and sixteen, trying it out for kicks. An accidental overdose of methamphetamine, the coroner's report had said, which translated to bad crank, something gone sour in the cooking. Lopez wouldn't have given a damn.

It had been three dead kids too many for Steven, who was working the schools. He had come back white-faced, his eyes flickering with the uneasy glitter of a man shoved over the edge of some private mental snakepit, and walked straight into the department shrink's office. When he had come out, he'd gotten into his car and gone. No one knew where, including the accounting department, which was frenziedly annoyed about the car, which was, strictly speaking, the department's. Then Philip Hull got a letter with a Virginia postmark saying that Steven had gone back to teaching, that he herewith resigned from the Fresno County Sheriff's Department and it could send him a bill for the car. Hull grinned crookedly as he swung the Lincoln down the ramp into the jail annex parking level. That had not squared things with accounting, which had no provisions for selling county cars to sheriffs' sergeants who had taken them to Virginia. They had sent Steven several annoyed letters about it, which he ignored.

Hull climbed out of the Lincoln and followed the backup deputies who were escorting a surly Lopez into the jail. That was typical of Steven, who was an enigma even to the men he worked with. Only Philip Hull, the other loner of the department, had had some idea of the restlessness and private demons that drove Steven Cullen. Maybe the demons had backed off a bit by now. And maybe they hadn't, Hull thought, but at least Steven was going to get the chance to decide. So, for that matter, was Philip Hull, who, like any cop who had been in the business for long, had a few demons of his own that surfaced from time to time. Starting with the prospect of getting shot at three days out of four, if you wanted to list them. Hull checked his gun in the gun locker, pocketed the key, and buzzed the door. How much did he want not to get shot at? He didn't know. Maybe he *liked* getting shot at. But now he had options, and so did Steven. The sword was going to buy them that.

Hull identified himself, and when the steel outer door opened, stepped in and waited for it to close behind him and the inner one to open.

The jail lobby had the usual strong odor of Pine-Sol overlying other, worse smells. The walls were khaki-colored, covered with graffiti, and the lobby was crowded with deputies and city cops ushering a day's catch of drunks, pushers, and the inevitable participants of a knife fight into the prebooking tank. One of the drunks was throwing up, and a trusty with a mop disgustedly pursued him. Edging away from the mess were a gaggle of hookers in miniskirts in which Hull thought it was a wonder they didn't freeze their working parts. There was a pretty stiff March wind blowing.

The arresting deputies and a uniformed jailer were running Lopez through the booking process. The booking officer sat at his desk on the other side of a glass partition and regarded Lopez wearily through the window. Lopez was protesting police brutality in the person of Philip Hull.

Hull started over to put in his two cents' worth about that and to make his formal report on the aborted buy, when he heard his name over the unsavory hubbub of the lobby.

It was Cahill, with a newspaper under his arm. Cahill spent most of his time reading the newspaper and worrying about Russia and the stock market; he owned ten shares which changed weekly and were never doing well. Hull clipped his ID tag to his jacket and threaded his way between a hooker with a split lip and an outraged customer with a missing wallet, each indignantly pressing charges against the other. He pushed open the partition gate and went to see what Cahill's ten shares were up to.

Cahill looked unnaturally subdued, even for him. Maybe it was Russia. "You find a missile in your backyard?" Hull inquired.

Cahill unfolded the paper to a back page and handed it to Hull. "It's the Professor, ain't it?" he asked. "I thought you oughta see it."

The Sheriff's Department was given to nicknaming its own. Steven Cullen had been the Professor. Hull took the paper silently and read the headline over the story, a cold pool spreading out in his stomach.

The story, under an AP byline, was short—three inches, with two lines at the end for Steven Cullen's obituary. The worst late-season storm in thirty years had caused millions of dollars in fruit tree damage, tied up air traffic over Washington, D.C., and claimed three lives: an elderly woman who had frozen to death, a Richmond man who had skidded off a bridge, and Steven Cullen, who had driven his car into a tree.

"Hull!" The deputy at the booking desk waved an arm

at him impatiently. Hull set the newspaper carefully back into Cahill's hands and turned away.

"Hull, dammit, come on!"

Lopez was being fractious, and one of the deputies on the lobby side of the booking desk had a grip on his arm. Lopez's face looked clammy, his eyes malevolent. "That's him!" He jabbed a finger in Hull's direction. "He tried to kill me, man!"

Hull crossed the space to the booking desk in two strides.

"Man, I'm goin' to press charges on *you*, man!" Lopez shrieked. "You broke my fuckin' ribs!"

Hull's arm shot through the window in the glass that separated the booking officer from the lobby. He grabbed Lopez by the upper arm and pulled. Glass splattered and Lopez slid through the shards of the partition onto the desk.

"Christ, Hull! Goddammit, you psycho!" The booking officer dumped Lopez off his desk onto the floor.

Hull grabbed Lopez by the collar. "You son of a bitch, if it wasn't for you, he wouldn't have gone out there. I'm gonna *feed* you your fuckin' ribs!"

The two arresting deputies came around the partition and pried Lopez loose from Hull. "Take my advice," one of them informed Lopez genially. "He means it. Now shut up and behave."

The booking officer stared at Hull warily.

"Possession, resisting arrest, and pulling a knife on *me*," Hull snarled. "I'm gonna go type my report."

He pushed his way through a crowd of interested looks, through the door that led from the jail annex into the Sheriff's Department offices, and sat down at a desk with his head in his hands.

By the time he got home, he still wanted to kill Lopez, but he was no longer actively thinking about how he could go back to the jail and do it. He got a beer out of the refrigerator and sat down moodily in an armchair.

The room was sparsely furnished, in keeping with the temple-roofed, Japanese theme of the apartment com-

plex's exterior. A low black lacquer table held a little
bronze horse and a jumble of receipts and income tax
instruction booklets. A stamped envelope addressed to the
IRS lay triumphantly atop the pile. A wooden sword stand
with two Japanese blades in it, temporarily displaced by
the claims of the Internal Revenue, sat on the floor beside
it, and the walls were hung with further fruits of the
collector's obsession that Hull had shared for nearly ten
years with Steven Cullen. A dozen swords, their ethereal,
deadly blades encased in lacquered scabbards or plain
wooden *shiro-saya*, were mounted in the dining alcove
and to either side of the front door. On the wall opposite
the door was a framed collection of *tsuba*—round, iron
sword guards pierced in graceful patterns or decorated
with small, exquisitely wrought scenes in silver and gold.
Two silk-lined boxes of *menuki*—hilt ornaments—flanked
them, and a *mempo*—the demonlike face mask to a suit of
sixteenth century armor—glared wildly down from a place
above the *tsuba*. There were no pictures on the walls,
except for a framed photograph of Hull and Steven at a
Japanese wedding. Susan Takaoka, who waited on them
nearly every lunch hour at her father's sushi bar on E
Street, and whose grandfather occasionally obliged them
with translations when their Japanese ran short, had been
married last fall and sent them an invitation. There they
were, unaccustomedly spruce in coats and ties, and looking round-eyed and a little silly among three generations
of Takaokas.

Hull lifted his beer at the photograph. "You shoulda
waited," he muttered. "Ah, Christ, Steven, you shoulda
waited."

They had found their lucky number, the sword that
would have bought Steven his options, in much the same
fashion that, on a Sheriff's Department sergeant's pay,
Hull had acquired most of his collection—nosing around
gun shops and flea markets in search of blades, and dealers who didn't know what they had, or tracking down
swords squirreled away in attics by men who had brought
them back from World War Two. Even a blade in military
mountings might be some family's ancestral treasure, lov-

ingly refitted over and over through the centuries. This particular one had been in a toolshed, where its current owner had been using it to cut kindling, since, as he said, the blade never seemed to get dull. All its fittings were gone, and the wrapping on the fraying sharkskin handle was torn and stained, but even under a coating of dust the blade was beautiful—slender and perfect, and the temper line that marked the cutting edge had a wonderful pattern like moonlight on the water.

Steven and Philip had bought it together because they both wanted it, and taken it gleefully back to Hull's apartment to translate the signature on the tang. That was when the sword had begun to give Philip Hull the fits. *Akinji kami ko-getsu-nami Sanjo saku.* "This sword was made for Akinji Lord of the Moon by Sanjo." The name Sanjo was enough to make them cautious. Sanjo was Sanjo Munechika, and anything he made was valuable, but there were a hell of a lot of forged signatures floating around, including some that had been counterfeited by lesser smiths in the twelfth century, when the real smith was still living. On the other hand, this blade looked good enough to be a real Munechika. But who in hell was Akinji Lord of the Moon? Susan Takaoka's grandfather had confirmed their translation and shrugged his shoulders. Who knew?

When Steven had left the department, Philip Hull had come home to find a pile of Steven's swords in his living room, with a note:

> *Keep these for me for a while, will you, buddy? I've taken a few of my best things, and the Munechika, since it's my month to have custody. I'll let you know where I am. Hang on to the rest till I figure out what the hell I'm going to do.*

Hull had sat staring at the Munechika often enough to know it by heart, and he had an *oshigata*—a rubbing of the signature. Driven by hunch, or just pure hope, he had taken the *oshigata* to other collectors, to meetings of the Southern California Sword Club, to anyone he could think of. No one could tell him anything about Akinji Lord of the Moon, but they pointed out that a real Munechika was more luck than Hull deserved. So Hull had gone back to the history books and read everything he could get his hands on about twelfth century Japan, and there he found Akinji Kobayasu, hero of the Gempi wars. Further digging had elicted the fact that Kobayasu's personal badge had been the moon before he had been rewarded for his efforts with other badges conferred by grateful lords of the Minamoto clan. It was the moon badge that had sent Hull scuttling back to the Fresno State library and a book leafed through casually over a year ago. And there it was, *photographed*, by God—*Ko-getsu-nami*, the Moonshine Blade, relic of Akinji Kobayasu, whereabouts unknown since the war.

Philip Hull put his beer down and began to prowl restlessly through the apartment. Steven had no family, which meant that the State of Virginia, in its kindly paternalistic fashion, was going to collar everything that Steven had owned if Hull didn't get there first. How could a man who took the risks an undercover cop did survive them just to go out and drive his car into a tree? Hull slammed his fist into the wall, looking over his shoulder at the photograph, missing Steven and cursing him for all the fun they could have had spending the money together.

Made by Munechika and once carried by a national hero, the Moonshine Blade was a national treasure, which the government of Japan would pay a very fat sum to have returned. The descendants of Akinji Kobayasu would no doubt like to have it too, but there were two rival branches of those descendants. One was not wealthy, and the Moonshine Blade had given Hull a bad case of greed. The other was something Hull had no intention of touching with tongs. The government was the best bet, the safe bet. For a man who had the sword, which Hull didn't. He stalked into the bedroom and began slinging shirts into a suitcase.

At seven o'clock on Monday morning Hull locked the door behind him, stuck a check for the month's rent under his landlady's door, and threw a handful of cat food to the *koi*—the fat Oriental carp that lived in the pool in the garden.

Downtown, he dumped his suitcase on the floor by the captain's desk. The captain looked at him warily.

"I want some leave time. I haven't got time to go through channels."

"Where the hell do you think you're going?"

"To a funeral," Hull said shortly. "A little late."

The captain sighed. "Yeah, I heard. Look, Hull, I wouldn't like to think burnout was contagious."

Hull shook his head stubbornly. "I am not burned out. And I am not, incidentally, crazy." The captain's look informed him that in light of Saturday's performance, he wasn't overly sure of that. "I just want some time. I'll go see the shrink if I have to, to get out." *Damn you, Steven. Damn you for dying, and damn you for having the sword, and damn you for screwing up all our plans.*

The captain snorted. "After Saturday it wouldn't break my heart if you lay low for a while. I never saw such a mess. Glass all over the place, and two reporters with long ratty noses just dying to know what happened about two minutes after you left. Christ, I suppose I'm lucky they weren't there to watch you."

"And the sheriff's up for reelection. Yeah, I know, I'm sorry. I lost my head."

"You'll lose your ass if you do it again. All right, go. They'll calm down by the time you get back. But I want to know what you're up to." He looked at Hull expectantly, waiting for an answer.

"Steven had something that was half mine," Hull offered. "I want it before the state claims it."

The captain fished gently. "It must be something pretty important." He didn't think he liked the fine-drawn look on Hull's face.

"Yeah." Hull stared out the window, wondering why good fortune always had an element of the lousy in it. "Yeah, it was pretty important. I guess it's important enough to go say good-bye for."

Denied any further information, the captain glowered at him. "Don't take another county car," he suggested.

2.
Past Persistent

". . . so as you can see, the techniques of biotechnology offer some startling, not to say unsettling, possibilities not only in improved agriculture and stock breeding, but in their natural extension into human research. I would be happy to see some of these problems explored in your final term papers, for which, incidentally, you should be choosing topics by now." Mary Rose pushed a few strands of hair back from her face and looked at the clock. This was her first day back in class. Her students had been unusually attentive, regarding her with a grave concern she found oddly comforting.

"I've scheduled a makeup lab for Saturday, for those of you who had to cut Friday's for the horse show. Are there any questions?"

A hand went up at the back of the room. David Hodges, a tall, brawny sophomore with a shock of unruly blond hair, stood up, glancing around at the rest of the class. "Dr. Cullen, I . . . we . . . well, we just wanted to say how sorry we all are about . . . about everything." He flushed, and went on doggedly. "I . . . I took Twentieth Century Lit from Professor Cullen, and I liked him a lot. We all did." He sat down abruptly.

"Thank you, David. You've been very understanding over the past few days, all of you, and I'm grateful to you."

19

The bell jangled outside the door, and they departed in a flutter of closing notebooks and an unaccustomed and embarrassed hush.

Mary Rose waited until they had gone, then made her solitary way down the Hopkins Hall stairs and onto the Quadrangle. It was the last day of March. The willows by the duck pond, across the sloping Quad from the Administration Building, were a bright yellow-green against the red brick of the Veterinary School. It was balmy, shirt-sleeve weather, and the gaggle of students on the Administration Building steps had emerged from their cocoons of parkas and ski caps into a jubilant display of Hawaiian shirts and hiking shorts. Behind them the white cupolas and balconies of the Administration Building looked newly washed against its red facade. Mary Rose regarded them fondly. She had always liked that building. In the late 1880s it had housed a finishing school, the Sarum Institute for Young Ladies. Now it sat between the utilitarian structures of Hopkins Hall and the college dining room in wild Victorian splendor.

Mary Rose crossed the Quad to the faculty parking lot with her keys in her hand. Nothing seemed to have changed. Her six-week courtship and two-week marriage was already more a lunatic interlude in an otherwise ordinary academic existence than any real part of her life. It saddened her that Steven's face was fading so rapidly in her memory. Sometimes at night she would stare at their wedding picture and then close her eyes, trying to conjure up the image of Steven alive, but it wasn't much good. There seemed to be nothing left but a wedding ring, the meager possessions that she hadn't had the heart to sort out yet, and his car. She climbed into the battered black Chevy and turned the key in the ignition. Her own Datsun had a flat tire, and she had begun to drive Steven's, still feeling too listless even to cope with a tire, and feeling that in Steven's car she might somehow be able to reach out and grasp the memories that were slipping away too fast.

Mary Rose swung the Chevy out of the parking lot and down the road toward the agricultural field offices. The car felt empty and uninhabited. Even in here he seemed to have vanished entirely.

The Piedmont Airlines plane touched down in Roanoke, Virginia, and Philip Hull looked around him dubiously. From there, the travel agent had told him, he had the choice of a Trailways bus to Lexington or a car. He had opted for the car, but staring at the network of little gray lines that spiderwebbed across the Virginia map she had dug up for him, he wondered if he knew what he was doing. He could find Lexington, of course. Any idiot could find Lexington: it was on the Interstate. But after that, with the exception of a few state highways that didn't go where he wanted to, the territory dissolved into a maze of pale gray lines which the map's key unoptimistically labeled "secondary state and county roads."

Hull slung his suitcase and his coat into the back of the rented Ford and headed it for the Interstate with much the same trepidation he would have had in sallying forth into the wilds of Arabia. Like many Californians, he had traveled abroad—in Hull's case, to Japan—but never to the east coast of his own country. There was something beguiling about it, he decided as the Interstate passed the outskirts of Roanoke and swooped up and down over a series of rounded hillsides. Weathered barns and white farm houses sat among patchworked fields of last year's stubble and newly plowed earth, and white pasture fences followed the curves of the hills. Willows drooped their branches over innumerable small streams, and even at the end of winter it was greener than California usually got.

At Lexington Hull left the Interstate and turned up into the mountains, among thick woods just beginning to leaf out. As he had predicted, he got well and truly lost. He crossed the James River three times, unsure whether the river was doubling back or he was. The third time he stopped the car and flattened the map out on the front seat, peering at it in exasperation while rain began to come down around him in sheets. It was after six o'clock when he drove through the town of Sarum and turned beyond its outskirts into the campus of Sarum College. He tried to envision Steven there, but with little success.

A sign to the left said Visitor Parking, and a map of the campus was posted next to it. Hull found the Administration Building with no trouble. He stared at it appreciatively, waiting for Scarlett O'Hara to appear on a balcony. There were still lights on the first floor, so he trotted up the steps and poked his head into the first office he came to.

He had a plausible speech prepared, but he didn't get very far with it.

"Yes?" the blond woman at the desk said brightly.

"My name's Philip Hull," he ventured. "I was a friend of Steven Cullen—"

"Oh, my goodness!" She bounced up from the desk and took his arm. "Oh, you poor man. I guess you've heard. It was just so awful, we were all so sad. Have you come all the way from California? That's *so* nice of you. I just know Dr. Cullen will be glad to see you."

"*Doctor* Cullen?" Hull stared at her.

"Why yes, they'd just been married two weeks, it was so awful. She's just over on Faculty Row, I'll point you the right way. Do you have an umbrella? It's going to rain again any minute."

"Uh, no."

"Here, I'll lend you mine, so you don't get soaked. I've got a spare in the closet. I'm Frances Cady, the dean's secretary. You can just bring it back any time."

She put a serviceable black umbrella into his hands, and Hull, unprotesting, let her lead him to the door. *Married*?

"You take that walkway at the end of the colonnade, and turn left when you get to the road. It's the last house on the right." She beamed at him. "We're all so glad you're here. I just know it'll be a comfort to Mary Rose."

The last house on the right was a one-story brick ranch with a concrete porch running the length of the front. Hull rang the bell and the porch light came on, revealing a black cat sitting motionless beside him, like a cast-iron doorstop. The door opened and a woman who might have been about twenty-five peered out at him. She was little, with a slim figure encased in blue jeans and a white lab coat.

She had blue eyes set in a rounded face, and wavy dark hair was pulled into a knot at the nape of her neck.

Hull scooped up the cat. "I think he wants in."

The woman shook her head. "That's MacArthur. He lives next door. He only wants in because of the mice."

Hull put the cat down, abandoning that ploy, and wondering, Why mice? He took a deep breath. "Mrs. Cullen? Uh, Dr. Cullen? My name's Philip Hull. I was a friend of Steven's."

The blue eyes opened wide.

"May I come in?"

Mary Rose stared up at him. He was tall, as tall as Steven, but broad-shouldered and muscular, with light brown eyes that were almost amber in color. He had an expressive, interesting face with a wide mouth and strong bones that gave him a faintly piratical look.

"Let me in, won't you?" Hull said gently. "I'm really not as shifty as I look." He fished in his wallet and handed her his department ID. "I worked with Steven."

"Worked . . . ?" The eyes opened wider. She backed away from the door a little, regarding him as if he were a Martian who had suddenly tunneled up through the concrete on the porch. "I guess you had better come in." She put out a foot to fend off the cat. "Go home, MacArthur."

Hull shook the water out of his borrowed umbrella, propped it against the doorjamb, and followed her inside. "Mice?"

"Experimental breeding. I'm a geneticist. MacArthur has no respect for science. Would you like some coffee?" She was still giving him that odd look.

"I'd love some." Hull looked around him while she fled into the kitchen. The living room was comfortably furnished with a pair of chintz-covered wing chairs, brass lamps, an overstuffed sofa, and a cherrywood coffee table. Books covered one wall from floor to ceiling, and there was an old rolltop desk in the corner with a framed photograph on it. Hull picked the photo up. Steven looked back at him, his arm around the dark-haired woman. They were both grinning at the camera.

"That was our wedding picture."

Hull put it back guiltily. "I'm sorry. I wasn't snooping." He took one of the heavy mugs out of her hand. "It's just that I didn't know Steven was married till I got here. Let's say it was a surprise."

Mary Rose sat down on the sofa abruptly. "This seems to be the day for them," she said. "Did you say you *worked* with Steven?"

"Uh-huh. Narcotics. He was a damn good officer." He stared at her. "You mean you didn't know?" Christ, no wonder she'd looked at him like that.

Mary Rose shook her head. She explained, feeling foolish, their courtship and marriage, which, as she talked, seemed a little insane to her now. "I . . . I knew he was a teacher. He said he'd been doing other things the last few years. I thought—oh, you know, different jobs," she finished lamely. "Insurance or something. Do I sound like an idiot?"

"Yeah," Hull said flatly. "That's how women marry serial murderers or psychotic rapists."

Mary Rose glared at him. "That didn't occur to me."

"Look, I'm sorry. But Steven was a little off the edge anyway. Do you want to know about it?"

She nodded, watching him warily. There was something about Philip Hull that reminded her of Steven, the same air of intensity, of controlled force. Maybe it went with his job. For that reason more than any other, she was prepared to believe what he told her.

"Steven was my buddy," Hull said slowly. "Drinking buddy, sword-hunting buddy. Japanese swords. That's how we got to be friends." He looked at her questioningly, and she nodded.

"He had a lot of them. They're still here," she said. "I didn't know what to do with them."

Hull let his breath out in silent relief. "He left some others with me," he said. "I'll ship them out to you when I get home."

Mary Rose curled her hands around the warm coffee mug. "How long did you know Steven?"

"About ten years."

"Ten . . . Go on."

"He started in the department when I did. He said once that when he was teaching and the kids started coming into his class stoned everyday, he figured he could do them more good as a cop. I don't know. Maybe he was just restless too, but I think he meant it. He damn near got killed a couple of times. And a little over a year ago he killed a guy." Hull stared into his coffee, wondering how much of this she could take. "But it was the kids that got to him in the end. Three dead kids. An overdose. Steven just got in his car and started driving. I didn't even know where he was till I got a letter from him about a month back, saying he was teaching here."

Three dead kids. And he killed a man. Mary Rose put her hands to her face, staring at this apparition out of Steven's past. Out of his real life.

"He burned out," Hull said. "He burned out and he started running. I don't know if he found what he was running to." He looked at her. "Maybe he found it." He didn't look as if he thought so. Christ, what had possessed Steven, whose taste in women had always run to the leggy beach-bunny type, to marry a woman with a back room full of mice?

Mary Rose stood up. She looked at Hull over her shoulder. "Coffee keeps me awake at night. I don't think I'm going to need that. Do you want a drink?"

"Yeah." She had more resilience than he would have given her credit for. He got up and followed her around the open counter that divided the kitchen from the long living room.

Mary Rose took a half gallon of Virginia Gentleman out of the cupboard and fished in the freezer for ice. "I'm not really a lush," she said. "Out here you have to buy it in the state stores and they're never open at night or on Sundays, so everyone keeps a pretty good supply. It used to drive Steven crazy." She handed him a glass. "I would have written you if I'd known who to write to. How did you find out?"

"Newspaper." Hull took a sip. Dr. Cullen mixed a pretty stiff drink.

"Oh. Oh, I'm sorry. That must have been awful, to find out like that." She looked puzzled. "I'm not sure why you came all the way out here."

Hull looked down at her. "Because one of those swords you didn't know what to do with, one of the ones he brought out here, is worth about a hundred grand. It's half mine. I guess the other half is yours now." He watched her expression with sardonic amusement.

"A hundred thousand dollars?" Mary Rose said faintly.

"At least. Maybe more."

"How much more?"

"Half again that. Maybe."

Mary Rose pointed firmly at the living room sofa. "Mr. Hull, I think you'd better tell me about that."

"It's called the Moonshine Blade. That's a rough translation. It was made by a very famous swordsmith in the twelfth century for a man who later became a Japanese national hero. I didn't know what we had until two days ago." He grimaced. "Just before I found out about Steven. It took me six months of research. What do you know about Japanese swords?"

"Nothing. Just that they were Steven's hobby. He used to spend hours taking them apart." Laying all the pieces and fittings out on the dining room table, a tedious, finicky process. "He'd do it when something was bothering him."

Hull grinned. "Yeah, I do too. Look, a sword like that, it gets passed down from father to son for centuries. They may give it new fittings to honor it, but it's the blade itself that's important. In Japan a sword like that has great significance, honor—face. And this one's a national treasure because of its quality and because it belonged to Akinji Kobayasu. That's the man it was made for—he's still a Japanese hero. The sword disappeared after the war. The Japanese government will pay a hundred thousand dollars to return a sword like that to Japan. I might even pry more out of them for this one."

"Why not the family it belonged to? Are there any of them left?"

"Yeah, but I think we'll bypass them. There are two branches of Akinji Kobayasu's descendants now. One's a nice, respectable family, college professors, but they haven't got any money to speak of."

Mary Rose sighed. "No, they never do. What about the other one?"

Hull shook his head. "Those you don't want to touch. Trust me."

"Why not?"

"They're *yakuza*. Gangsters. The Japanese equivalent of the Mafia. Very unhealthy to associate with. They'd want the sword all right, but they wouldn't be inclined toward paying for it. They'd be more likely to just take it. And they wouldn't be above killing for it."

"Good God." Mary Rose stared at him. "You know nice people."

"I don't know *yakuza*," Hull said. "I don't want to. No, what we want is a nice, safe, quick sale to the government. Before the *yakuza* have a chance to find out we've got it."

"Could they?"

"Not if we don't make a noise about it."

"I think I'm going to be a lot happier, Mr. Hull, when *you* have that sword." A buzzer went off from another room, and Mary Rose stood up.

"What's that?"

"The mice."

"They ring bells?"

"Bring your drink. You can tell me what I'm looking for while I deal with them. Steven had a lot of swords. I don't know one from the other."

He followed her curiously into a small room that opened off the kitchen. It was fitted out as a laboratory, with neatly arranged cages and a long table full of seedlings under Gro-lights.

"I'm babysitting a senior student's project," Mary Rose

said. "Her mother's sick and she's had to be off campus. She's put a lot of work into her mice. These little devils have to be measured every day. The buzzer's just so I don't forget." She picked up a set of calipers, reached into a cage that was set apart from the rest, and fished out a young, gray-furred mouse.

Hull peered over her shoulder. "Who's he?"

"This is Normal Mouse." Mary Rose made deft measurements and recorded them on a clipboard that was pegged to the cage. "That's his brother Godzilla in there."

Hull bent over the cage. The second mouse was already more than twice as big. Mary Rose put Normal Mouse back in the cage and extracted Godzilla. "They're litter mates, which makes Normal Mouse a very good control. We inserted a human growth-hormone-producing gene into the embryo that produced Godzilla. As you can see, it works on mice too."

"That's a *student* project?"

"She's a very advanced student. The University of Pennsylvania has already done this. And the University of Washington. They were the first. Genentech has been mass producing the hormone, using bacteria, for use in children born with a deficiency of it. Our application here will be with livestock, when we get that far. Ideally, I'd like to artificially split the embryo, which would give us identical twins, and then insert the gene into one of them. Colorado State has already done embryo splitting and transfer with cattle. We may take a crack at it. But this is all pretty advanced for Sarum. It's hard to get the money for it. And we have to convince the Board of Trustees that we aren't all mad scientists who'll try cloning people next."

"Could you? Clone people?"

Mary Rose grinned at him. "Think of all the people you know. Can you think of any that you could use two of?"

Hull chuckled. "None that come to mind."

"Me either. And this is an agricultural college. I can leave the ethics of human research to someone else, thank God. We have to be aware of it, and so do the students, but right now all I want is the money to split a calf embryo. They don't come in litters like mice."

"Would your half of a hundred G's run to something like that?"

"Oh, no." Mary Rose chucked Godzilla under the chin and put him back in the cage. "Probably not nearly, and in any case, I'm not that generous. I've never in my life had any money to speak of," she said wistfully. "I can think of an awful lot of other things to do with it." She locked the cage and washed her hands at a sink beside it. "Just exactly what does this solid-gold sword look like?"

"It's a *tachi*, a two-handed sword, curved blade." He held his hands apart. "About, oh, four feet long, including the handle. It's probably in *shiro-saya*—that's a storage scabbard, plain wood."

"There's one about that long, but I don't remember a wooden scabbard."

"He could have changed the fittings. Where is it?"

"In the bedroom, I think. Steven—well, he *hid* things. Important things, or things that were important to *him*. Not to hide them from *me*, just to hide them. He—"

"Never mind. I know. He always did." Hull saw her look of distress. "It was a kind of compulsion. You didn't do it to him."

She nodded and went back into the kitchen, heading for the hall. Hull stared after her thoughtfully. She was nice. Maybe it was as simple as that, the answer to what Steven had seen in her. There was a matter-of-fact wholesomeness about Mary Rose that might be almost addictive to a man who had spent his professional life among the doomed, the hopeless, and the evil.

A crash and the splatter of breaking china from the kitchen startled him out of his wits. He pushed the door open to find Steven's wife crouched among the shards of an overturned drainer of dishes. "Who are you? Get out of my *house!*" Her voice was hoarse. The man who had overturned the drainer advanced on her, and two others followed him menacingly. The front door stood ajar.

Christ, where did they come from? One of them dived for Hull as he came out of the lab. Hull twisted out of the man's grasp and elbowed him hard in the chest. The man had on a thick red parka, but Hull's elbow connected hard enough to slump him against the kitchen cabinets with a grunt. A second, in an oil-stained denim jacket, jumped Hull before he could back away. Out of the corner of his eye Hull saw that Mary Rose was clawing at the face of a third, who had her by both arms and was shouting at her.

The man forced her arms behind her back. "Now you jus' settle down."

Mary Rose glared up at him, angry and frightened. He was a tall, lanky man in nondescript boots, jeans, and jacket, but there was something about all of them—their straw-colored hair and their faces, blue eyes slightly watery, teeth crooked or going bad—that made Mary Rose think of the mountains, the isolated hollows where the same families might live for generations, interbreeding. "What do you want?" she gasped, twisting in the man's grasp.

"Jus' call off your boyfriend an' act nice an' we'll tell you."

Horrified, Mary Rose saw Philip Hull at the bottom of a pile of thrashing, grunting bodies. The topmost body sailed off him propelled by a well-placed kick. The second man got his hands around Hull's throat. Hull brought his knee up into the man's groin and slammed the side of his hand hard against the back of the man's neck. The fingers on Hull's throat loosened, and Hull rolled away, drawing in a ragged breath as the man in the parka came after him.

"Stop it!" Mary Rose said. "They'll kill him!"

"He ain't got no business here anyway," the man who was holding her said with a grin. He was the eldest of them. The father, maybe? They looked related. "An' you only jus' a week a widow. Now I tol' you, call him off."

Mary Rose didn't think Philip Hull looked like a man who could be called off. And she had encountered the mean-adder look that these men had about them before. You didn't reason with this kind of man, you struck back from a position of strength, whether you had one or not.

"There's an alarm on that door you broke open," she said. "You'll have every security guard on the campus here in about two minutes."

"Naw there ain't." The man's fingers dug into her arms. "We checked."

"You wouldn't know it if you saw it!" Mary Rose snapped, lying furiously.

Philip Hull and the other two men were still rolling on the floor, and Hull had blood on his mouth. Mary Rose opened hers to scream and the older man clapped his hand over it. "Now you jus' shut up!" Mary Rose sank her teeth into a finger and he yelped. She wrenched one of her hands free, stooped and snatched up a small cast-iron skillet from among the wreckage of the dishes. She swung it without aiming and caught him across the shins. He lurched off balance and Mary Rose fled into the living room.

Hull's fist connected with an unshaven jaw and his attacker stumbled backward into the man pursuing Mary Rose. Hull heaved himself to his feet as the man in the parka came back at him again. Hull caught the man by the wrist and flipped him. As the man struggled to rise, Hull caught him in the jaw with his boot and the man crumpled. This time he didn't get up. In the half-second breathing space before they could jump him again, Hull dived for the holster in his boot. His hand came up with a gun in it. "Hold it!"

The man he had kicked was going to give no further trouble, but the other man's hand reached inside his denim jacket in a quick movement like a snake's.

"No!" the older man bellowed. "You a fool, Jem? Get outta here!" He lunged for Mary Rose and wrested the skillet from her. He flung it at Hull across the open counter and grabbed the unconscious man by the collar. The skillet glanced off Hull's wrist into his ribcage.

Hull yelped, nursing his ribs. He staggered toward the gun he had dropped.

Jem hesitated a moment. He had a thin, pinched face like the others, and his pale eyes glittered malevolently as he pulled out his own gun.

The older man shouted at him. "Jem! Not here, you goddamn fool!"

Jem aimed the gun at a terrified Mary Rose. "Shoot me

an' I'm gonna shoot her," he told Hull. He and the older man dragged the limp body of the third out the door.

Hull shoved Mary Rose down behind the sofa and ran after them. An engine started and wheels spun in the road. Hull crouched and fired at the disappearing tail-lights, but they were out of range. The shot reverberated like a cannon in the quiet road. Lighted doorways popped open all down it as if they had been operated with one switch.

Hull went back in the house, locked the door behind him and slumped against it. Unless the wholesome Dr. Cullen had been up to something totally unexpected, those country-boy thugs had been his fault. Worse, with a single gunshot he had violated the sanctity of Faculty Row, and he had a pretty good idea they were going to be in for considerable nosiness as a result. Agitated voices and the patter of running feet came up the road.

Mary Rose got up off the floor, her eyes wide. Hull dumped the gun down on the table and sat her on the sofa.

"Look, don't tell anyone *anything*. Are you all right?"

Mary Rose nodded. She stared at Hull's gun. *He had that with him the whole time he was here. My God.*

"Mary Rose? Mary Rose, are you all right?" Three or four people seemed to be knocking on the door at once.

"Yes . . . yes, I'm all right." She looked up at Hull. "You've got blood on your mouth."

Hull dived down the hall to the bathroom and scrubbed his face with the first washcloth he found, while she opened the front door. Anxious voices filled the living room.

"Was that a gunshot?"

"What's goin' on here?"

"You're as white as a sheet!"

They crowded around her, suspicious and concerned. Louise Evans's hair stood wildly on end and she clutched a blow dryer in one hand, its cord trailing behind her. Bill McGinnis and Harold Robley had apparently been drawn from their nightly game of chess. Anne Ogilvie looked motherly and worried, and her husband Peter, in tuxedo pants and a half-fastened dress shirt, appeared to be trying to check Mary Rose for bullet holes, an exercise hampered by his fistful of shirt studs—the dean was dining with the president and the Board of Trustees tonight.

"*What* was that noise?"

Mary Rose managed to make them quit prodding her for holes, and pushed her hair back out of her face. Her hands were shaking. If Philip Hull thought that the very proper faculty of Sarum College had any dealings with the sort of men who had just been here, he was even crazier than he looked, but she didn't feel up to explanations and speculation.

"I . . . was going through some of Steven's things, and I found a gun," she said. "I didn't know it was loaded. It just went off." She picked it up from the table and exhibited it to them, holding it between thumb and forefinger by the handle, the way someone would carry a dead rat.

"Here, let me have that." Hull took it away from her and put it back on the table, and they turned their amazed attention from the gun to him.

"This is Philip Hull," Mary Rose said. "He was a friend of Steven's."

"Oh."

"He's going to help me decide what to do with some of Steven's things."

Louise Evans inspected him much as she might a surprising culture in a petri dish.

"You might start with unloading that gun," Bill McGinnis said.

"Good idea." Hull shook the cartridges out deftly and stuck them in his pocket.

Mary Rose made a feeble attempt at introductions, aware that Hull still looked like a man who had been in a brawl. She suspected that she did too, and the kitchen was a shambles. She didn't even want to think about what the crowd in her living room was going to decide that she and Philip Hull had been doing together. "I'm really all right now," she said firmly, trying to shepherd them toward the door. They eyed Hull askance and trooped out, but the sound of interested murmuring drifted back through the open window.

"Goddammit, they know!" Hull muttered.

"They think they do," Mary Rose said grimly, "which is probably worse."

"Not your friends," Hull said, folding himself gingerly into a chair. He stuck the cartridges back into the gun and put it back in his boot. "Go get the sword. The sooner we get that thing out of here, the better."

3.
That Man

"That's not it." Hull had the sword only halfway out of the black lacquer scabbard before he was sure. He drew it the rest of the way out and laid it on the coffee table in disgust.

Mary Rose studied it doubtfully. "It looks just like you said."

Hull shook his head. "Uh-uh. Look. This is a *katana*, not a *tachi*. The shape of the blade's all right, but it's a little too heavy. And the temper line's wrong." He picked it up by the handle and held it carefully to the light. "See those little half circles? That's *gunome*, 'priest beads.' What we're looking for is *midare*, it looks like waves with little bits of spray coming up from them. And the *kisaki*, see where it goes out from the *yo-kote*?" He pointed carefully at the tip of the blade. "This is *chu-kisaki*. The *tachi* has *ko-kisaki*, which is smaller."

Mary Rose gave him a look that she would have accorded to someone who had suddenly started to speak Arabic.

Hull grinned. He used to have much the same glassy-eyed feeling in his college calculus class. There was a certain satisfaction in trotting out his expertise for a woman who made her living doing things like sticking human genes into mice. He wondered if he was showing off. "Where's the stuff Steven used to take the fittings off?"

"You mean a little brass hammer?"

"Right. And a bottle of clove oil, and some rice paper. In a wooden box."

Mary Rose produced them, and Hull carefully knocked out the peg that pinned the handle to the tang of the blade. He set the handle and the other fittings aside and pointed to the tang. "This is a fish-belly tang. See how it curves up toward the end? The sword we're looking for has a pheasant leg. It makes a little jog about halfway up."

Mary Rose considered. "I think I *have* seen that."

"Well, thank God." Hull peered at the inscription on the tang, momentarily diverted. "Hey, this is a good sword. I didn't know he had this one. The date's fifteenth century. 'Made on a lucky day in October.' They always say that, even if it was July—October's luckier. It's been tested by a professional cutter. See that? 'Cut through three bodies and lodged in the sand.'"

"*Bodies?*"

"Uh-huh, that's how they tested a blade. Stacked them up and—"

"Never mind." She edged away from the sword and Hull both.

"Right." Hull started putting the fittings back on, positioning the pieces deftly and delicately. "Now where's the other sword?"

"I don't know. I just saw Steven taking it apart one night, the way he did. I wasn't paying much attention. They all look like knives to me."

"Knives! Christ!"

"Well, nobody told me they were worth money. *Or* would have people barging in here, waving guns. That *was* what those men were after, wasn't it?" She looked at him accusingly.

"Yeah, probably," Hull admitted. "I may have been a little too noisy about it when I was trying to track it down."

"Oh, lovely." Mary Rose stood up. "Mr. Hull, I'm going to get you every sword Steven had. You pick the right one and get out of here with it, and they can shoot at you someplace else."

"They were after you, not me," Hull said mildly. "They weren't expecting *me*. This is where the sword is."

"Not for long." Mary Rose picked up a step stool from the kitchen and marched down the hall with it. Hull followed, and she began to put swords in his hands, from the tops of closets, under beds, in dresser drawers. "Just supposing you tell me who that was who was here tonight."

"*Yakuza*," Hull said grimly. "Not those men, but I'm willing to bet there's *yakuza* behind them." He looked at a short sword and tossed it on the bed in disgust. "That's not even the right *length*."

Mary Rose gave him a malevolent look. "Just tell me when we come to the right one."

"You want to know about the *yakuza*?"

"No," she said frankly, "but I think I'd better or I'll start imagining things that are even worse."

"You couldn't," Hull said.

"Mr. Hull, if you don't want me in screaming hysterics, just *tell* me."

"Well, it isn't so much *yakuza* as it is Sadao Akaishi. He's a big *oya-bun*, that's a boss, sort of like a Mafia don. He's a descendant of Akinji Kobayasu, the guy who owned the sword, just like the nice college professor in Tokyo is. If we're up against *yakuza*, it's because Sadao Akaishi wants his ancestor's sword."

"Why?"

"I thought I told you. It'll give him a lot of power to have Akinji Kobayasu's sword. A lot of face. Consequence. The Japanese don't operate the way we do. Things like this matter."

"Enough to kill for it?"

"Hell, yes."

"Mr. Hull, you're making me very nervous."

"I'm making *me* nervous," Hull said.

He followed her into a room that was apparently her office and watched her stand on tiptoe on the stool to poke around in the top of a long closet. Two curtain rods and a shoebox full of old bank statements came down with a crash. Mary Rose fished out another sword, wrapped up in half a sheet.

Hull unwrapped it. "That isn't it."

"It's got to be. It's the last one."

"Well, it's not. God damn it." Hull considered the sword, a very pretty *wakizashi* of entirely the wrong date, style, and everything else. "There've got to be more."

Mary Rose got down off the step stool. "Not in this house. I've been through everything here."

"Then somewhere else. You know what Steven was like. It'll be somewhere on the campus, I'd guess."

"Oh, that's great." Mary Rose pulled a swivel chair away from a desk laden with neatly stacked papers. She sat down and pointed a finger at him. "Do you have any idea how big the campus of an agricultural college is? You can borrow Steven's car if you want to go look for it. You're going to need it."

"Steven's car? I thought he wrapped it around a tree."

"No, he was driving a rented car," Mary Rose said. "We never did know why." Her face softened, irritation fading. Steven seemed to be slipping through her fingers, growing more mysterious and shadowy by the hour.

There was another chair in the room, a black recliner. Philip Hull sat down in it suddenly. "Oh, Christ." He put his face in his hands.

Mary Rose looked at him with concern. "What is it?"

Hull lifted his head. In the light from the desk lamp his amber-colored eyes were anguished, hard, almost as yellow as a cat's. "They killed him. The sons of bitches killed him for the goddamn thing."

Mary Rose stared at him. "*What?*" she whispered.

"They thought it would be easier to get it away from you than Steven," he said.

"It would have been if you hadn't been here," Mary Rose said. She felt as if something cold were crawling up her back. The men who had been here tonight wouldn't have stopped looking when she ran out of swords. They would have torn the house apart. And when they didn't find it . . . She shivered, trying not to think what they might have done if they hadn't found it. And Steven . . .

"Why?" she asked desperately. "*Why* do you think they killed him?"

"Did Steven ever drive anything but his own car?"

"No."

"None of us do," Hull said. "It's a professional obsession. These bastards probably rented the car in his name, forged his signature to the papers." He tried to stop thinking about Steven, so he could explain to Steven's widow in the matter of fact tones in which he would make any report, how Steven had been murdered. "Then they caught him somewhere, dragged him into the car, doped him up or knocked him out, and *killed* him for the damn thing!" His voice rose in spite of himself. He stared at her, his eyes haunted. "It was my fault."

"No, no!" Mary Rose said forcefully. "It wasn't. You didn't know what the sword was until it was too late to be quiet about it." It wasn't fair that he should torment himself. "Maybe you're wrong," she ventured. "Why should they bother to rent a car? Steven's would have done just as well."

Hull gave her a crooked smile. "One of these days I'll show you a few things about Steven's car," he said. "But just take my word for it, Steven wouldn't drive anything else, and not even the *yakuza* would try to take him in it if there was an easier way. The *yakuza* are very . . . practical." He looked at her, sitting there being sorry for *him*. He didn't know what he had been expecting. Hysterics, or accusations. Certainly not words of comfort. "You know, you're a particularly nice person. I'm gonna nail those bastards. But first you find that sword. I'll take it from there. If you don't find it, they're gonna come back. I want to get the thing as far away from you as I can."

"No," Mary Rose said. An hour ago she would have thought she had lost her mind, but now— *They killed him*, she thought. *Just to make it easier*. She looked at Philip Hull stubbornly. "I'm in this now."

"On account of Steven?" Hull asked.

Mary Rose bit her lip. "Partly. I never really knew him, did I?" she said sadly. "And if you're right, I don't think we can prove it. The car rental in Roanoke just remem-

bered someone tall and blond. And the rental agreement
was in the wreck with him. The signature on it looked like
Steven's to me. If they killed him, I can't just let that go
by. And I want that sword. I want the money. I can't let
you take all the risks and then just collect my share."

"Most people would," Hull ventured.

"No."

"Dr. Cullen—Look, can I call you Mary Rose? 'Dr.
Cullen' makes me think of Steven a little too much."

"Sure. Mary Rose."

"You're a very pigheaded person, Mary Rose."

She didn't say anything. She just sat there looking at
him, as stubborn as hell, with her chin jutting out. She
looked like some nice country girl, no makeup, with her
hair pulled back in a nice practical knot, and those round
blue eyes. And there she sat, saying she was going to take
on the *yakuza* with him. "What do you think you're going
to do?" Hull asked her in exasperation. "Slap them with a
slide rule?"

Mary Rose stood up. "For now, I'm going to make up
the bed in the back room for you. Then you can do any
slapping that's required. You seem to be pretty good at
it."

Philip Hull leaned in the doorway while she put an
extra blanket on the bed and fluffed up the pillow. "I'm
going to go and get my car," he said. "It's got my suitcase
in it. Thanks for letting me stay."

"I'm terrified to have you leave," Mary Rose said frankly.
She went back to her office and got a Guest Parking
sticker out of her desk. She scribbled her name across the
bottom of it. "Put this on your car, or it'll get towed if you
park up here for long. Here's my spare house key. I'm
going to lock the door behind you and try to go to sleep. I
have an eight o'clock class in the morning."

"I'll talk to you tomorrow, then," he said. "And tomorrow you tell anyone you can think of that you found out
from me that Steven had some things—don't say what—
that you haven't found, and you're trying to figure out
where he might have stored them. Those guys are gonna
be back, but with me here, they'll nose around some first

and keep their ears open. Maybe that'll keep them off for a while, if they think you don't know where the sword is either."

"All right." Mary Rose looked at him vaguely. "I'm so tired. I feel like I could just lie down on the floor and go to sleep. All of a sudden."

"It's the adrenaline," Hull said. "A bad time uses up a lot of it. Then, when the effects wear off, you drop. You go to bed. I won't be gone a minute."

He pocketed the house key and walked down Faculty Row toward the parking lot. The night air was only faintly cool and it smelled wet. It smelled green, he thought. Spring out here seemed to have an almost overpowering life to it. Clumps of daffodils fluttered in the night breeze, and some kind of flowering tree was blooming already, clouds of white petals floating in the glow of a muted streetlight. In some ways it reminded him of Japan, all that green, but Virginia was more unruly. Its spring had a restless exuberance.

Hull got into the car and turned its nose back up the hill, worrying a bit at the problem of what they were going to do with the sword when they found it. He decided that he'd better just concentrate on finding it, before the *yakuza* got better organized. As long as the *yakuza* stuck to working with local talent, he and Mary Rose had a chance.

She was asleep when he got back to the house, but she'd left the hall light on for him. There were clean towels laid out in the bathroom. The washcloth he'd cleaned the blood off his face with had vanished, and she'd shoved her comb and brush and cosmetics, neatly arranged in a little plastic tray, to one side, to make room for his shaving things. Hull smiled. So she did wear makeup. On state occasions maybe. He wondered what she'd look like dressed up, and told himself to quit that. She was his buddy's widow, and he wasn't in the market for a woman anyway. Not a woman like Mary Rose, who was cut out to be somebody's *permanent* woman.

He left the bedroom door ajar, stuck the gun on the night table, and climbed into bed. His muscles were already beginning to tighten up. By morning he was going to feel like he'd been run over by a truck.

He woke at six-thirty because there was a woodpecker trying to drill a hole through a tin rain gutter outside his window. There was bacon frying, and better yet, a strong smell of freshly ground coffee.

Mary Rose was in the kitchen, barelegged, in a terry-cloth bathrobe, flipping eggs in a skillet. She looked chipper. An oldies station on the radio was playing Frankie Laine singing "The Girl in the Wood."

"Good morning," she said. "If you can stand to eat this early, I'll fix you some eggs."

"You look better than last night."

"It wasn't a good night," she said after a moment. "After I went to bed, I thought about Steven and how nothing in his whole life seemed to have been fair. Maybe not even his marrying me. But I can't do anything about that. The best I can do for him is to find his sword. The men who killed him are *not* going to have it. So where do we start looking?"

"Where did Steven spend his time?"

She handed him the eggs she'd been cooking and cracked a couple more into the skillet. "Well, in his classroom. Most of his classes were in Gower Hall. But we can't go poking around in there until tonight, when no one's using it. He had an office there too, on the first floor. I've got the key. Maybe we could start there. I promised Bill McGinnis I'd clean it out."

"Great. When?"

"I've got an eight o'clock class and a ten o'clock department meeting, but the afternoon is clear. I don't keep office hours on Wednesdays."

"You *sound* like a doctor," Hull said, amused. "What do you do, play golf?"

"Wednesday's just the day I keep to catch up on loose ends," Mary Rose said. "I grade papers. I go to the dentist. Assuming that I need to."

"Or have your hair done?" Hull suggested, grinning.

"Does it need it?" She looked at him distractedly, flipping eggs.

"No. It looks fine." Out of its prim chignon, it hung in soft little waves around her face.

She caught him looking at her and brushed it back over her shoulders, embarrassed. "I think it would make sense if you did take Steven's car," she said. "There's no point in having a rented one eating its head off while you're here. But I'll have to change a tire on mine first. I've been driving Steven's."

Hull put his plate in the kitchen sink and walked through the living room. In daylight he could see the carport through the south window. Mary Rose's Datsun sat on its flat tire, with Steven's black Chevy behind it. "I'll change the tire for you," he volunteered.

"Thanks. I'll give you a map of the campus. You knew Steven better than I did. Maybe if you look around, you'll get some idea of where he might have been likely to put the sword." She studied his tall back, silhouetted against the window. Something about Philip Hull still reminded her of Steven, but she thought that he seemed somehow more solid than Steven—not physically, but emotionally. Philip Hull looked like a man who had always known exactly what he wanted. She put her own plate away and disappeared abruptly into the bathroom.

When she emerged, clad in a khaki skirt and a striped shirt, her hair combed rigorously into its usual knot, he was already in the carport, taking the tire off the Datsun. She put the map and the keys to the Chevy on the Datsun's hood. "I'll be back around noon."

He grunted in agreement, wrestling with the spare tire. Mary Rose watched him indecisively for a moment and then set off at a brisk pace down the hill.

"Mary Rose, *where* did that man come from?" Louise Evans buttonholed her determinedly as the department meeting broke up.

Mary Rose looked around for some place to dodge and found none. Louise had the tenacity of a bull terrier, and the same general courage of her convictions.

"He used to work with Steven," Mary Rose said.

Louise snorted. "That man is no professor."

"Will you quit calling him 'that man'? I never said he was a teacher. He's a police officer. So was Steven."

Louise's eyebrows shot up into her hair. "What sort of police officer?"

"Narcotics," Mary Rose said. She was going to have to tell them eventually. She might as well tell Louise and save having to tell everyone else. "I gather it's a fairly intense job. Steven decided he just couldn't handle it anymore."

"And this Hull person can? If you ask me, he looks more like someone the cops ought to be chasing. Are you sure about him?"

"For God's sake, Louise, he showed me his identification."

"Well, what's he *doing* here?"

"I told you, he's helping me with Steven's things. There are some I can't find, that he may have put in storage somewhere. I'm hoping Philip can help me figure out where."

"Philip?"

"Philip Hull," Mary Rose said patiently. "His name is Philip Hull."

"Where's he staying?"

"With me," Mary Rose said firmly. She dodged around Louise and out the door while Louise was digesting that.

"Well, I think you're taking a big chance," Louise called after her.

She wasn't joking about the size of the campus, Hull realized, as the car rolled along between flat fields, newly plowed for whatever it was they learned to grow here. At least he could eliminate those, he decided, since he was pretty sure Steven hadn't buried the damned thing. Around the fields the mountains rose up like the rim of a bowl, and the main campus itself sat on a series of hills at the mountain's foot. Beyond the Quadrangle, the classrooms, and the Veterinary School, were the field offices and barns. Those might be a possibility, he thought, but only a last-ditch one. The sword would be somewhere where Steven spent some time. Hull couldn't picture Steven in the barns, cozying up to cows.

He found an Avis office in the town of Sarum, definitely a small-scale operation, tucked in between the Red Top Café and a gas station, and firmly returned the car, which they didn't want. But negotiations concluded, the proprietor was inclined to be chatty. He apparently didn't have much else to do. Hull grew more sure than ever why the car that Steven had died in had come from Roanoke. Anyone renting a car in Sarum would be remembered.

He hitched a ride back to the college with the proprietor's nephew and got out at the main gates, watching with some amusement while a girl in pigtails and a burly blond boy tried to coax a bull through a pasture gate. The bull didn't seem annoyed about it, he just didn't want to go, and stood there, watching them with mild bovine indignation while they pushed and tugged at him.

Hull walked up Faculty Row to Mary Rose's house and went inside to find Mary Rose at the rolltop desk, paying bills, with the radio on. The strains of "Stardust" were just fading out. With her dark head bent over the stack of envelopes in front of her, the light from the window beside the desk emphasized the dark sweep of lashes across clear, pale skin. She had taken off her shoes, and her stockinged feet were crossed over each other and tucked underneath her chair. It was a pose at once both innocent and oddly seductive.

"Now I TELL you my friends, that you must put SIN from your HEARTS, because if you have sin in your heart, why then Jesus knows what you've been thinking of—"

Mary Rose lunged for the radio and turned it off.

"Where did *he* come from?" Hull said.

"He's on at noon every day for an hour. He's probably what keeps the station afloat. They don't seem to have much advertising. Did you get any lunch?"

"I had something called a Dixieburger at the Red Top Café," Hull said.

"Good Lord. You'll poison yourself."

"I think I already have." He clutched his throat dramatically and crossed his eyes, and she giggled. "Look," he said, "I can't let you go on cooking for me. Why don't I buy some groceries and we'll take turns?"

"Can you cook?" she asked suspiciously.

"You'll find out." He motioned her toward the door. "Let's go and sift through Steven's office. I want to find that thing. I've felt like someone was breathing down my neck all morning."

As he opened the front door, a flash of movement caught his eye.

"Hey, you!" Hull shoved Mary Rose back inside and jumped over the porch railing. A man in a denim jacket ran around the side of the house and sprinted diagonally up the street to dive over a stone retaining wall and slither down the hill, out of sight behind the faculty houses on the other side of the road.

Hull peered over the wall in disgust. Sarum's students had just come out of their last class of the morning, and the Back Quadrangle below was jammed with them. By the time Hull caught up with him, the lanky form and denim jacket would be lost in a crowd of several hundred others.

Mary Rose emerged indignantly from the house. "You aren't the Lone Ranger. Will you quit pushing me out of the way?"

"It's a reflex," Hull said. "Department conditioning. We have to pass a test in shoving helpless civilians through doors before we get hired." He looked gloomily over the wall at the mob of students in the Back Quadrangle. "You couldn't have picked a worse place to live," he informed her.

"What's wrong with it?" Mary Rose prepared to do battle for the honor of Sarum College.

"How many students have you got here?"

"About fifteen hundred, counting the graduate students."

"You know all of them?"

"No." She looked at the mob in the Back Quad. "I see what you mean."

"All they need is someone young enough to be a plausible student, and they can watch us with a pretty good chance we won't be watching them back. I don't know who that was, but he wasn't one of the ones who was here last night."

"Well, where are they *coming* from?"

"All Rabbit's friends and relations," Hull growled.

Mary Rose chuckled. Any man who had read *Winnie the Pooh* scored points with her. But she was interested that he had the same impression of the men who had been there last night as she had—that they were related.

"Come on," Hull said. He took her arm and hustled her down the road. "I want to go over that office before he spots us again."

Steven's faculty office, on the first floor of Gower Hall behind the Administration Building, yielded, on the face of it, very little. Mary Rose unlocked the door and looked dispiritedly at the contents of the desk. There were some freshman English papers that ought to be handed over to Bill McGinnis, the usual jumble of pens, paper clips, odd bits of string, an empty coffee cup, and not much else. Gower Hall was old, the original classroom building of Sarum Institute, and the offices were twelve-foot cubicles, their outer walls red, unpainted brick. There didn't appear to be any place to hide a penknife, much less a four-foot sword.

The wall beside the door was lined with bookshelves, and Mary Rose slid her hand behind the few books that were there, to see if there was room for anything behind them. There wasn't. Philip Hull had turned the threadbare rug back and was inspecting the floorboards.

"Aren't you being a little melodramatic?" Mary Rose inquired.

"Not necessarily. I've known Steven to find squirrelier places." He got up, dusted off the knees of his slacks, and began prodding with a pocketknife at the bricks in the outer wall. "Aha."

"Aha, what?"

"Aha, look here." He poked with the pocketknife at the mortar between the bricks. "This is new mortar. See, it's a different color, and the old stuff is starting to crumble. This isn't."

Mary Rose peered at it. A long rectangle of brick,

suspiciously sword-shaped, did look different. "I can't believe he'd brick it up in a *wall*."

"I can," Hull said. "I told you, Steven was a little off the edge. More so lately. How much attention is it going to draw if I start knocking bricks out of this wall?"

"Plenty."

"Then we'll have to come back tonight. I'll go into town and get some mortar to put these things back in with. Let's go look at his classroom now. There won't be anyone in it till one, will there?"

Mary Rose shook her head faintly. What kind of mental state made a man brick up his possessions in a wall?

She led Hull upstairs and showed him Steven's classroom, but they turned up nothing there, although Philip Hull went over it with the swift and thorough expertise of a man who has spent years learning where people hide things.

"I've found dope in some of the damnedest places," he explained.

"But dope is little, isn't it? I mean, it doesn't take up much room."

"You'd be surprised. I busted a guy once who had enough pills to fill a bathtub, very neatly tiled into the bottom of one of those stoves in the middle of the kitchen. Islands, they call them. We started pulling the tiles off when we tried a burner and it didn't work."

"Where did he cook?" Mary Rose inquired, giving this notion practical consideration.

Hull looked at her. "You ask the damnedest questions. *I* don't know where he cooked. He probably ate at McDonald's." He looked more closely. "Hey, are you crying?"

"No," Mary Rose said firmly. She sniffed. "I just feel so sorry for Steven. And guilty, I guess. I keep wondering if the man I thought I was in love with was even there."

"Maybe he wasn't," Hull conceded. "But I told you, you didn't do it to him."

"What did?"

"I wish I knew. Even before he took off, he never stuck with anything for very long—except the department, and the swords. The swords were a passion. He was worse than I am. Maybe that's why he had this thing about hiding them. I guess searching other people's houses makes you paranoid about your own."

"Do *you* hide your swords in walls?" Mary Rose demanded.

"No." Hull grinned. "I keep 'em handy. They're sharper than hell. Anyone who wants to try lifting one is welcome to come and get cut in half with it."

Mary Rose looked at him sideways, trying to decide how serious he was.

"Mary Rose!"

She jumped. Bill McGinnis was standing in the doorway. "I was just seeing if Steven had left anything up here," she muttered, shoving the Freshman Lit papers at him. "Here, these were in his desk."

"Uh, great." Bill stuck them in his jacket pocket and eyed Hull with an expression that said plainly, *You still here?*

"I went through Steven's office," Mary Rose said hastily. "I'll bring a box or something and clear everything out tonight." *While I'm taking the bricks out of the wall.* If Bill knew about that, he'd think *she* didn't have all her bricks.

"Nice to meet you again," Hull said genially. He escorted Mary Rose firmly out the door. On their way down the stairs he asked her, "Why do I get the impression he doesn't care for me?"

Mary Rose sighed. "Everyone on the faculty always knows what everyone else is doing. I told Louise Evans you were staying with me. I guess Bill thinks I need protecting."

"From what?" Hull said indignantly. "What do I look like?"

"I don't know," Mary Rose said, "but you don't look safe."

He looked even less so in Steven's office at midnight, with blankets tacked over the windows, methodically prying bricks out of the wall by the light of a flashlight. The sharp shadows it cast over his face accentuated the piratical look, and the precautions he'd taken getting them from her house to Gower Hall had done nothing to dispel that impression. Hull had piled her into Steven's Chevy with the blankets, a sack of mortar, a bucket, a gallon jug of water, and a crowbar. Then he had driven clear into Sarum at a speed that unnerved Mary Rose totally, dodged three times through the town by different routes, and finally driven back to the campus with the lights out. He had parked in the student parking lot at the end of Back Quad and then they had slunk through the dark to Gower Hall, carrying the bucket and everything else. It was a wonder, Mary Rose thought, that the campus cops hadn't spotted them and hauled them off for being up to no good.

"Got it." Hull set the last brick on the floor and wriggled his arm through the hole. "Something's in here, wrapped up in some kind of cloth."

"Maybe it's a body," Mary Rose said sarcastically.

"Not unless there's nothing left of him but one thigh bone," Hull announced cheerfully. He pulled it out and laid it on the floor. "Ah, shit."

"What is it?"

"Another dud. Christ, how many do you suppose he hid?"

"I don't know." Mary Rose looked at the sword. It looked like all the rest of them to her. "I don't even know how many he *had*."

Swearing, Hull began to cement the bricks back into the wall.

They drove back to the house on Faculty Row in moody silence. As they pulled into the carport, Hull motioned for Mary Rose to stay still. He opened the driver's door, got out, and closed it again. As the interior light went out, he crouched by the car and looked up the road. Headlights came on and a car pulled into the street. It drove slowly past the house and then down the hill, picking up speed.

Hull stood up and opened the passenger door. "Our shadow's back," he said. "He's probably been sitting up here since we ditched him in town."

"But why come back here?"

"To see if we do. If we come back here, we haven't split

with the sword. What I want to know is where the *yakuza* got these people. They aren't professionals, not at this kind of business."

"Then why use them at all? If these *yakuza* people are what you say they are, why bring in someone who's not a professional?"

"Cover," Hull said. "There are millions of Japanese in California. Out here they're gonna get noticed."

Mary Rose gave the darkened street an edgy look. The idea of being watched made her skin crawl. She took her keys out of her jacket pocket.

"Just a minute," Hull said. "You get back in the car and lock the doors. I'm gonna look inside first." He pulled his gun out and took the keys out of her hand.

In a few minutes he reappeared. "All clear. I don't think they'll try anything here again, it's too public, but I'm not gonna take any chances. Can I put a long distance call on your phone?"

"Yes, sure." Curious, she followed him into the house. Hull was already punching out numbers on the telephone.

"Sunny, this is Philip Hull. I hope I didn't get you up— what is it out there, eleven? . . . Oh, good . . . I'm in Virginia . . . No, just a vacation. Listen, is Mike around? . . . Thanks." He looked at Mary Rose. "I've had a bright idea." He turned back to the telephone. "Mike? Listen, I need a favor. Just some quiet information. Very quiet. Can you find out who out there in the *yakuza* has a connection with someone out here, and who the hell the guy out here is? . . . Yeah, I know. I'm not expecting anything concrete, just scuttlebutt. I'll give you the number." He read it off. "No, I'm not getting in over my head. Just something that's come up. One of my swords turns out to be something they're interested in. I just want to know which way to dodge. . . . Yes, I'll watch my ass. Thanks, I appreciate it."

He hung up. "That was Mike Kawasaki. He's with the San Francisco P.D. If anybody can ease a little information out without blowing it, Mike can."

4.
In Debt to the Devil

"I'm going to have to sit here and wait," Hull said the next morning, jerking his thumb at the telephone. "I don't know how long it'll take Mike to snoop out what I want."

Mary Rose regarded her houseguest dubiously. Hull was stretched out on the living room sofa, reading the morning paper, his bare feet crossed at the ankles. The holster around his right ankle showed under the cuff of his tan slacks. Mary Rose pointed a finger at it. "Do you always wear that thing?"

"It seems like a good idea at the moment," Hull said. "It's my off-duty weapon; I'm supposed to wear it. At home, anyway. I just feel a little naked without it. I kind of suspect I need a Virginia permit out here, but I don't think I'll bother, because it would be a little awkward if they wouldn't give me one."

"How'd you get on an airplane with it?" Mary Rose asked.

"I put it in a suitcase in the baggage compartment," Hull said. He looked at her over the top of the newspaper. "I don't think I ever met a woman with such a passion for irrelevant details."

"Most of my friends don't wear guns on their feet," Mary Rose said.

"Most of your friends probably don't need to," Hull

53

muttered, looking at the paper. "Not in a state where they just gave a guy thirty years for rape."

"We take a dim view of rape out here," Mary Rose said.

"So do I. I take a dim view of a lot of things guys get sent up for out of my department, and then paroled three years later because some shrink, who wasn't around when the creep blasted his way through four people in a gas station, says he's 'rehabilitated.' I could learn to like this place."

Mary Rose sat down on the edge of the sofa and Hull moved his feet over to give her some room. "I expect I'm very insular," she said. "I never really think about that sort of thing happening. Oh, in D.C. maybe, but not here."

"Nothing wrong with that," Hull said. "It's a fine thing to live in a place where you feel safe."

Mary Rose was beginning to suspect that if Philip Hull lived in a place where he felt safe, he'd get bored. "I don't feel very safe at the moment," she informed him. "Why don't we just call the police and let them handle this?"

"Because they couldn't do diddly-shit," Hull said. "How do you think they're gonna find the clowns that broke in here—advertise?"

"What *I* think," Mary Rose said, "is that you've got a bee in your bonnet about telling anybody about this sword."

"That too," Hull said. "Not till I know who's after us and what their connections are."

"You're the most suspicious man I ever met."

"I'm also still alive, if you'll notice. I want to find out what Mike Kawasaki has to say before we talk to *anybody*."

"How on earth is this Mike person going to find out something like that?"

"He's going to exercise his subtle Oriental charm on the Japanese community, for starters. Round-eyed cops who barge in asking tactless questions get frozen out pretty fast," Hull said. "The Japanese look right through you, and they're so sorry but they've never heard of *yakuza*. Then they tell all their friends, and *nobody*'ll talk to you."

"But they'll talk to your friend in San Francisco?"

"Mike's *nisei*, first generation American-born. He knows

how to handle them. He'll also sift out the law-enforcement scuttlebutt for anything that sounds useful. *Yakuza* keep to themselves. If they've had dealings with Caucasians, it's unusual enough for someone to have picked up on it."

Mary Rose picked up the armload of books she'd dumped on the coffee table and held them indecisively in her lap.

"You go teach your class," Hull said, halfway wishing she'd stay instead. "Go on, get. No one's going to chase you until they think you've found the sword. It's obvious it isn't concealed on your person." Hull's eyes lingered for a moment longer than he meant them to on the soft contours clad in blue jeans, boots, and a short-sleeved jersey.

Mary Rose gave him a thoughtful look. "I'm less worried about them than I am about you," she informed him. "You give me nightmares. Last night I dreamed that you'd decided to take up the floorboards in the president's office, and I had to help you, and people kept coming in to ask us what we were doing."

Hull sat up, laughing. "We'll skip the president's office," he promised. His eyes strayed to the slim legs perched on the sofa beside his. "Those aren't your classroom clothes," he said, trying to divert his thoughts into safer channels. "What are you doing this morning, grooming the giant mice?"

Mary Rose looked at him gravely. "Not at all," she said. "I'm helping Harold Robley artificially inseminate a cow."

Hull choked. His lip started to twitch. He lay back down and put the newspaper over his face. "It's spring," he said from beneath it. "Romance is everywhere."

"Mary Rose, dear. How nice to see you." Anne Ogilvie put her lunch tray down next to Mary Rose's and slid into the chair beside hers. She looked plump and motherly in a beige spring suit; like a nice hen, Mary Rose thought.

"Tsk. The soup's cold again." Anne gave her bowl a reproving look and fixed her brown eyes on Mary Rose instead. "Are you beginning to feel more recovered, dear?"

"Yes. Thank you for asking. Maybe it's the spring weather," Mary Rose said. "Things always seem less gloomy when the dogwood's out."

"Louise Evans, who always talks too much anyway, tells me that Mr. Hull is still staying with you," Anne said.

Mary Rose paused with a forkful of salad halfway to her mouth, said "Uh-huh" quickly, and stuck the fork in her mouth, hoping that would provide sufficient excuse for not elaborating further. Philip Hull had been pacing through the house for three days, swearing and waiting for the phone to ring, and she was sure that by now everyone on campus was aware of his presence.

Anne took a mouthful of soup. "Of course, Frances Cady thinks he's wonderful," she commented. "Frances lent him her umbrella and seems to regard that as a recommendation of his character. I expect she took to him because he's so handsome. Which is probably why Louise *doesn't* like him. He really seems to be a most unsettling man."

"He certainly seems to be unsettling all my friends," Mary Rose remarked, but she gave Anne an affectionate look. Anne was obviously worried about her, and it would be rude of Mary Rose to go on wolfing salad so she wouldn't have to talk to her. "Anyway, I don't think he's all that handsome," Mary Rose added doggedly.

"Not as handsome as Steven," Anne conceded. "Not in the same way. But this man has something. He looks like a pirate to me. I wouldn't be surprised to see him with an eyepatch and a ring in his ear."

Mary Rose couldn't find anything suitable to say to that, since she thought so herself.

"How long is he going to be staying with you?" Anne inquired gently.

Mary Rose poked at her salad. "I'm not sure."

"Dear, I don't want to be an old busybody, but do be careful, won't you? You're still in a sort of shock over Steven, and one does tend to, well, leap into things in that state of mind. And you're rather an impulsive person, you know."

"I'm *not*," Mary Rose said. "The only impulsive thing I ever did in my life was marry Steven, and, oh, Anne, I'm beginning to think it was an awful mistake. I don't know what it would have been like if he had lived." Two tears rolled down her cheeks into her salad. "Poor Steven."

Anne looked at her sympathetically. "You didn't know him very well, did you? That's what I mean, dear."

"Don't do it again?" Mary Rose said. "I don't think I'm in much danger. Steven was running away from things. I just happened to be what he ran into." She made a face. "The college and I. We made a great place to hide." She pushed her salad bowl away, wiped her face with her napkin, and stuck her fork in her fried chicken. "Philip's just here to help me sort out those old swords of Steven's." She hesitated. "Some of them turn out to be worth some money, and he's going to help me sell them. His intentions toward me are so respectable they're nonexistent."

"And I can tell Louise Evans to put that on her needles and knit it?" Anne suggested. "Well, I will, but I hope you're sure, dear."

Mary Rose grinned at her. Her glance took in the rest of the faculty dining room, which had all the electricity of a well-ordered museum. Some of the elderly professors looked as if they ought to be dusted. "I honestly can't see Philip Hull settling in at Sarum. Now, can you?"

"Frankly, no, dear," Anne said. "That's why I'm worried."

She finished her soup and stood up, eyeing Mary Rose's chicken wistfully. "I'm so tired of being on a diet. It would be such a relief just to get fat as a pig and not worry about it." She picked up her tray. "I'm going to go speak to the kitchen about this soup. There's not much *to* soup, but at least it ought to be hot."

She trotted away and Mary Rose hastily propped a book up in front of her. She didn't mind Anne, but she didn't think her nerves would stand anyone else coming along. It was bad enough keeping one eye cocked over her shoulder for Japanese gangsters without adding a steady parade of busybodies.

Mary Rose sighed. Anne wasn't a busybody, Anne was just a nice worried friend with the impression that Mary Rose was not, at the moment, in complete possession of all her marbles.

Mary Rose glowered at her chicken. Maybe she wasn't.

She couldn't think of any reason other than temporary insanity to have let a man like Philip Hull into her life.

Hull hung up the telephone and made a face at it. Every time it rang he jumped on it, and it was always someone looking for Mary Rose, who wanted to know who the hell *he* was. This time it had been that Evans woman, who knew damned well that Mary Rose was in class, Hull thought. She just wanted to see if he was still here.

He prowled around the living room and looked at the newspaper with disgust because he'd already read it three times. He had found a few books that were old favorites among the incomprehensible biology and genetics texts in Mary Rose's bookcase, and in another mood he would have settled down happily with James Thurber or Saki, but his mind wasn't on it. He kept trying to figure out where Steven might have been loony enough to have put that sword. Mary Rose had said she'd been over the whole house, but she was an awfully literal-minded woman. She'd lived here a long time. Hull wondered if there was any place she hadn't looked simply because *she* had never gone there and it hadn't occurred to her that Steven might.

He stalked restlessly down the hall and stared at the basement door. No, she'd been down there, and so had he. There was nothing there but a monstrous furnace, and the hot water heater, and an impressive accumulation of dried-up cans of paint. Hull began opening the other doors that led off the hall: Mary Rose's office, his bedroom, and, feeling a little furtive, her bedroom.

He stared into it dubiously. He didn't want to go pawing through her things, but it was the only room he hadn't been in. There was a double bed, neatly made up, a marble-topped dresser with a starched dresser scarf, and an overstuffed chair beside a table full of books. Hull poked his head tentatively into the closet. Clothes and shoes were tidily arrayed, with sweaters and purses stacked on the shelf above them. Hull peered up at them. She would certainly have gone through all that and not missed a four-foot sword if it had been there. He looked at the ceiling.

Thirty seconds later he was wrestling a dining room chair into the closet, with a flashlight stuck in his back pocket. There was an access panel in the closet ceiling, just big enough to squeeze through. The woman had said she didn't have an attic, he fumed, shoving at the panel. Just because you couldn't get to it through a goddamned *door* . . . The panel was stuck, and he knocked it loose with the handle of the flashlight, showering himself with dirt and chips of old paint. He slid the panel sideways onto the attic floorboards and stuck his head through the hole. The attic floor was just level with his nose, and he played the light over it.

Dust and cobwebs gleamed desolately in the beam of light. Hull shone it slowly back and over the floor and walls again. It wasn't really an attic, only a crawl space, but big enough to get into if you wanted to. Apparently no one had. The boards were bare of anything but dust. Hull panned the light over them one more time and a bit of something white leapt up in the light and then vanished again. Hull swung the flashlight back. Whatever it was, he could only see a corner of it, hanging below one of the roof beams, but it looked like cloth. He put the flashlight down on the attic floor and hooked his elbows over the edge of the hole. Dust swirled up in his face as he wriggled through the hole, sneezing.

Halfway through, the flashlight rolled out of reach and, lunging for it, he kicked over the chair beneath him. Hull made a grab at a brace that slanted upward from the wall to the rafters and hauled the rest of himself through the hole, ducking his head as cobwebs plastered themselves across his face. The crawl space clearance wasn't much more than three feet, even in the middle, and only about two where the access panel opened into it. Hull wormed his way across the boards, sneezing again, and trying to ignore the fact that a spider had gone down the back of his collar. He had just pulled his feet over the edge when the telephone rang.

*   *   *

"What on earth have you been doing?" Mary Rose stared at Philip Hull with interest. He was sitting cross-legged on her living room carpet, taking a sword apart on the coffee table. Strands of cobweb clung to his brown hair and there were streaks of gray dust on his face and the front of his white shirt. One knee of his khaki pants exhibited a large triangular tear.

"Why the hell didn't you tell me you had an attic?" he said accusingly.

"I don't, just a crawl sp—" She looked at the sword. "Do you mean you *found* it?"

"No, you idiot woman, I didn't find it," he snarled. "I found another goddamn ringer, that's what I found. But if I'd known you had an attic, *you* could have gone up there instead of me, and *you* could have crawled through ten years' worth of dirt and crud and got a spider down your back and then had to drop down again out of a two-foot hole onto a chair that fell over and had all its legs sticking up at you when the goddamn telephone rang."

He looked so outraged that Mary Rose sat down on the sofa and put on the most sympathetic face she could muster under the circumstances. "Who was on the phone? Was it your friend Mike?"

"It quit ringing about the time I got to it," Hull informed her. "Maybe it was your friend Robley and his cow. Maybe they've got another hot date." He picked up the pieces of the sword and began to fit them back together. "Then I had to go back *up* there and get the frigging sword."

"Is it valuable?"

"Not particularly," Hull muttered.

"Then why did Steven go to all that trouble to put it up there?"

Hull spread his hands out. He looked at her and shook his head. "Goddamned if I know. It was wrapped up in another piece of that sheet and hung up on a couple of big hooks on the back of a rafter. On *hooks*. That's old wood up there, and it's about as hard as a chunk of railroad track. He'd have had to use a drill just to get the hooks in it. He must have hauled about forty feet of extension cord up there."

Mary Rose bit her lip. "Philip . . . was Steven crazy? I mean, literally?"

"Nah, he was just . . . Yeah, maybe he was. I don't know." Hull dropped his troubled gaze to the sword again and sat fidgeting with the pieces.

"Poor Steven," Mary Rose said. That seemed to be the only way she could think of him now. She watched Hull's long fingers pick up the sword fittings and then put them back again on the coffee table. The bare blade lay beside them. "It looks like what you described to me," she ventured. "Are you sure it's not the right one?"

"I am positive," Hull said with elaborate patience. "Now, look. The tang's all wrong, not to mention the fact that it hasn't got the right signature, which incidentally I'm beginning to see in my sleep. The blade's not long enough and it has too much curve. And the temper line doesn't look like moonlight, it looks like shit to me. This isn't even a good blade. Are you paying any attention?"

"Uh, not much. I'm sorry," Mary Rose said. "My eyes just start to glaze over when you start telling me what all the different pieces are. And it's even worse when you do it in Japanese."

"I'll bet." Hull pinned the handle back on the tang and slipped the blade back in its scabbard. The telephone rang. He pointed a finger at her. "You get it."

"Hello. Yes, he's here." She held the receiver out to Hull, who was already halfway across the room.

"Mike? Yeah. Yeah, I'm still here . . . No, I know it takes time. Thanks. What have you got?" He listened intently, and after a minute gave a low whistle. "Sounds like it. Christ, what an asshole. Well, they've got a good handle on him, then; he's got to be our boy. Thanks." He hung up the phone, shaking his head.

"Did you find out something?"

"I think so. I can't believe anybody'd be that dumb, but I guess the world's full of 'em. Mike says the word out there is that a country boy named Jem Shale who grows pot up in Humboldt County has got himself in debt to the *yakuza.* If it were me, I'd just jump off a pier before I messed with the *yakuza,* but Humboldt County's pretty strange. It's a nasty place. Outsiders tend to get shot there, and cops only go in in teams of about fifty. Maybe this Shale just got too big for his britches and figured he could handle the *yakuza.* I don't know. Anyway, he made a big mistake. Word is that this Jem Shale has kin in Virginia and the *yakuza* have put the arm on him to help them with something that's going down out here. I don't know how much closer that gets us, but at least we've got a name."

Mary Rose cocked an eyebrow at him. "Drugs and moonshine," she said decidedly.

"Huh?"

"Moonshine. The liquid kind. This is bootlegging country. It always has been. But some of the old mountain families that used to make their living off liquor are running drugs now. There's more money in it. I expect that's what the Shales are doing if this Jem has been growing pot in California."

"How do *you* know all that?"

"For goodness sake, I grew up here."

Hull eyed her with respect. "You're a very surprising person."

"No, I'm not," Mary Rose said. "You can't live here and not know what goes on. And I thought those men who broke in here looked like they came out of the mountains. People up there get a certain look when they're too isolated. Too much in-breeding. My mother used to call it 'that pink-eyed look.' You know, washed-out and not quite healthy."

Hull studied her, trying to decide if she knew what she was talking about. He thought she probably did. "Well, at least we know who's after us. That may help. If we ever find the damn thing." He gave the sword on the coffee table a disgusted look. "I'd like to know who's putting the Shales through their paces, though. It'll be one of Sadao Akaishi's *ko-buns*—lieutenants—but Mike couldn't get a name. They keep a pretty low profile. Sadao Akaishi's a big *oya-bun,* a boss. He probably doesn't leave Japan, but he may have sent a top *ko-bun* from there when his people in California gave him the word."

"What do the *yakuza* do here?" Mary Rose asked him. "In this country, I mean?"

"Believe it or not, we aren't really sure," Hull said. "They set up shooting ranges sometimes. Guns aren't legal in Japan. This way they have trained shooters to send back over there. And we find evidence of their presence, you might say. There was a body that turned up in the Sierras that gave the department fits when they figured out what killed him. He turned out to be the loser in a duel. With swords. We caught the winner when he started sending money to the loser's parents."

"Good God."

"We could never prove *yakuza* involvement, but we were pretty sure. The loser was missing a finger. They cut off a finger sometimes to atone for mistakes. Maybe it wasn't enough. Or maybe he just stepped too hard on someone else's turf." Hull walked over to the window, leaned his hands on the sill and looked out at the street. "They aren't somebody I would have picked to mess with," he muttered. "I'd like to know who they've sent after us." He stared out the window as if trying to conjure up the shadowy face of the *yakuza* agent. Now that Mike Kawasaki had confirmed Hull's suspicions, Hull could practically feel the man out there, somewhere in those damned mountains. He didn't like the sensation.

Hidehiko Ota regarded Jem Shale and his brothers with immeasurable disgust. "You have made everything immensely more difficult," he said. Ota's English was accented but clear, and the Shales shifted uncomfortably from foot to foot in front of him. Ota sat on a camp stool and glared at them balefully from black eyes that were narrowed like a hawk's. He wore a pin-striped suit and his polished shoes reflected the last of the afternoon sunlight, but he was wiry and as tough as whip leather, as the Shales had already discovered. They looked back at him sullenly, their pale eyes reflecting the dislike that one vicious animal holds for another, stronger one.

"You were told to find the sword," Ota said. "You were not told to throw in fancy touches. I have no use for men who cannot follow orders."

"You jus' said to get the sword," Jem said. "You didn't say nothin' about how."

"I overestimated your intelligence!" Ota snapped. "It is not a mistake I will make again! If you had left Cullen alive he would have *led* you to the sword. Instead, you killed him, because you are cowards and thought that it would be easier to take the sword from the woman. Now no one knows where it is and we have this Philip Hull to deal with."

"Now you look here," Jem said. "No one calls me a coward."

"I have just done so," Ota pointed out. "I am paying you for the privilege."

"Then maybe you oughta jus' take your money an' clear out, Mr. Ota." Ben Shale ambled forward out of the shadow of the barn to Ota's left. He was in his fifties, of the same age as Ota, but tall and angular, with a weathered face and a hooked nose. "We got work to do here. Maybe we're through wastin' our time on your sword."

"It is not my sword," Ota said. "It is the sword of Sadao Akaishi, and it is very unwise to cross him. I thought that I had made that clear. Find me the sword and you will be well paid for it. Otherwise, we will take back the value of the money that your son has been so foolish as to steal from us—in whatever fashion seems suitable to us."

Ben Shale glowered at Jem. "Goddamn fool."

"Pa—"

"Shut up." Ben Shale studied Ota and considered. Jem had offered to supply one of those damn *yakuza* with a load of guns, and then had taken the money and put a load of bricks in the bottom of the box where a third of the guns should have been. When Jem had come yelping home with the *yakuza* on his tail, it was plain that he hadn't known what a wasps' nest he was sticking his head into. He did now, and Ota had been in their camp ever since, poking his nose into their lab and slinking around like a goddamn cat. He made Ben Shale nervous, aside from Ben's natural reluctance to have any outsider in his camp. "All right," Ben growled at Ota. "But this is the last time I get your ass out of a sling, boy," he informed Jem. "Next time I'll just let the bastards have you."

"Your family loyalty is commendable," Ota said. He stood up, sniffing the twilight breeze fastidiously. Their lab stank. "Keep watching Hull and the woman until they have found the sword. When they have, bring it to me. If you wish to kill someone then, I will not particularly care. I am going where the air does not smell like a cesspool, if such a place is to be found here."

Ota stalked away upwind of the lab to the ramshackle cabin that had been allotted to his use. Ben Shale's camp consisted of a weathered barn that served as garage and workshop; two cabins, one of which—Ota's—had until recently been used to store gasoline for a small airplane; and the lab, a long cinderblock box with four high windows. The camp was reached by an unobtrusive dirt road and screened by trees. The open space between the buildings was littered with rusting car parts and the leavings of a clan that rarely went to the trouble to throw anything away. Ota entered his cabin with distaste. It had been swept and cleaned, according, at any rate, to the Shales' definition of clean, but Ota brushed the seat of the single chair with his handkerchief before he sat down. He took a sheet of rice paper and a brush from his suitcase and uncapped a bottle of ink. He began to write with neat, precise brushstrokes, allowing the beauty of the characters to supersede the stink of the Shales and their drug lab, while he considered.

Ko-getsu-nami, the Moonshine Blade, *that* was what mattered. The sword of Akinji Kobayasu meant honor and power for Sadao Akaishi, and Ota had served the *yakuza* and Sadao Akaishi since he was fifteen, with the same fervent loyalty that monks gave to their temples. He was *yakuza*. There was no other life for him. To be entrusted with the sword was honor in itself. Thus there was no other center to his life but the sword until he brought it to Sadao Akaishi. Ota sat back to admire the poem he had composed to set his thoughts in order.

The circling hawk above the loft,
Seeing the cat bring out its mouse,
Eats both the hunter and its prey.

The Shales were worthless, stupid, but he was conspicuous here and they were not. Ota was a professional
soldier. He made use of what was at hand.

Mary Rose stuffed Godzilla back into his cage and entered his measurements on his chart. "Mama will be home
soon," she informed him. "You're a damn nuisance." She
watered the pots under the Gro-light and looked around
the lab, wondering if there could be any place in here that
they had missed. The lab had originally been the garage.
It had a concrete floor and walls. Surely not even Steven
at his most paranoid could have hidden anything here.
Mary Rose hung her lab coat on the hook over the door
that opened into the carport. What could he have *done*
with it? Buried it in the backyard? There was a new bed of
hybrid lilies which she had lovingly planted this spring.
Mary Rose wondered with some annoyance if she was
going to have to dig them up. It was a miracle that Philip
hadn't suggested it already. *I'm getting as crazy as he is*,
she thought distractedly.

The sword that Philip had found in the attic was still
lying on the coffee table, since both of them had been too
disgusted with it to put it away, and everytime she saw it,
she found herself mentally measuring it, thinking of places
where something that size would fit. She wondered if she
was beginning to appear a little wild-eyed. Certainly the
students in her afternoon lab had shown a tendency to
look at her sideways, but that could have been because by
now, thanks to the unstoppable campus grapevine, they
all knew she had That Man still staying with her.

David Hodges, looking earnest and embarrassed, had
come up to her after lab and, after much hemming and
hawing and staring at his feet, told her that if she ever
needed help with anything just to let him know. Help
with chores around the house, David had added hastily—he
thought she hadn't been looking well lately. David was

nineteen, just the right age to develop a crush on a young widowed teacher. Mary Rose was fairly certain that what David had meant was help with Philip Hull, who David apparently suspected of taking advantage of her in some sinister, unspecified way, judging by the look David had given him when he had met them walking across campus this morning. Mary Rose had thanked David gravely and assured him that she could manage.

Mary Rose pushed open the door into the kitchen, wondering where Philip was. He was supposed to be cooking tonight. She had discovered that he *could* cook, and had gratefully let him do so. As she stepped through into the kitchen, she froze, her heart thudding under her ribs. There was someone in the living room, and she knew with certainty that it wasn't Philip. Suddenly a wave of pure fury washed over her. How dare those thugs come in her *house*? She picked up a bread knife out of the knife block on the kitchen counter. The shadowy form in the living room straightened up, startled eyes meeting hers. The sword that had been on the coffee table was tucked under his arm.

"Put it *down*!" Mary Rose screamed at him. "Get out of my *house*!"

Jem Shale backed toward the front door. Mary Rose advanced on him purposefully. A wild peal of bells came suddenly through the open windows—the chapel carillon announcing Wednesday evening services. Startled, Jem spun toward the door as the sound rang and clattered through the house. The sword slipped from under his arm.

Mary Rose came toward him. The look on her face and the bread knife in her hand refocused Jem's attention on her. "Get away from me!" he warned her.

"Get out!" she screamed at him again.

Jem snatched a gun from under his jacket and fired. He caught up the sword and ran, out into the wild pealing of the bells.

Philip Hull, climbing out of the Chevy with an armload of groceries, heard the shot that cracked across the clamor of the bells and saw Jem Shale running from the house. Hull dropped the bags on the concrete. He let Jem go and sprinted for the door into the lab, which was the closest.

"*Mary Rose!*" The door into the kitchen stood open, and Hull burst through it, screaming her name.

Mary Rose was slumped against the living room wall, staring at a bullet hole in the wallpaper a foot away from her. Hull grabbed Mary Rose and pulled her to him, oblivious to the bread knife in her hand. His arms were shaking. "Oh, Jesus, I'm sorry," he said into her hair. "I never should have left that sword out. I should have known they'd think— Are you all right?"

Mary Rose nodded, her face against his chest. He didn't let go of her, and she didn't move. "They took it," she said. Her voice was tight with anger. "God damn them, they took it."

Hull hugged her tighter. "It's all right," he said soothingly; then he felt the bread knife. "Jesus Christ, what's that?" He stepped back and looked at the knife.

Mary Rose looked up at him. "I got mad."

Hull snatched the knife out of her hand. "You mean you went after him with *this*? You idiot woman, that sword wasn't worth anything, not even a hundred bucks."

"It was *mine*," Mary Rose said.

Hull went into the kitchen and put the bread knife back in its block. "It wasn't worth getting shot for!" he turned and shouted at her. His face looked gray.

"I didn't think about that," Mary Rose said. "Stop yelling at me."

"I'm not yelling at you!" he shouted. "I thought that bastard had killed you." He lowered his voice and glared at her. "That's a fine thing to have on my conscience," he muttered.

Mary Rose followed him into the kitchen and sat down on the step stool. Her knees were shaking.

Hull looked down at her. "I can't figure you out," he growled. "I can't even figure out why Steven married you, but he must have had rocks in his head."

Now that her fury had worn off, Mary Rose thought

about Steven and felt forlorn. "He said I was restful," she said, sniffling.

Hull's mouth began to twitch. As Mary Rose glowered at him, he sat down on the floor beside her and started to laugh. After a minute he reached up and put an arm around her. "Don't do that again, okay?"

5.
No Bed of Roses

"This does it." Mary Rose poked a forefinger at Hull's chest. "You're coming with me and explain your *yakuza* to the county sheriff. Or the State Police, I don't care. But someone."

"Look, I thought we settled that," Hull protested.

"We *need* the police," Mary Rose said. "We could get killed."

"Yeah, sure, they'll just be charmed to know we want to be protected from somebody we can't even name."

"We can name the Shales," Mary Rose said.

"On pretty dubious grounds. Look, I know cops. I *am* a cop. If I actually get shot, they might sit up and take notice, but until then—"

"Well, *I* got shot. Shot at, anyway, in case you're forgetting you were almost fainting at the thought a minute ago," Mary Rose said indignantly.

"We can't prove it was the Shales," Hull said. "Not this time or the last. You're just gonna look silly."

"Not half as silly as you'll look explaining my dead body to the rest of the faculty. You just don't want to tell anybody about that sword."

Hull looked at the stubborn set to her mouth and decided that he'd better pacify her. But the county cops

71

weren't going to listen, he thought gloomily. It all sounded pretty farfetched to him too.

The next morning Mary Rose appeared at breakfast still determined, and announced that she had canceled her eight o'clock class for pressing personal business. Hull eyed her respectfully. She was obviously dressed for war. The blue jeans and country-girl khaki skirts were gone. She wore a blue silk dress, a pearl necklace, and blue kid shoes with heels. There were pearl buttons in her ears, and she had on makeup—lipstick and some kind of eyeshadow that made her round blue eyes look even larger under a dark fringe of lashes. A faint whiff of lilac perfume drifted past him as she strode purposefully toward the coffeepot.

"Going to charm the force into a little protection?" he inquired genially.

Mary Rose gave him a dignified look and ignored this sally, but she noted that he had on a coat and tie himself. "I'm trying to look businesslike," she said. Her heels clicked on the floor as she brought her coffee to the table. She caught sight of herself in the mirror over the sideboard and appeared to waver. "Don't I look all right?"

Hull smiled at her. "You look fine." He sighed and moodily poked a spoon around in his coffee. "But they aren't gonna listen to us."

This litany was repeated as they drove into Sarum, which was the county seat. They pulled up in front of the county sheriff's office, a small boxlike building of the same red brick that everything was made of here. All the small towns were painted from the same palette, Hull thought: red brick and white clapboard and the gray of tin roofs and weathered wood. Even the dirt was red, the clay color of the bricks they made out of it.

Inside, a uniformed woman who seemed to be the entire staff at the moment sat listlessly typing. She looked up with interest as Hull and Mary Rose appeared. Asked for the man in charge, she buzzed an office whose door opened to their right. It was inscribed in tarnishing gilt letters, LT. SAWYER. Lieutenant Sawyer, she informed them, would be happy to see them.

"No, he won't," Hull growled.

Happy or not, Lieutenant Sawyer graciously waved them to a pair of vinyl-cushioned chairs opposite his desk and folded his hands on his desktop. He was a pleasant-faced man in his thirties with sandy hair and a neatly starched uniform. He had a sunburned face, ears that stuck out a little, and gray eyes that reflected a shrewd intelligence. He greeted Hull politely and Mary Rose with gallant deference.

"Now what can I do for you folks?"

"It's awfully nice of you to see us without an appointment, Lieutenant," Mary Rose said before Hull could get them off on the wrong foot. Californians, like Yankees, seemed to want to get to the point right away, without passing the time of day first, and Southerners, especially country Southerners, were insulted by it.

"No trouble at all, ma'am," Sawyer said. "The sergeant's called in sick today—he really runs the place. But I'll be glad to take care of you. Where are y'all from? California?"

"Oh, no." Mary Rose noted the direction of Sawyer's glance. The Chevy with its California plates was parked outside the window. "We're from the college, or at least I am. That was my late husband's car."

"Oh, yeah, I remember." Sawyer's face was sympathetic. "You doin' all right now, Mrs. Cullen? No trouble up at the college, I hope."

"Get to the point," Hull suggested.

"Well, I am," Mary Rose said. She gave the lieutenant her most confiding expression and began to explain. As she got to the *yakuza*, she was uncomfortably aware that Lieutenant Sawyer's expression was fading from benign helpfulness into skepticism.

"And where do you come into this?" The lieutenant looked at Hull.

Hull presented his credentials and Sawyer inspected them with an experienced eye. Hull gave him a brief background on the *yakuza* and such information as he had gleaned from Mike Kawasaki in San Francisco. Sawyer leaned back in his chair and laced his fingers together. The glance he gave Hull was eloquent.

"Well, Sergeant Hull, I don't want to question your reasoning here, but we went over Mr. Cullen's accident pretty thoroughly. And it seems to me that a man who'd burned out on his job might just want to steer clear of a car he associated with that job, so I'm afraid I can't see eye to eye with you on the significance of that rental vehicle. As for your Jap gangsters and that sword that nobody seems to be able to lay their hands on . . ." Sawyer's expression said plainly what he thought, and what the sheriff was going to think about an out-of-state cop barging in and stirring up dust with nothing to go on but rumors out of California. "I'm just a hick lieutenant"—Hull decided that Sawyer was no hick—"but if there was a Japanese running around these mountains shooting people, I can promise you I'd have noticed him. You actually see this guy?"

"No," Hull said shortly.

Sawyer looked at Mary Rose. "Ma'am, I'm awfully sorry you're having all this trouble." He plainly felt that her troubles included Philip Hull. "And I'm mighty sorry about your break-in. I'll be glad to send a man up to take a look around, but you got to report these things right away to give us much chance of catchin' an intruder. You want me to send one of the boys up? Be happy to anyway."

"Don't bother," Hull growled.

"What I want—what *we* want," Mary Rose said as Hull and the lieutenant eyed each other balefully across the lieutenant's desk, "is to keep it from happening again."

"Ma'am, I don't see how to do that," the lieutenant said patiently, "not when we don't know who they are. Not conclusively," he added as Hull opened his mouth. "Ma'am, Sergeant Hull oughta know he hasn't given me enough evidence even to go lookin' for somebody named Shale, much less to back up a warrant."

"You find 'em," Hull said, "and I'll identify 'em."

Sawyer smiled. "Sergeant Hull, you ever been up in those mountains? *If* these folks are what you say, which I'm afraid I'm just not convinced of, they've had nearly twenty-four hours to go to ground. I couldn't find 'em with dogs. Now, ma'am, I'm mighty sorry about this, but there's just not much I can do for you." He smiled. "Except maybe recommend you not read thrillers at night."

Mary Rose stood up. "Thank you, Lieutenant."

Sawyer escorted her to the door. "Now if you have any more trouble, you just call me right away. I'll be happy to come right over."

"All right," Hull said as he slid behind the wheel. "I'm waiting."

"For what?" Mary Rose said.

"Probably for hell to freeze over," Hull said. He put the Chevy into gear. "You're too pigheaded to say I was right."

"You were right," Mary Rose said.

Hull raised his eyebrows. "Did I hear you clearly?"

"You heard me. I felt like the most awful fool in there. 'Don't read thrillers.' He must have thought I was a moron."

"Don't blame Sawyer," Hull said. "I wouldn't have believed our story either, if I'd been him. Especially with some out-of-state cop muscling in and telling me I'd overlooked a murder."

"Then why couldn't you have been polite to him?" Mary Rose said, exasperated. "It might have helped."

"It wouldn't," Hull said. He was still smarting from having sat there in Sawyer's office looking like a horse's ass while Mary Rose batted her mascaraed lashes at Sawyer and Sawyer practically patted her on the head. "You were polite enough for two." Hull dodged the Chevy around a woodchuck that was sitting in the road, and turned the car toward the college. "I told you so," he announced gloomily.

"I got it." Jem Shale dumped the sword across Hidehiko Ota's knees. Jem rocked back on his heels, thumbs stuck in his belt loops, grinning. "I damn near had to shoot me that woman—she come after me with a bread knife. But I got it." Jem felt good. The weight of the *yakuza*'s relentless harrying had been lifted with the presentation of the sword to Ota. And the fear and anger that his encounter with Mary Rose had aroused had faded, leaving him convinced that no stupid woman was a match for Jem Shale. His thin, pale face was pleased with itself and cocky.

The other Shales gathered around, punching Jem in the arm and slapping him on the back. "Shit, didn't we tell you he'd get it?" they inquired of Ota.

Ota, seated on his camp stool, ignored them. He slid the blade reverently from its sheath and wrapped a handkerchief around his fingers to hold it to the light. His masklike expression broke into sudden fury.

The Shales took a step backward and then stood their ground, dogged and angry with Ota for the reaction he had forced from them.

"You are fools." Ota remained seated, his eyes narrowed at them, his voice never rising, as he told them in detail what fools they were. He could feel their fear of him, and he had fostered it carefully. It was all that kept them from killing him. They were too stupid, he thought with disgust, to understand what the *yakuza* would come and do to them afterward if they did. It was a stupidity that made them dangerous, but also manageable. It was a very fine line he was walking just now.

"Wait here." Ota stalked to his cabin without looking back to see that they obeyed him. Behind him the Shales stuck their hands into their pockets and muttered after him.

"We oughta shoot us that sumbitch."

"I don' let nobody talk like that to me."

"Shut up, all o' you," Ben Shale growled. His enterprise was strictly a family affair. He had his sister's boy Sulie and three sons of his own, counting Jem, in the camp with him. "You ain't gonna shoot nobody less I tell you to. We get him that sword an' get us the money he's willin' to pay for it, then I'll think about it."

Ota came back with a polished wooden box, from which he took a small brass hammer of the same sort that Philip Hull had used, and methodically began to take the sword apart. "The blade I want is shaped in this fashion," he began, and described it from tip to tang, in English and in Japanese.

The Shales stared at him, uncomprehending.

"Sounds 'bout like that sword there," Ben Shale ventured. " 'Bout the right length, ain't it? You sure that ain't it?"

"You are as stupid as that woman!" Ota spat at him. "You have been told, and shown, and you still cannot see. Are you *blind*?" He made an exasperated movement with his hands. "Watch them closely. Not the woman only, but this Philip Hull who is with her. He will know the sword when he finds it." Ota stared at Jem. "And he will not be such a fool as to leave it lying on a table for you." Ota gritted his teeth, staring into the gathering dusk. Philip Hull would know *Ko-getsu-nami*, Ota thought. Philip Hull would know the Moonshine Blade as he knew his own face in the mirror, as Ota did. Philip Hull and Ota and no one else.

"Philip, do we have to? I just planted those." Mary Rose looked at her lily bed with dismay.

"I wouldn't put anything past Steven right now," Hull said.

Mary Rose sighed. "All right." She disappeared into her lab and returned with a pair of pink-flowered gardening gloves and a trowel.

"Christ, haven't you got a shovel?" Hull demanded.

"Well, I don't want to damage them."

"You can't dig up a twelve-foot flower bed with a spoon. Where's your shovel?"

Mary Rose pointed back toward the lab. Hull fetched the shovel. He set his foot on it and began to dig, while Mary Rose snatched the clumps of newly sprouted lilies and tried to repack the earth around them.

"How deep did you spade this up?" Hull said.

"Only about a foot."

Hull nodded and dumped another shovelful in her lap. "But you left the bed overnight before you planted these things. He could have dug a little deeper and put the sword in, and you'd never have noticed."

Mary Rose wiped dirt out of her hair with the back of her glove, leaving a streak across her forehead, and glared at him balefully. "If he went at it the way you are, I'd have noticed," she assured him.

"Sorry." Hull brought the next clump out more gently and deposited it at her feet.

"*Why* would he put it in a flower bed? With all the other places to hide it, why put it where he'd have to dig up a flower bed to get at it?"

"It's the sort of thing that would occur to him, that's all. Except for his work, Steven did damn near everything on impulse. Same way he fell in love with women." Hull looked at her. "Ah, shit. I didn't mean to say that. I'm sorry."

"It's all right," Mary Rose said wearily. "I *was* beginning to wonder. Did he fall in love a lot?"

"In and out," Hull said. "It was always a grand passion while it lasted. But they weren't women like you," he added, trying to sound comforting. "I mean, they were—"

"Tarts?" Mary Rose suggested acidly.

"No, not exactly." Hull leaned on his shovel and grinned reminiscently. "Leggy and blond, usually, and smart, some of them, but well, lightweight, not permanent." He looked at her kindly. "You're different enough that I suspect he really *was* in love this time. Permanent-type, I mean."

Mary Rose put the lilies down. She drew her knees up and wrapped her arms around them. She put her chin on her knees and looked broodingly into the lily bed while Hull, embarrassed, went back to his digging. *Would* Steven have stayed in love with her? She didn't think she wanted to bet on it now. And what about herself? As she knew him better, and his mania for hiding things and the scars left on him by his job became more evident, would *she* have stayed in love? Dear God, what a mess.

"Well, they aren't going to get away with it," she said abruptly.

"Huh?" Hull looked up from his excavations.

"He was my husband, and those bastards killed him. Poor Steven, he had enough wrong with his life. They aren't going to get away with it, whatever that Lieutenant Sawyer thinks."

"Atta girl." Hull gave her a look of approval that was faintly startled. Something sure as hell had come over her in the last couple of weeks. He looked at her brooding face with the dark cloud of hair around it and her blue eyes shadowed by a sweep of black lashes. Somehow she didn't look so innocent to him anymore. "You're different," he said quietly. "What is it?"

Mary Rose sat up and began packing her lilies into a box full of wet newspaper. "There's nothing like finding out your husband was mentally unstable, and probably murdered by the mob, to change your outlook on life," she snapped.

Hull gave her a rueful look. "I suppose that was a dumb question. There's more of this flower bed than there looks like, isn't there?" It was warm for an April day, and his hair was plastered to his forehead with sweat. He stood the shovel up in the turned earth and peeled his shirt off.

Mary Rose watched him out of the corner of her eye. His chest and back were tanned and muscular, with a couple of old scars crisscrossing each other just below the breastbone. Her expression softened. In some ways he was blessedly uncomplicated. Any scars that Philip Hull had got from his work were literal, not dark patches in his mind.

Hull inspected his palms. "I have blisters."

"Here, I'll take a turn." Mary Rose waggled the pink-flowered gloves at him. "That's what these are for." She put her foot on the shovel. Beyond the split-rail fence that separated her yard from the one next door, she could see Bill McGinnis settled on his patio with his evening martini, regarding them with interest.

"I think the old party next door thinks we're burying a body," Hull muttered.

"I wouldn't doubt it." Mary Rose unearthed another clump of lilies while Hull obediently packed them in wet paper. "The college hasn't had so much to talk about in years."

Hull looked up at her. "Am I making you a scandal?"

"Probably. But with half the student body doing heaven knows what in coed dorms these days, it isn't nearly the scandal it used to be, so don't worry about it. My students seem to find it rather dashing."

Hull put his head in his hands. "Oh, Lord."

"And the faculty 'simply don't know what's come over me,'" Mary Rose went on relentlessly. "That's a quote from Louise Evans. *She* thinks you're dangerous."

"Dangerous to what, for Christ's sake?"

"Oh, don't mind Louise. She just doesn't like men. She holds them all personally responsible for women being oppressed."

"I'm liberated enough to let you dig."

"Louise doesn't make distinctions. Men are men. Haven't you noticed that the people who are the most dedicated to a good cause are the ones with the least sense of perspective?"

"What are you dedicated to?"

"Getting my lilies back in the ground before they die," Mary Rose said. "I developed this strain myself. They're pets."

Hull sat back and watched her dig. The late afternoon sun filtered through the white flowers of the dogwood and cast a gold glow around her dark hair. Mary Rose's garden was lush and damply scented with the smell of lilac and new grass. The cat MacArthur came around the side of the house to see what was up, and sat beside Hull. A bird skimmed across the lawn in a flash of brown and white and lit in the dogwood. It cocked an eye at MacArthur and meeowed at him.

"That's a mockingbird," Mary Rose said. "I think they do it to be funny." MacArthur flicked an ear at the bird and turned away with immense dignity.

Mary Rose dug up the last of the lilies and gave the shovel back to Hull. "It had better be in there," she informed him. "I'm going to go start dinner. I have a faculty meeting at nine."

Half an hour later she came out the back door to find the lilies neatly replanted and Hull washing his hands with the hose.

"Did you find anything?"

"Cat shit," Hull said. MacArthur gave him a look through half-closed eyes. Hull leaned the shovel against the wall. "I'm going to take a shower and sulk," he announced.

*   *   *

Bill McGinnis fell into step beside Mary Rose as they left the faculty meeting, plowing their way through their fellow professors, most of whom were still arguing. "Don't know why they want to conduct a post mortem," McGinnis said. "Nothing's new. The college wants us to volunteer for a lot of unpaid extras—and I draw the line at chaperoning their blasted May Day dance. With the license allowed to students these days I don't know what they think the chaperones are *for*."

"Probably to keep them from doing it on the dance floor," Mary Rose murmured.

"No doubt. And as for the department budget requests, I could have told you how those would come out without leaving home—nobody's getting what they wanted, and the English Department is getting less than anybody."

"You'll give yourself an ulcer," Mary Rose said. "I thought you didn't want to do a post mortem."

"You wouldn't know whether I was or not," McGinnis said. "You couldn't tell me one word that went on in there if you had to. You looked like one of those whatchamacallems that are supposed to go floating off into space and leave their bodies behind."

"Astral projection." Mary Rose chuckled. "I had things on my mind."

"That's what I mean," McGinnis said. "I know Steven's death was tough on you, but you seemed all right. Then ever since this Hull character started staying with you, you haven't had your mind on your work."

No, it's been on Japanese gangsters and whether my husband was crazy or not. She couldn't tell Bill that. "Why is everyone around here so interested in Philip Hull?" Mary Rose said. She could at least defend her privacy.

"He's an unknown quantity," McGinnis said. "In a place like this, the unknown quantity is always viewed as dangerous."

"Oh, for heaven's sake."

"We knew where we were with Steven. He was part of our world, whatever he'd been doing before. Hull's different. And nobody's sure why he's still here. Those of us

who care about you"—he gave her an avuncular glance—
"are naturally concerned."

"And speculating like mad," Mary Rose said dryly. "I'd
take it as a favor if the faculty would kindly stop trying to
figure things out when there's nothing to figure."

"You've been teaching long enough to know that the
gossip factor in an academic community is unsuppressable,"
McGinnis said. "If you want to stop the speculation, you'll
have to bring him around some—make social chitchat
and look ordinary and boring. There's that idiot Will. I'm
going to go tell him I absolutely will not stand around like
a gorgon at his blasted dance."

He departed in pursuit of the dean of students before
Mary Rose could answer. She turned moodily toward Faculty Row and let her mind drift back to the problem of
where Steven could have hidden the sword, which it had
been doing all through the faculty meeting. They had
exhausted all the possibilities that she could think of. The
next step would have to be the public buildings or somewhere in the fields. Maybe the library, if they could figure
out what would be a likely place. She walked along the
colonnade, wrestling with the architecture of the library,
and was nearly knocked flat by a hurrying student as he
came down the steps from the road above.

"Excuse me!" It was David Hodges, his round face
creased into a frown. "I'm awfully sorry. Dr. Cullen!" The
frown turned to embarrassment. "Oh, Lord! I *am* sorry.
Here, let me help you." He retrieved her briefcase from a
hedge and put it back in her hands. "Did I hurt you? I
didn't mean to be such an ass, charging along like that,
but I was looking for you." He waved the book he was
carrying. "I took this up to your house." His face red-
dened. "Just to thank you for lending it to me. But you
weren't there." His voice sounded a little aggrieved.

"You could have left it with Mr. Hull."

"Yeah, but he *said* he didn't know when you'd be back."
David's blue eyes flashed angrily. "I wanted to give it to
you in person, you've been so awfully nice to me, but he
. . . well, he wouldn't let me in and . . ." His sentence

slithered to a halt, and he stood looking at her, stubborn and embarrassed.

"That's all right, David. Thank you." Mary Rose held out her hand for the book.

"Yeah." David handed it to her. He stood indecisively in the dim light of the colonnade. "Well, he was just making himself at home," he blurted. "He made me so mad. He didn't even have clothes on."

Mary Rose blinked at him. "None?"

David's face flushed. "No, I didn't mean he was . . . well, he had on a bathrobe. He shouldn't be answering your door in a bathrobe," he said angrily. "All the kids think it's so damn funny, but I don't, and . . ." He paused, apparently gathering courage, and put a hand on hers. He was a good six inches taller than she was. "Dr. Cullen, if you need a man around—to help with things, I mean— couldn't you let me . . . I mean, you know how I feel about you—"

"David—" Mary Rose said warningly.

"Dr. Cullen—" He grasped her other hand. "Mary Rose— you must know how I feel. I'm not that much younger and—" Mary Rose tried to pull her hands away, and he leaned closer. "Mary Rose—" He tried to kiss her and succeeded in banging his chin on the top of her head. Mary Rose stamped her heel down on his instep and he yelped and let go of her hands.

She took a step backward and put her briefcase between them. "I think you'd better go home, and we'll just pretend this didn't happen."

"Oh, hell." David rubbed his foot, passion and humiliation plainly warring with each other for possession of his emotions. "I suppose you think I'm too young," he said miserably.

"You are a bit," Mary Rose agreed.

"If you'd just let me show you—"

"You've shown me quite enough," Mary Rose said. "David, go home. I never date students," she added with as much kindness as she could muster.

David scowled at her. "I suppose I look like a fool. I'm

sorry I bothered you. I wouldn't have if *he* hadn't poked fun at me!" He fled in the direction of the dorms.

Mary Rose fled herself, up Faculty Row, hoping no one had seen them. Neither she nor that poor boy would ever hear the end of it if they had. In her living room she found Philip Hull stretched out on the sofa in a silk kimono, with his bare feet propped on a cushion and a crossword puzzle in his lap. His expression was truculent.

"What did you say to my student?" Mary Rose demanded.

Hull looked up. "Oh, you ran into him, did you? What's a word for underground temple in nine letters?"

"Mithraeum," Mary Rose said. "What did you say to him?"

Hull whistled. "Damned if you aren't right." He filled in the spaces.

"Philip!"

"I said I didn't know when you'd be back."

"That's all?"

"He asked me what I was doing here, so I told him it was none of his business. He got kind of shirty about it. He seems to have a crush on you," Hull observed.

"What *else* did you say to him?"

Hull made a face. "I suggested he find someone his own age. That was when he offered to punch my nose in."

"Oh, good God. You didn't—"

"What do I look like? I told him if he tried it, I'd take him by the ears and turn him inside out. Then he went home."

Mary Rose sat down. "Oh, fine. Very subtle."

"I wasn't feeling subtle," Hull growled. "Do you always carry on with undergraduates?"

"I'm not carrying on with anybody, if that's any of your business, which it's not. And certainly not with nineteen-year-olds. But you didn't have to pick a fight with him."

"*I* didn't pick the fight."

"Certainly not. You were a perfect gentleman. You offered to turn him inside out. So he salved his pride by declaring his passion for me in the colonnade just now."

Hull hooted with laughter.

"It wasn't particularly funny." Mary Rose gave him a much-tried look. "I have enough to cope with."

Hull looked repentant. His mood was beginning to improve, although he was strangely reluctant to consider closely why Mary Rose's lovestruck student had irritated him so thoroughly. "All right," he said, "I'll try to be respectable."

"You can chaperone a May Day dance with me," Mary Rose said. "It's hard to get more respectable than that."

She thought at first that he was going to balk, but he just raised his eyebrows at her. The day before the dance he drove dutifully into Lexington and rented a tuxedo, every garment in the local shop in Sarum having been reserved weeks before. He left Mary Rose with instructions to cajole the maintenance department out of a flashlight strong enough to show up any discoloration in the basement floor.

"I suppose he could have knocked out a chunk of the concrete," Hull said, spread-eagled on the floor, shining the light into a murky corner. "It's the only idea I've had lately." They had drawn a blank in the library; in the science building, where Mary Rose held her laboratory classes; and in the barns, where Hull had been stepped on by a Clydesdale.

"What about a safe deposit box? Are they big enough?"

"Some of them, but you would have found the key by now. And if he'd had it on him, the *yakuza* would have found it and wouldn't still be chasing us, which they are." He straightened up and his eye caught a flicker of movement outside the basement window, which opened onto the back lawn. "Get lost!" he shouted. There was a faint stirring in the aqueous shadows under the dogwood tree, and then silence.

Mary Rose fidgeted in the gloom of the basement while Hull played the light over the ceiling for good measure. "I hate this feeling of being watched," she whispered.

"I'm not fond of it." Hull flicked the light off. "Go get dressed. We'll take care of your collegiate duty at this dance, and maybe we'll think of something."

Mary Rose closed the bathroom curtains and pinned

them together before she sank into the tub. The sensation of having her every movement observed was making her edgy. She felt the Shales' eyes on her every day, even in bed in a darkened room. She scrubbed the basement grime off her hands and face and hoped the Shales got thoroughly sick and tired of sitting outside the Hot Springs Hotel all night.

Bathed, she wrapped a robe around her and padded into the bedroom. From the other bathroom she could hear Hull's voice cheerfully raised in song. Singing-in-the-shower music: snatches of old Kingston Trio songs, and the Captain's song from *Pinafore*. Mary Rose slipped her evening dress over her head and looked dispiritedly into the mirror. It looked, she thought, as if her mother had picked it out. It had a prim little eyelet bodice, and a bow in the back. After a moment's indecision, she peeled it off again and put on the dress she had bought to be married in. It was a deep marine-blue taffeta, with short accordion-pleated sleeves that dropped slightly off the shoulders, and a flounce of the same pleats that swept up the skirt from her toes in the front to the hip line in the back. It was a rakish-looking dress, dashing and a little flighty. Philip Hull, coming down the hall with a handful of shirt studs, found her considering herself in the mirror, and whistled admiringly.

"That's your wedding dress, isn't it?"

"Yes. I'm just wondering if people will think I ought to wear it."

"The hell with 'em. You look great." Hull, who seemed to have got stuck on the score of *Pinafore*, struck a pose.

"A maiden fair to see, the pearl of minstrelsy,
* A bud of blushing beauty,*
* For whom proud nobles sigh, and with each other vie*
* To do her menial's duty!"*

Mary Rose giggled, and sang back at him:

"Refrain, audacious tar, your suit from pressing!
* Remember who you are, and whom addressing."*

"Hey, that's great. Are you a Gilbert and Sullivan fan?"

"Absolutely." She took the studs out of his hand and began putting them in his shirt for him. "We're going to hate the music at this dance, but that's the traditional function of chaperones, to stand around and say how much better the music was in their day."

"I'm not as old as Gilbert and Sullivan," Hull protested.

"If you can remember the Kingston Trio, that's old enough. Most of these little devils won't even have heard of them."

"Where do you come in?" She would have been in high school in the early seventies, he thought.

"I'm a throwback." She put the last stud in and straightened his tie for him. "There, I think we look elegant."

They admired themselves in the mirror for a minute. "I haven't worn a tuxedo since my brother got married," Hull said.

Mary Rose looked up at him. He did look good. Tall and elegant, in a solid, muscular sort of way. "It pains me to admit it," she told him, "but you're a prince of a fellow to do this. I hope you don't die of boredom."

"I thought that was the general idea," Hull murmured.

When they got to the hotel, however, he seemed to Mary Rose to be having a fine time. He said good evening to David Hodges with a formal politeness that did much to soothe that young gentleman's ruffled feelings, discussed the Washington Redskins and the situation in Libya with Lee Bowling, the president, and Peter Ogilvie, the dean, and chatted affably with their wives. Mary Rose noted that he had unaccountably adopted the Southern habit of saying "ma'am" to any woman senior to himself, and that it did not sound forced, but on the contrary, as if he had been born with it. How many times had he slipped on another skin with the facility he was showing tonight? she wondered.

When the band changed to a slow dance and the gyrating bodies on the floor took a breather, Hull held out his hand to her. He guided her expertly around the student couples who, their feet barely moving, were now clinging to each other like drowning victims to their rescuers, and spun her in graceful circles in the center of the floor.

"You're very unexpected," she commented.

Hull looked down at her. "Just because I chase dope dealers for a living doesn't mean I live like one. I, too, had a mother who made me go to dancing class."

Mary Rose chuckled. The music ended, and they found Anne and Peter Ogilvie beside them. "Goodness, it's nice to see someone who can dance," Anne said. "I wonder if these children know any steps at all between uninhibited frenzy and passionate embrace."

Hull laughed. "Oh, I danced like them when I was in college. At that age you don't pass up a chance to get a good grip on a girl."

"There's champagne punch at the bar," Anne said. "If you want something stronger, Lee Bowling seems to have a private stock of bourbon on the veranda. Just follow the trail of paper cups."

Peter Ogilvie grinned. "A privilege of age and rank is not to have to drink champagne punch. Just follow me."

They sat on the hotel veranda under a full moon and drank the president's Virginia Gentleman out of Dixie cups. The Hot Springs Hotel was a turn-of-the-century building, with white columns and wisteria. The veranda had a flagstone floor and white wrought iron benches, and the music from the dance floor was blessedly muted. Most of the chaperones seemed inclined to join them, lured partly, Hull suspected, by the president's flask, and partly by the chance to give Hull the once-over. Hull, who didn't care for being inspected any more than the next man, thought briefly of giving them something to worry about, but decided that Mary Rose had enough to try her. Frances Cady, the dean's secretary, sat down on his other side and questioned him with cheerful determination about his travel plans. Even Frances seemed to feel that Hull had been comforting Steven's widow for an unusually long time.

Hull was uncomfortably aware of Mary Rose's presence beside him. In her slim, elegant taffeta, she looked like a John Singer Sargent painting, and she smelled of expensive perfume. He was no longer wondering why Steven had married her, but only how he himself was going to get out of Virginia in one piece. He knew it was a mistake to go on staying in her house—just about the most dumb-ass thing he had ever done, when he was starting to lie awake at night imagining her in bed beside him—but he couldn't see any way around it, not with the Shales prowling around.

Hull sipped his bourbon moodily, listening to Frances Cady with half an ear and dodging her questions. There was no place for him in a place like this, and he knew Mary Rose well enough by now to know that there was no place for her in California, not in the life he led. And if ever there was a woman who wasn't cut out for a one-night stand, it was the one sitting beside him.

Frances, balked of any information, drifted off, leaving Hull and Mary Rose alone in the shadow of the wisteria. "Come on," Hull said abruptly. "Let's dance."

When the dance ended at two A.M., they drove home, following the little parade of faculty cars up the road toward Faculty Row and the president's house. The campus was eerily deserted—most of the students were probably going off somewhere to neck—and Hull cut the engine a hundred yards from her driveway and let the Chevy drift silently into the carport. He felt for the holster around his ankle, and the moonlight gleamed faintly on the snub nose of his gun.

"Good Lord, have you been wearing that all evening? Who do you think you are, James Bond?"

"I think I'm careful." He motioned for her not to get out, and switched off the interior light so it wouldn't go on when he opened the door. He slipped past Mary Rose's Datsun and through the door that opened into her lab.

Mary Rose crouched apprehensively in the darkened car and waited for him to come back. Hull's caution was an unpleasant reminder of their situation, which she had managed to forget about for most of the evening. For a long while there was no movement in the house. No lights came on. She was beginning to panic when the front door opened and Hull appeared, sticking the gun in his tuxedo pocket. He flicked the porch light on and bent to pick up something from the doorsill.

It was a piece of paper. He stood looking at it for so long

that Mary Rose got out of the car and came to peer past his shoulder at it. The characters were meaningless to her, stylized calligraphic squiggles that she recognized as Japanese and nothing more.

"What is it?" she whispered.

"It's a . . . suggestion," Hull said. "That we find the Moonshine Blade and leave it where it can be taken unobtrusively. If we do that, he'll guarantee our safety."

"He? Who's he?"

"*Yakuza*," Hull said quietly.

"Does he say so?"

Hull shook his head. "No more than he needs a name. He knew I'd know."

"Find the sword and hand it over and he'll guarantee our safety!" Mary Rose said indignantly. "He's got a nerve."

"It's not that nicely put," Hull said. "Look, I'm not making a pass or anything, but leave your bedroom door open tonight. I want to be able to get to you in a hurry if I have to."

6.
Tennessee Waltz

Mary Rose sat up in bed and looked dispiritedly at the light streaming through the window. She might as well get up. She obviously wasn't going to sleep anymore. She had slept only in patches all night, trying without much success not to translate every noise outside her window into the footsteps of the *yakuza*, and uncomfortably conscious of the fact that all she had to do was yell and Philip would come and keep her company. She wondered if that thought had kept her awake as much as the *yakuza*, but when she wrapped a robe around her and padded into the kitchen, she was immensely grateful to find him there, pottering among the dirty dishes and concocting a breakfast of scrambled eggs and toast.

"Get any sleep?" he inquired. He probably knew she hadn't.

"Not a lot." Mary Rose began putting last night's dinner dishes in the dishwasher.

"Here, I'm not through with that." Hull retrieved a spatula as it disappeared into the dishwasher. "And those are clean plates over there. Leave them alone. You're the tidiest damned woman I ever saw. I bet you clean up half-full coffee cups and empty ashtrays people are using."

"I just hate looking at yesterday's food." Mary Rose dumped his eggshells into the trash and leaned across him

91

to retrieve a dirty fork. "I meant to do this last night, but I ran out of time "

Hull watched her with amused exasperation. If he went off and left her, she'd probably try to tidy up the *yakuza* and get killed for her pains. He handed her a plate. "Quit washing things and eat your eggs."

Mary Rose took her plate to the dining room table and propped the Sunday comic section up in front of it.

Hull looked over her shoulder. "I bet you read them all, even the ones you don't like."

"It's kind of a compulsion. Don't you?"

Hull chuckled. "Yeah, but I usually won't admit it." He sat down across from her and reached for the local news, but his eyes strayed from the newspaper to the window. "We've got to find that thing," he muttered, "before they get sick of waiting and start looking too."

Mary Rose looked at him soberly across the comics. "What do we do when we've found it? How are we going to get out of here with it?"

"I'm working on that," Hull said. "I'll figure something out." He was damned if he knew what.

"You aren't very reassuring."

"Let's just find it first."

Mary Rose decided she could resist the compulsion to read Judge Parker this morning. The Judge wasn't having nearly as many problems as she was. "I'm fresh out of places to look."

"Well, we've tried all the offices. What did you and Steven do when you weren't in class—when you were together?"

Mary Rose blushed. She opened her mouth and closed it again.

"Besides that," Hull growled. "You can't have spent the whole day in bed."

"We'd only been married two weeks," Mary Rose said defensively. "Uh . . . we went on picnics a lot."

"Any special place?"

"There was one we went to three or four times."

"Could he have hidden the sword there when you weren't looking?"

Mary Rose considered. "Maybe. We were together most of the time."

Probably screwing on the picnic table, Hull thought sourly. *Christ, am I jealous?* He stood up abruptly. "Let's go look anyway. How do we get there?"

Mary Rose gave him a wicked smile. "On horseback. Do you like horses?"

Hull inspected his mount, eyeball to eyeball. "I used to have a girlfriend who had a horse," he announced. "When I was in junior high. It liked scraping me off under trees." The horse snorted at him in contempt. Hull swung himself onto its back. "I know more now," he informed it. "Don't get cocky."

Mary Rose laughed. "Sylvester has better manners than that." She sidled her own mount, a bay mare named Carmen, up beside him. "We really could have walked," she said in a low voice, "although Steven and I always rode. I just thought that if we find the thing, it might be better not to be on foot."

Hull looked at the open pasture that stretched out ahead of them and the steep slope of the woods beyond it. "Yeah." They would be vulnerable enough as it was, but at least Sylvester and Carmen could outrun the Shales. He looked over his shoulder. Nothing so far, but he'd bet one of the Shales was back there somewhere, trying to figure out how to get across that pasture without being spotted.

Beside him Mary Rose was humming happily. It was a beautiful day, warm and thick with the smell of grass and wildflowers. Bees zoomed at knee level over the ground and butterflies floated above them like scraps of black and yellow paper in the breeze. There were ham sandwiches and a bottle of wine in the canvas bags behind Mary Rose's saddle, and a collapsible camp shovel unobtrusively rolled in a rain slicker behind Hull's.

When they came to the pasture fence, Mary Rose maneuvered Carmen up to a gate and held it open for Sylvester and Hull. Beyond the fence the trail went into the cool dampness of the woods. Sylvester snorted again as a chipmunk darted across his path into the pale green of the new ferns unfurling beneath the trees. Hull, who was used to a landscape that was already turning dry and brown by May, began to think that the seduction this place had worked on Steven was mostly Mary Rose, but also in some part the land itself.

"It's beautiful, isn't it?" Mary Rose said, making Hull wonder uncomfortably how much else of what he'd been thinking was obvious to her. If it was, he decided, she seemed intent on ignoring it.

"We were lucky to get the horses on such short notice," she said cheerfully. "I expect most of the students are still recovering from last night. And this place is worth seeing even if we don't find anything."

The trail came out on the top of a rise, and they turned the horses down a track that ran along the crest beneath overhanging oaks. "There used to be a road here," Mary Rose said, "about two hundred years ago. There's a spring farther on, and there was an 'ordinary,' an inn for travelers. You can still see the chimney. See? Look there."

The gray stone of the chimney rose from a tangle of wild blackberries, and beyond it someone had made a table out of the cross section of a tree. The spring splashed from a crevice in the limestone hillside into a rock basin, and a wooden dipper hung from a peg beside it.

"Who comes up here?" Hull asked.

"Nobody much," Mary Rose said. "It's not college land. The old boy who owns it is picky about trespassers. He's been known to shoot at them. Maybe he'll shoot the Shales."

"What makes you think he won't shoot us?"

"Because my father used to get Shirley Simkins out of jail every Saturday night, when Shirley was still young enough to raise hell. Daddy was the only lawyer in town who'd bother with him. We've always picnicked up here."

"Shirley?"

"That's his given name," Mary Rose said. She climbed out of the saddle and tied the horses to a tree. "It's not that uncommon out here. I wouldn't snicker if I were you, because he's six feet tall and still about as broad in the beam as that horse."

"Certainly not," Hull said piously. "Would old Shirley notice if someone had been digging up a patch of ground up here?"

"Probably. He gets his water from the spring. The chimney's probably a better bet; it's so overgrown."

Hull headed purposefully for the tangle of briars around the chimney.

"Get a stick and poke around some," Mary Rose said, unpacking ham sandwiches. "There're copperheads up here sometimes."

"Nice." Hull found a piece of dead wood and poked gingerly at the blackberries. No snakes appeared, so he waded into the jungle and ran his hands over the stones, feeling for openings. The blackberry vines pulled at his pants legs and lacerated his hands. "I've decided this is a dumb idea," he said, his grievances a running commentary as he kept on looking anyway. "Who'd bring a sword all the way up here and get eaten alive by this stuff? Ow! God *damn*!" He stuck his thumb in his mouth and tried to push the vines out of the way with his boot. "Wait a minute. There *is* a hole here. Down at the bottom."

Mary Rose jumped up and wriggled her way through the vines to look.

"What the hell?" Hull fished out a gallon milk jug, half full of pale liquid.

Mary Rose sighed. "Put it back. That's probably Shirley's private stash." She pushed her way back through the blackberries and sat dejectedly on a rock beside the table. "It's hopeless, Philip. If Shirley's been keeping his liquor here, nobody could hide anything without his noticing." She bit into a sandwich. "We might as well eat."

"Would Steven know Shirley had his booze here?"

"No, but—" Mary Rose looked up from her sandwich. Her eyes met Hull's.

"That's too good a hiding place for Steven to resist. What if he left the sword here and this Shirley *did* notice?"

"I don't know," Mary Rose said.

"Do you know where he lives?"

"Yes, but we can't go there. Half the time he's not home, and I'm not going to sic those *yakuza* on him without warning. They'd follow us and be waiting for the poor man. He's got a cousin who works in town. We'll have to find him and get him to get hold of Shirley for us."

"I suppose it was too much to hope for that this old coot had a telephone," Hull muttered.

"Way too much," Mary Rose said. "I don't think he's even got indoor plumbing. Furthermore, the cousin works the night shift, and I don't know where *he* lives, so we'll have to catch him at work. He's the bartender at Delilah's Tavern, but they won't be open tonight because it's Sunday, and you can't buy liquor in Sarum on a Sunday."

"We had a drink in that restaurant," Hull said. "A week ago. That was on Sunday."

"That was in the next county over," Mary Rose said. "They're all different."

"Christ Almighty," Hull said. "This isn't a state, it's the twilight zone."

The Chevy slid into the parking lot of Delilah's Tavern, under a neon sign which sputtered fitfully from the roof. The parking lot leaned heavily to pickup trucks with gun racks in their rear windows, and the two girls who had pulled their car up next to Hull's giggled and winked at him as they got out. They wore blue jeans and very high heels. Hull cocked an eyebrow at Mary Rose. "You come here often?"

"Just when I want to impress my guests." Mary Rose got out and beckoned to Hull to follow her. Inside she slid onto a stool at the bar. The air was loud and smoky, and the bartender peered at her through it with surprise.

"Dr. McCaskey? Ah, hell, I guess it's Cullen now, ain't it? Dr. Cullen, you know this ain't a nice place. Your daddy, he'd have a fit."

"I'm just trying to get hold of Shirley, Jim," Mary Rose said. "I don't like to leave a note up at his cabin—you never know who's going to read things."

If Jim's curiosity was aroused by that, he showed no sign of it. "I'll be glad to tell him you're lookin' for him," he said, "but ol' Shirl's gone off to a funeral all this week. Won't be back till Friday."

"Sounds like a hell of a funeral," Hull said.

"That side of the family does tend to go on." Jim gave Hull a look of appraisal and returned his attention to Mary Rose. "You keepin' all right? We was real sorry to hear the news." He flicked an eye at Hull again.

"Yes, I'm fine, Jim, thank you. This is Philip Hull. He was a friend of my husband's."

Jim stuck a hand out and Hull shook it.

"I'll tell ol' Shirl you wanta see him."

They climbed back into the Chevy. "I'd buy you a drink," Hull said, "but I wouldn't want your daddy to have a fit."

Mary Rose laughed. "He would too, if he wasn't in Richmond. There are three or four fights a week at Delilah's, and sometimes some idiot gets shot. Delilah's isn't exactly uptown."

Hull pulled the Chevy out of the parking lot and hesitated. He was feeling restless. "We could go do something else," he suggested. "I think those jerks are on our tail again. I'd just as soon they thought we were bar-hopping as chasing that sword. Or we could see a movie."

"There's only one theater in town," Mary Rose said dubiously, "and mostly they play old stuff because they can't afford the first-run films."

"What have they got this week?"

"*Key Largo*."

"Hey, that's great. You ever see that?"

"No."

"Come on." He found a parking place across from the theater just in time for the first, and only, showing. There weren't more than ten people in the place, Hull decided, which would make it easy to keep an eye out for the Shales. And vice versa, of course, but the hell with them. He bought a box of popcorn and they settled down companionably in the back row.

"The first time I saw this," Hull said while they waited for the lights to dim, "I was in high school, but I missed a lot of it because I took a girl to it and spent most of my time trying to get her to let me put my hand under her sweater. Then I saw it again later."

"I always thought it was a waste of money to neck in a movie," Mary Rose said. "There were plenty of places you could do that for free."

"I'll bet you were fun on a date."

Mary Rose chuckled. "Probably not much."

The lights dimmed. Hull took a handful of popcorn from the box in her lap and draped his arm across the back of her seat. He didn't seem to notice that he'd done it.

Mary Rose looked at his profile out of the corner of her eye. He appeared to be engrossed in the movie, but there was a tension about him that was almost tangible. Mary Rose thought that part of it stemmed from whatever emotion was developing between them, but also that part of it stemmed from some other source. He looked watchful. After a few more minutes the arm across the back of her seat slid down until his hand just brushed her shoulder, but the watchful look didn't leave his face. They sat poised in some delicate balance, desire and fear in overlapping layers—desire for each other and for the sword, the Moonshine Blade, fear of their own desire and fear of the man, also desirous, who stalked them.

When the lights came on again, Hull stood up, stretched, and looked across Mary Rose at a slouched figure on the other side of the aisle. "Go tell your boss I said to go to hell," he said. The figure disappeared.

Mary Rose was angry to find that she was shaking. "Has he been watching us the whole time?"

"Yeah. You get so you can feel 'em."

Mary Rose put her hand, almost imploringly, on Hull's arm. "Let's go home," she whispered.

"Sure." Hull patted her hand. "Don't let 'em get to you."

"No." Inexplicably, she wanted to cry. She sat silently on the drive back to the college.

This time it was Hull who glanced sideways at Mary Rose as he drove. She was on the edge of coming apart tonight, he thought. And it wasn't only the *yakuza*. He didn't feel so solid himself. The sooner he got the hell out of Sarum College, the better off they'd both be. He just hoped he could remember that until he *could* leave. *I've got to go home*, he thought desperately.

Mary Rose unlocked the front door and stared vaguely at the pile of envelopes on the hall table: that afternoon's mail, collected from her box at the college post office and forgotten in her eagerness to track down Shirley Simkins at Delilah's. Mechanically she began to sort it into neat stacks: bills, sweepstakes notices and junk, and letters. There was an envelope with Hull's name on it. He opened it while she swept the junk into the wastebasket and stuck the bills into a drawer with her bankbook.

"Ah, shit."

She spun around. "What is it? Not another—"

"No." He gave her a crooked smile, and stuck the envelope in his pocket. "It's from home. My promotion came through. I'm a lieutenant." He smiled again, even more crookedly than before. "If I get home before the captain gets so pissed off that I'm out on my can instead."

She stared after him silently as he strode down the hall toward his bedroom.

It was Friday afternoon before Jim Simkins from Delilah's called her to say that Shirley was home. It had been a real wingding of a funeral, Jim said, and everybody had got drunk as owls at the wake. He reckoned ol' Shirl must of stayed till the booze run out, then they'd poured him on a bus. Anyway, if Dr. McCaskey wanted to come visitin', ol' Shirl would be pleased to see her.

"Cullen," Mary Rose said, and Jim corrected himself, but she didn't really mind. Married names never counted for much in a town where everybody had known you since you were born. Jim always used the "Doctor" though. His sister had been Mary Rose's mother's dressmaker, so he felt entitled to be proud of her.

Philip Hull came through the door with an armload of groceries as she hung up the phone. His somber, reticent mood of earlier in the week had gradually faded, although he still looked tightly strung and had spent the last three evenings methodically taking a sword apart and putting it back together again, a silent ritual that Mary Rose recognized as a sign that something was on his mind. Now, though, he smiled at her as he set his groceries down. "Great. We'll celebrate, just in case the old boy really has it. And I'm going to introduce you to Japanese cooking."

Mary Rose peered suspiciously into the sacks. "What's that?"

"Squid. I won't make you clean it, but you have to give me moral support while I do. And that's seaweed. And rice vinegar." He spread his purchases out on the counter. "Tempura batter, and shrimp. And sea bass for sashimi. I had to go clear into Lexington for this stuff. They didn't have everything I wanted, but it'll do."

He took an apron out of the cupboard and Mary Rose watched him, bemused, as he put the frozen squid into a pan of warm water to thaw. The squid looked back at her with frozen, malevolent eyes. Hull unpacked a second sack, this one vegetables. "Snow peas. Daikon radish. Cucumber for the salad." He added a wrapped parcel from the meat counter. "And sirloin for the teriyaki."

"Thank God," Mary Rose said faintly. "Something I recognize."

"You'll like the teriyaki," Hull said. "It's full of sugar. As far as I can tell, Southerners put sugar in everything. It's a wonder you don't all have acne and no teeth. Here." He handed her the cucumber. "Slice it as thinly as you can, and leave the skin on. Put it in a bowl."

Mary Rose obeyed and watched him deal expertly with the other vegetables. When the squid were thawed, he took them to the sink and proceeded to turn them inside out, dropping the heads and gelatinous insides into the garbage can. The flat, tubelike bodies and the tentacles went into a bowl.

"Philip, I'm not going to eat that."

"Sure you are." Hull fished a little pot with a long handle out of a saucepan of boiling water on the stove. "Especially if you have some sake first. I couldn't find any sake cups, but those little coffee cups of yours'll do. Go get a couple."

Mary Rose produced two of her mother's Limoges demitasse cups and watched dubiously as Hull poured hot sake into them. She took a tentative sip. It was strong and faintly sweet. Odd, but nice. She took another sip.

"Go easy on it," Hull said. "It's potent stuff." He drained his own cup and refilled it. His amber eyes had a reckless look that made her put her cup down.

It took him nearly two hours to put everything together, and when he was through, Mary Rose wasn't sure what any of it was, but it was arrayed on her best china with artistic flair. The squid had been dipped in tempura batter with the shrimp and deep fried, and was surprisingly good, although Mary Rose couldn't quite bring herself to eat the tentacles. Hull wolfed them down with no squeamishness, along with what Mary Rose thought was his seventh or eighth cup of sake. The seaweed had been sliced and wrapped around pickled rice to make sushi. It tasted just the way she would have expected pickled rice and seaweed to taste.

"That's a very trendy thing to eat in California right now," Hull said reprovingly.

Mary Rose laughed. "You don't strike me as the trendy sort."

"I'm not, I just like the stuff. Try the sashimi."

"Which is that?"

"This one here. You dip it in soy sauce."

Mary Rose peered at the plate. "Philip, that's raw fish."

"Well, you eat raw oysters, don't you? Try it."

"Can't you catch something horrible from eating raw fish?"

"Not that I know of. In Japan, if you're very daring, you order sashimi made with fugu fish, which is poisonous. It's a great delicacy. Of course, if the chef hasn't fixed it right, you fall down dead. This is sea bass," he added.

Mary Rose burst out laughing, and Hull grinned at her. "Are you chicken?"

"Yes," Mary Rose said firmly. She pushed the raw fish across the table to him. "But the teriyaki is great, and so is the tempura and the salad. And I think I could acquire a taste for sake."

"Good." Hull refilled her cup. They were such little

cups that you didn't really feel as if you were drinking anything much, but she suspected that that was erroneous. His face loomed above her by candlelight, reckless and piratical, with a dark glitter in his eyes. "Turn the radio on?" he suggested.

"Sure."

He flicked the knob to the oldies station and cocked his head at the speaker. Patti Page was singing "The Tennessee Waltz."

"A sappy song if ever there was one," Hull said. He held out his arms to her. "Let's dance to it."

Mary Rose got up a little unsteadily, wondering just how much sake she'd had. Hull's arm around her waist did nothing to sober her up, but she was acutely aware of every movement of his body.

"I'm kind of sorry I let you in for this," he said, his mouth against her hair. "The fix we're in, I mean." He wasn't sure if he meant the *yakuza* or the fix of wanting someone you couldn't, or shouldn't, have.

"It's all right," Mary Rose said. "I always wanted an adventure."

He drew her closer and his lips touched her face. The music faded out and she stepped back a little unsteadily. "I think I've had too much sake," she whispered. She crossed to a chair in the living room and sat down in it, feet tucked under her.

Hull stood where he was for a moment, his face brooding and uncertain. Then he followed and sat in the chair opposite her. The lamplight made harsh shadows about his mouth and eyes.

"What will you do with the money?" Mary Rose asked. "When we get it." They had to talk about something.

"I'll go places with it," Hull said, his voice even again. "Back to Japan first. Then maybe South America. How about you?"

"England," Mary Rose said wistfully. "I've always wanted to see England. Or go down the Mississippi River on a steamboat."

"A steamboat's small change." Hull smiled. "You'll be

able to do a lot more than that with it. I thought you
wanted an adventure."

Mary Rose laughed. "A carnival in Rio? Maybe I will at
that."

"We could go together," Hull said. His eyes met hers.

Mary Rose stood up suddenly. "I think I'd better go to
bed," she whispered. "You were right about the sake."
She fled down the hall and he heard the bedroom door
click behind her. On the other side of it she leaned her
face against the cool plaster of her bedroom wall. If she
ever let herself go with Philip, when he went home to
California she would be bereft, emptier than she had been
over Steven's death. She undressed shakily and slid into
bed.

In the living room Hull sat staring at his feet for a long
time. Then he got up and got one of Steven's swords down
from the closet shelf. He laid it on the coffee table and
slowly and carefully began to take it apart.

7.
Diplomatic Tango

When Mary Rose got up the next morning, she found a fresh pot of coffee on the kitchen counter and Hull stretched out in the carport under Steven's car.

He heard her footsteps and extricated himself from the Chevy's underpinnings. "Just checking things out." To Mary Rose's critical eye he looked a little embarrassed. She thought she wasn't the only one who had had too much sake the night before.

"What things?" She inspected the Chevy suspiciously. "It was running fine yesterday."

Hull dusted himself off. "There're a few fine points you don't know about."

"You said there was something funny about that car," Mary Rose said accusingly. "But I forgot about it. You never told me what you meant." Her head ached. She put her hands to her temples.

"I thought maybe you didn't want to know," Hull said. "Every time I tell you anything, it gives you the creeps. But we may need 'em, so look here." He opened the driver's door and slid into the car, leaning down to run his hand under the passenger's seat. "This fits under here," he said, exhibiting a red light, which, switched on, flashed ominously. He put it away again and took her hand. He ran her fingers along the underside of the dashboard.

105

"Feel those switches? This one cuts out your brake lights, this one the running lights, and this one knocks out one headlight."

His manner was brisk and determinedly impersonal. Mary Rose drew her hand back. "What on earth for? I mean, I understand why no brake lights, if you don't want someone to see you, but if you turn out all the other lights, doesn't that turn off the running lights, too? And why one headlight?"

"Think. You're tailing someone and you think they've made you—or maybe they're just getting antsy. You drop back, cut out one headlight, and you look like a different car. Or you knock out the running lights for the same reason. Older models don't have running lights. If someone's tailing *you*, the principle's the same."

"And you think someone's going to be."

"Hell, yes. Now, pay attention. If something happens to me, I don't want you to throw up your hands and say, 'Oh, Lord,' and let the *yakuza* walk all over you." He produced two more items with a professional air. "This is a microcassette recorder. If you want any evidence for that ass Sawyer at the sheriff's office, it may help. And this thing broadcasts as well as receives." He showed her a handheld radio. "You push this button here."

"What makes you think something's going to happen to you?" Mary Rose demanded.

"I don't. I hope to hell it isn't. But I better be practical. We're in deep shit."

He slid out of the car and walked her around to the trunk, where he produced a set of road flares and a previously unnoticed box of license plates. "These may not be much use because they're mostly California plates, which are pretty conspicuous out here, even with the wrong numbers on them, but there're a few out-of-state ones too. Those might come in handy. Now get in and memorize those cut-off switches." He settled himself in the passenger seat and fiddled with the handheld radio. It emitted a series of squawks and wheezes.

"What are you doing?"

"Finding the local police bands. Just in case."

"I wish you'd quit saying that," Mary Rose said morosely.

Hull continued to tinker with the radio. "I'm just glad Steven never got around to decommissioning his car."

"Decommissioning it?"

"An activated cop car is illegal as hell, if you don't happen to be a cop. Nothing wrong with a few fancy switches, but Sawyer wouldn't like that light. Let's just hope he doesn't take notice of it."

"But you're a cop."

"Not out here. Move your feet a second." Hull reached into his pants pocket and produced a gun that Mary Rose had never seen before. He slid it deftly past her ankles into a slot under the driver's seat.

"Has that been there all this time?"

"Yeah. It's Steven's spare."

"Is it loaded?" she demanded.

"Well, what the hell use would it be if it wasn't?"

Mary Rose got out of the car. "Do you mean to tell me I've been driving around sitting on a loaded gun?"

"They don't go off of their own accord, you know," Hull said. He moved over into the driver's seat. "There's also a lot more engine in this thing than it looks like, which I expect you've noticed."

Mary Rose didn't say anything.

Hull looked up at her. "By the way, this is the department's car. I haven't done anything about getting it back to them because I thought we might need it. But if you don't ship it back eventually, you're going to start getting some nasty letters."

Mary Rose edged away from the car. "They can have it," she said flatly.

Hull nodded. He replaced the radio and gave the switches under the dash a final flick. When he climbed out of the Chevy, Mary Rose was still staring at it, but her expression had grown grimly thoughtful.

"This was why you were so sure, wasn't it?" she said. "All these things. They're why the *yakuza* wouldn't go after Steven in his own car. Why they rented another car to kill him in."

"Yeah." He looked at her face and his resolve faded. He

slid an arm around her. "Look, don't let it get to you. We're gonna nail those bastards, I promise you." He gave her a brief hug, as avuncular as he could make it. "Come eat breakfast."

When they had eaten, they walked to the stables to collect Sylvester and Carmen. It was possible to get to Shirley Simkins's cabin by car, but it was hard on the car. Shirley's old Ford was held together with string and bubblegum anyway, Mary Rose said, so he didn't care. But if they rode the horses, the Shales, with any luck, would decide they were just amusing themselves and leave them alone.

They rode past the spring and the picnic table, deeper into the cool leafiness of the wood. The mountain laurel was beginning to bloom, and occasionally a newly awakened turtle sat sleepily by the path, thinking about going somewhere. The first sign of human habitation was a hand-lettered board that said: PRIVATE PROPERTY. Then the path dropped onto a rutted road. At the end was a weathered cabin with a television antenna atop it.

The cabin's front porch was a jumble of old washing machines and refrigerators, none of them in use. There were two ancient easy chairs beside the door, one occupied by an old man who looked a lot like a turtle himself. A dog was asleep on its back in the other.

Mary Rose tied the horses to the porch railing as the old man heaved himself out of his chair. He was enormous, tall and broad, running to fat in the belly but hardly anywhere else. He was dressed in an undershirt, a pair of olive drab trousers held up with suspenders, and a dilapidated hat. He removed the hat, apparently out of respect to Mary Rose, revealing a bald head.

"How do, little sister. Jim says you been lookin' for me." His eyes rested thoughtfully on Hull.

Mary Rose nodded. "Shirley, this is Philip Hull. He's a friend of my husband's. We've got something we want to talk to you about. Something private."

Shirley appeared to consider that. "Private from who?"

"Private from anybody," Mary Rose said firmly.

Shirley nodded. "I reckon I know how to keep my

mouth shut." He looked disgusted. "Been doin' it all last week. I never saw so much fussin' over who was gonna get what, when there wasn't nothin' *to* get 'cept a TV what don't work an' a buncha furniture ain't worth the powder to blow it to hell. But there they was, all the sisters an' aunts, squabblin' like a buncha hens."

"And what were the men doing all this time?" Mary Rose asked, interested.

"Doin' what you're supposed to do at a funeral," Shirley said. "We was gettin' drunk."

"How *are* your sisters?" Mary Rose asked him.

"Tootie, she's keepin' pretty well," Shirley said. "Live to be a trial to her great-grandchildren, I reckon. Alma's not so good. Got somethin' the matter with her stomach, doc wants to take a piece of it out."

"You tell Alma I'm sorry to hear that," Mary Rose said. "If she wants another opinion, I could get you the name of someone reliable there." She could feel Hull fidgeting behind her, but she couldn't rush Shirley.

"Obliged to you," Shirley said. "I'll tell Alma. She sent me back with a bottle of her blackberry wine. Come up and set an' I'll get you a glass." He picked his way through the debris on the porch and disappeared through a screen door into the cabin.

"Who do you think you are," Hull hissed in her ear, "Scarlett O'Hara's mother? Just find out if he's got the sword and skip the good works."

"You can't do it that way," Mary Rose said, "so be patient. And you'll have to drink his blackberry wine."

"Oh, for—" Hull followed her onto the porch. Mary Rose shoved the dog over and sat down, while Hull leaned against the porch railing with some care. It didn't look any too solid.

Shirley reappeared with a pair of plastic glasses, ominously full of purple liquid. Under Mary Rose's eye, Hull drank his, stone-faced.

"You tell Alma that's good wine," Mary Rose said.

"I'll do that." Shirley resettled his bulk in the other chair. "Your daddy keepin' okay?"

"Just fine," Mary Rose said. "He asks after you." She

glanced at Hull, who had the look of a man who couldn't take much more blackberry wine. "Shirley, I'd better tell you why we're here. I'm afraid there may be some trouble."

"What kinda trouble?"

"Bad trouble, I'm afraid. My husband Steven—I'm beginning to think he was a little crazy. Before he died, he started to hide things. He had a lot of weapons. Not guns—old Japanese swords—and he hid them all over the house, and even behind a brick wall in his office. It was some kind of compulsion, I think."

"What do these Jap swords look like?"

"They're long, about like this. . . ." Mary Rose held out her hands. "With a curved blade."

"A handle like this one," Hull said, suddenly alert. He pulled a sharkskin-wrapped handle from his pocket. Shirley turned it over in his fingers.

"There's one sword missing," Mary Rose said carefully. "And there's someone who wants it who's dangerous. I've looked everywhere and it's nowhere on the campus. Steven and I used to go up to the picnic table a lot, and now I wonder if he might have hidden it there. In the chimney maybe."

"You wait right here, sister," Shirley said.

"Do you mean you've got it?" Mary Rose gasped.

"Reckon I do. I figured whoever put it there would be along back for it one o' these days. I wanted to know who was messin' with my chimney. Didn't figure on it bein' you."

He vanished into the house again, and Mary Rose looked at Hull excitedly.

"If it's another ringer," Hull informed her, "I'm going to cut my throat with it. Then I won't have to drink any more of this stuff." He looked at his glass with ill-concealed loathing.

"It's *got* to be the right one," Mary Rose said. She slumped in her chair. "I don't think I can stand it if it's not."

The screen door creaked and Mary Rose jumped up. "Wait a minute, Shirley. I don't want anybody to see it. They've been following us. I'm about to go crazy from it."

"Ain't nobody follow you up here without I know about it," Shirley said. "But y'all come inside if you want to."

The interior of the cabin, which served as kitchen, bedroom, and anything else Shirley needed, smelled of mildew, as un-air-conditioned houses tended to in warm weather, but it was reasonably tidy. Apparently Shirley kept all his junk on the porch. There was a rag rug on the floor and an ancient console television in front of another easy chair. He ran it off a portable generator, Shirley informed them proudly. The light was dim, and the old man lit a kerosene lantern and set it on the table. The sword was tucked under his arm, sheathed in an old, nicked scabbard. He handed it to Mary Rose. "This what you're after?"

"Philip?"

Hull took the sword and held the blade to the light. Then, almost without breathing, he unpinned the handle. "This is it." He felt almost sick with relief. He took a scrap of silk from his pocket and cradled the blade gently. *Ko-getsu-nami.* The Moonshine Blade. The watery temper line rippled down its length with a fierce silver beauty. *I'll never have another sword this good.* It was achingly, heart-stoppingly beautiful.

Mary Rose came to stand beside him. "I wish I could see what you see in it," she whispered.

"I could teach you to," Hull said. "It's there." He shook his head as she put a hand toward it. "The oil from your skin will leave a rust spot." He wrapped her fingers around the silk where he had held it. "There. But be careful. It's still sharp."

"How old is that thing?" Shirley asked him while Mary Rose tilted the sword toward the light, trying to see in it the beauty that so bewitched Philip.

"About eight hundred years," Hull said.

"Jesus, ain't that somethin'? What you gonna do with it?"

"I'm going to send it back where it belongs," Hull said. "We shouldn't even have it. It belongs to Japan." He decided not to mention money.

"Philip, how are we going to get it home with the

Shales probably right behind us? Maybe we ought to leave it here."

Hull frowned. He had given all his concentration to finding the Moonshine Blade. Now that he had it, he was violently reluctant to let it out of his hands again.

"Shales?" Shirley looked interested. "Them boys up on Blue Mountain? That's a no-account bunch by anybody's reckonin'. The law's gonna get 'em one o' these days, an' I personally wouldn't lift a finger. What do they want with a Jap sword?"

"They're just the hired help," Hull said. "But we don't want them coming after you."

"Don't you worry about that," Shirley said. "You all just make like you been visitin'. Everybody knows little sister here comes to see me sometimes. And I reckon them Shales know enough to stay offa my land. Long as they don't see no sword, they won't go lookin' fer reasons to come an' get shot."

"Shirley's right," Mary Rose said. "If we don't *act* like we found it, and they don't see us with anything that *looks* like it, I think it'll be all right. They can't break into every house we visit."

"I don't know." Hull took the sword from Mary Rose and put it back in its scabbard. He regarded it possessively. What would happen if he kept it? *I must be nuts.* He thought of a hundred fifty thousand dollars versus the *yakuza* chasing him for the rest of his life.

"Don't you worry, sonny," Shirley said. "You leave that sword here, it ain't gonna go nowhere till you're ready for it."

Hull eyed Shirley respectfully. Nobody had had the nerve to call him sonny in a long time. If there weren't too many of them, old Shirley was probably a match for the Shales.

"All right." Hull handed Shirley the sword. "We'll leave it with you until I figure out how the hell to get it out of here." He wondered if the Japanese government would kindly come and get it. "But don't mention it to *anybody.* No relatives, no pals, *nobody.*"

Shirley looked at him with scorn. "I ain't no fool."

"No, I don't expect you are," Hull conceded. "Mary Rose, we ought to get home or our shadows are going to be wondering what the hell."

"Philip, how *are* we going to get it back?" Mary Rose asked as they turned Carmen's and Sylvester's noses toward home. "A four-foot sword is pretty conspicuous."

"I'll think of something," Hull said. "I've got to make a few phone calls first. I suppose you'd think I was out of line if I asked if you're sure that old boy isn't going to double-cross us."

"I would," Mary Rose said firmly. "You have to understand people like Shirley. He—"

"I'll take your word for it," Hull said. He was willing to trust Mary Rose's instincts about the local people. She had the kind of intuitive knowledge that came from growing up in a place where everybody knew everybody else, and where everybody's fathers and grandfathers had known each other too. Hull found that notion faintly claustrophobic, but it had its uses. And they had the sword. They had the Moonshine Blade. Now that the first shock of relief had worn off, he felt self-confident, cocky, and a little reckless. As they came out of the woods through the pasture gate, Sylvester appeared to realize that he was going home. He quickened his pace and Hull let him have his head. A warm, grass-scented wind blew across Hull's face, and he grinned over his shoulder at Mary Rose. She leaned forward in the saddle and let Carmen gallop, and they raced, suddenly laughing, across the open ground.

When they got back to Mary Rose's house, they saw no sign of the Shales, although Hull would have bet they were still around. He had that hand-on-the-back-of-his-neck feeling that being watched always gave him. He gave the house a thorough going-over, ferreting through it like a retriever. When closets and basement produced no Shales, he started turning the furniture upside down.

"Philip, what are you—?"

Hull shook his head at her. He set the coffee table right side up on the rug again and ran his fingers across the underside of the telephone table that stood beside one of the wing chairs. A vase of dried flowers on it caught his eye. He shook the flowers out and investigated that too. With a grunt of satisfaction, he shook a small plastic bug into his hand. After a moment's consideration, he took it into Mary Rose's lab and stuck it to the top of Godzilla's cage.

"If I smash it, they'll just come stick another one somewhere while we're gone," he said when he had closed the lab door and motioned Mary Rose back into the living room. "This way, they'll just think there's something wrong with the transmission. Get me a screwdriver. I think that's all, but I want to be sure."

Mary Rose produced the screwdriver and watched him apprehensively as he took the base off her telephone. "How long has that been here?" The idea of the Shales having listened to their conversation of the night before made her embarrassed and furious.

"Since this morning, I think," Hull said. "After we left for Shirley's. The house didn't look right when we got back. They poked things around a little."

Mary Rose gritted her teeth. The thought of having her possessions pawed over by the Shales was nearly as unpleasant as having her conversations listened to.

"This phone's clean," Hull announced. "I'm going to look at the extensions, but I doubt the Shales have got enough brains to tap a phone. The *yakuza* man probably gave them the bug they did plant."

Mary Rose sat down on the sofa, trying to remember if they had talked about Shirley last night, just in case. She didn't think so. They had had other things on their minds. She looked sideways at Philip Hull as he came prowling back down the hall and picked up the telephone again.

After some thought, Hull punched out the number for long distance information and asked for the Japanese embassy in Washington. At the embassy a polite young woman managed to convey that it was an honor merely to speak to him, while deftly ascertaining his name and business. She connected him with a cultural attaché who, after a few moments' conversation, hastily passed him on to another, presumably higher up. The higher-up also listened intently and transferred the call again. Hull grinned. The words *Ko-getsu-nami* seemed to constitute a magic formula. The progression ended with a man who introduced himself simply as Mr. Ohmori and asked gently if Mr. Hull were quite sure of what he had.

Hull described the Moonshine Blade in terms that produced a small, thoughtful silence at the other end of the line. After a moment, with an unusual directness that Hull decided was a mark of how badly the Japanese government wanted the Moonshine Blade back, Mr. Ohmori tentatively named a figure. Hull grinned again and settled in to drive the price up.

Since the conversation, after its initial stages, was conducted largely in Japanese, Mary Rose gave up listening and slumped brooding against the sofa cushions, watching Philip Hull. His long legs were stretched out in front of his chair, the tan leather of the holster just showing under the cuff of his jeans. The telephone receiver was cradled between his ear and shoulder and he listened as intently as a cat, amber eyes half closed.

"For a blade such as this," Mr. Ohmori was saying, "I have the authority to offer one hundred and fifty thousand dollars, provided it is genuine. Of course, *Ko-getsu-nami* is priceless, but I am very sorry, my government will not go higher."

"I understand," Hull said. "Still, it is sad to be so shortsighted, because naturally for this blade an American collector would pay much more."

Mr. Ohmori sighed. "That is true, Mr. Hull. Very sad. But of course one must consider the honor attached to returning a treasure like *Ko-getsu-nami* to Japan, as opposed to purely monetary gain." He made monetary gain sound disgraceful. "You have lived in Japan, Mr. Hull, you speak our language with great skill. These things cannot be without meaning to you."

"Certainly not," Hull said piously. Mr. Ohmori was right. However much he itched to keep it, *Ko-getsu-nami* belonged to Japan. To sell it to an American collector was, to Hull's mind, damned near as bad as letting the *yakuza* get their hands on it. Japan had been raped of enough good blades after the war. Family treasures, some of them centuries old, confiscated and dumped by the shipload into the sea—those that hadn't gone home as souvenirs in some soldier's kit. Whatever the military justification for that, the destruction of so much beauty depressed Hull every time he thought about it. He dickered a few minutes more just to be sure that Mr. Ohmori really had hit his limit, and then conceded.

Financial negotiations concluded, Hull decided that now was the time to break the news to Mr. Ohmori that he wasn't the only bidder. "I am very sorry, but there is one more pressing problem which we must solve."

There was a small alert silence at the other end of the line.

"I don't wish to embarrass you," Hull said politely, "but it must be known to you that of the descendants of the famous Akinji Kobayasu, a certain element today are not . . . law abiding."

"Regrettably. Yes." The long distance line suddenly crackled with unspoken caution. Hull had a mental picture of Mr. Ohmori holding the telephone with his fingertips.

"They know about the sword, Mr. Ohmori. We would be most lucky to go more than a mile away from here with it before they tried to take it. Your government must call them off."

Mr. Ohmori sighed. "It is very unfortunate, Mr. Hull. I regret exceedingly, but that is not possible."

I'll bet you do, Hull thought. "Mr. Ohmori, your government will never see *Ko-getsu-nami* if Sadao Akaishi's *ko-bun* gets his hands on it."

"You are very knowledgeable, Mr. Hull." Mr. Ohmori sounded more regretful yet.

"I know when I'm likely to get killed," Hull said, reverting to English for emphasis. "I get a good healthy fright when it comes to tangling with *yakuza*."

"We prefer most strongly not to use that term," Mr. Ohmori said. "Officially, *yakuza* do not exist, particularly in your country. They are . . . an embarrassment."

"Well, I don't like to embarrass you," Hull said, "but I've had one in my hair for the last six weeks."

"You must understand that I am a diplomat, Mr. Hull. Matters of trade between our countries are somewhat touchy just now. I cannot take any action that might jeopardize those relations."

Such as admitting to a few *yakuza* among their exports, Hull thought grimly. He gritted his teeth and was polite in Japanese again, polite being a matter of phrasing rather than actual meaning. "It is unfortunate that your government has lost control over its criminal element. It must make life very difficult for you, since your embassy seeks to avoid embarrassment." He endeavored to sound sympathetic, but Mr. Ohmori wasn't biting.

"Embarrassment is a matter of form, Mr. Hull. If we do not admit to *yakuza*, we do not admit embarrassment. Thus everyone retains honor. But for us to fight with *yakuza* here, in your country, where your press is so likely to take notice of it—this would make great scandal. Scandal is what I am employed to prevent."

"It won't make a scandal if an American citizen is killed by these nonexistent *yakuza*?"

"Americans are killed constantly. Your murder rate is really most disgraceful. But if my government is involved, it will be an 'incident.' There will be stories in your press, and letters to the editor, and your president will make unfortunate speeches. That must be avoided at all costs."

"I see. Then what do you suggest, Mr. Ohmori?"

"I am not at liberty to suggest anything, other than that I have never talked to you. However, for me to acquire this sword for my country would be most beneficial to me. So I will mention that my government keeps a condominium in Virginia Beach. For the use of our staff, you understand. If these men that you speak of should come there, it will be less embarrassing. And fortunately the concept of diplomatic immunity is transferable to official residences. Most helpful. If you bring *Ko-getsu-nami* to Virginia Beach, Mr. Hull, I will have your money. It is a very great sum of money," he added hopefully.

"All right, I'll call you. Thank you for your time, Mr.

Ohmori. It's been enlightening." Hull hung up the telephone and glared at it. "The bastard won't even admit
there are *yakuza*," he informed Mary Rose. He snorted.
"They're a diplomatic embarrassment. We've got to get
the sword to Virginia Beach."

"That's two hundred fifty miles," Mary Rose said.

"Well, we'll just have to do it," Hull said. "I got a
hundred and fifty grand out of him, and I'm starting to feel
very proprietary about it."

Mary Rose stood up, her blue eyes resting on him
appraisingly. "And when you've got it, you'll take your
half and go home to California with it, damn you, won't
you?" she said. She looked at him, stricken. "I'm sorry,"
she whispered, and fled.

Hull looked after her. "You're a hell of a lot of help," he
shouted. There was no answer, so he sat scowling at the
empty sofa instead. He should have gone home a month
ago. He should have run for his life before he started
falling in love. Hull put his head in his hands. After a few
minutes he sat up and punched out another Washington
telephone number. He didn't need to ask Information for
this one.

8.
Up the Hollow

Mr. Ohmori hung up the telephone and sat looking at its dozen little buttons. Fate had dropped Philip Hull and the miraculous sword in his lap. It was a great pity that fate had seen fit to add Sadao Akaishi. *Karma*, Mr. Ohmori told himself firmly. What will happen, will happen. Strive for balance. Mr. Ohmori, who was also a devout Episcopalian, added a brief prayer that Philip Hull could outrun Sadao Akaishi, and ground his teeth. Unfortunately, Mr. Ohmori had meant what he said about *yakuza*. The American government was already unhappy over the *yakuza* presence in their country at all, and seemed to feel, illogically to Mr. Ohmori's mind, that the Japanese government could do something about it. The Americans couldn't control the Mafia, or their own street gangs; how did they expect Japan to control *yakuza*? But certainly there must be no scandal. Mr. Ohmori ground his teeth again and then reminded himself not to; an unfortunate habit which annoyed his wife.

Mr. Ohmori picked up the telephone again and buzzed his secretary.

It took the embassy secretary a while to politely convince the Modern Languages Department secretary at the University of Tokyo that the call was a transpacific one and that nothing good would come of it if she did not immedi-

119

ately locate Professor Masayuu Noguchi, who was probably still at his breakfast, and personally instruct him to return Mr. Ohmori's call.

While he waited, Mr. Ohmori arranged his paper clips in his desk drawer in neat little lines, according to size, a habit which he was aware drove his secretary into a near screaming frenzy. At home he did it with rubber bands, and it had the same effect on his wife. When the paper clips were arranged in regimental rows, he closed the drawer carefully so as not to shift them. By the time he had measured his desk with a ruler and positioned the blotting pad in the exact center, Masayuu Noguchi, politely suspicious of his government's interest in him, was on the line.

"You are most kind to interrupt your breakfast to speak with me," Mr. Ohmori said.

"I am very sorry not to have returned your call more quickly," Noguchi said, "but I was taking a bath. I do not have a class this morning until ten." The implication being that he had not yet got to his breakfast, and what the hell did Mr. Ohmori want?

"Ah? I am sorry to have interrupted that. But we have received some information which, as the head of your family, we felt it was most important for you to know."

"And that is?"

"*Ko-getsu-nami* has been found," Mr. Ohmori said, and smiled, satisfied. The silence at the other end of the line was most attentive now. "Of course, the government will use all of its financial resources to return your honored ancestor's treasure to our country."

"That is most kind of the government," Noguchi said, a touch dryly. "I fear our own resources are limited," he added before the government could suggest that he should help pay for a sword which he was aware the government had no intention of allowing him to keep personally.

"I beg your pardon, but there is one resource that you possess that we do not," Mr. Ohmori said. It was a matter that had to be approached delicately. "Even with money at our disposal there is a problem that we may be unable to solve. The circumstances of the discovery of your ancestor's sword are . . . unpleasant." Mr. Ohmori outlined them. "I fear that the safety of *Ko-getsu-nami* will depend on whether this Philip Hull is a match for his adversaries. Officially, you understand, we can do nothing. The chance of embarrassment is too great. But family ties are like a spiderweb." Mr. Ohmori was pleased with his analogy, which he had thought up while arranging his paper clips. "Thin, sometimes invisible, but possessing great strength. And I had the happy thought that perhaps your influence on a distant kinsman—"

"I have none," Noguchi snapped.

"It is very sad." Mr. Ohmori clucked sympathetically. "One understands . . . an unfortunate connection, from your point of view. But there is no one else with any hope of intervening."

"My distant kinsman's mere existence brings shame and disgrace on my family and on the name of our mutual ancestor," Noguchi said. "I do not know him."

Mr. Ohmori clucked again, gently disbelieving. "Japan is a very small island."

"I have not seen Sadao Akaishi since I was a child," Noguchi said. "Even then he was a disgrace. We do not acknowledge his existence. Even if I were willing, there is no hope of his acknowledging mine."

"The spiderweb—" Mr. Ohmori said.

"No. It grieves me," Professor Noguchi informed him with a sarcasm that was not lost on Mr. Ohmori, "that I cannot help the government acquire my family's treasure. But no."

Mr. Ohmori knew when to give up. *Yakuza* in the family, like an inherited and disgraceful disease, tended to make one touchy. He hung up with reluctance and the good wishes to wife and family which politeness required, and prepared to requisition $150,000, on the slim chance that Philip Hull could get to Virginia Beach without getting killed.

Professor Masayuu Noguchi stared haughtily at the Tokyo end of their erstwhile connection. It was unthinkable that he speak to *yakuza*. And unspeakable of his government, in the person of Mr. Ohmori with his fat little air of cajolery, to suggest it. Particularly, the professor reflected, since his government had not suggested that he should receive custody of the sword, only that he should help them to get it.

Masayuu Noguchi hadn't seen Sadao Akaishi since they were both eight, at one of those sprawling family gatherings —the funeral of an aged great-aunt—to which everyone with a family connection had to be invited, for the sake of doing proper honor to the deceased.

Sadao had been as vicious as a shrew even then, in a schoolboy cap and pants, and holding the hand of a surly older brother. Their father, dark-eyed and heavy with power, had watched the funeral from the rolled-up windows of a black car. Eight years later Masayuu Noguchi had not been surprised to learn that the older brother was dead of unnatural causes and Sadao, at sixteen, was sitting firmly in the seat recently occupied by his father, whose finally failing health had sparked their brief fraternal war.

The connection of Akaishi to the family of Masayuu Noguchi was not a thing that was ever mentioned by the respectable side of the family, nor within their hearing. But Japan, as Mr. Ohmori had said, was a small island. Everyone knew. Akaishi and his life had tainted Masayuu Noguchi's. Even descent from the legendary Akinji Kobayasu was a silent pride, not to be spoken of, because Sadao Akaishi also claimed it. And now some foreigner, some *gai-jin* with a collector's passion, had found Akinji Kobayasu's sword.

Masayuu Noguchi got up and began to pace about his office: quick, unvarying steps, three paces to the window, six to the door, three to the desk again. Brooding on Sadao Akaishi was not a habit with him. During most times Akaishi was an unpleasantness at the back of his mind— there, but not thought of. But now the government had thrust family honor under his nose. *Ko-getsu-nami*, the sword of Akinji Kobayasu, belonged in the family. Not to the government, which was a race of bureaucrats spawned by bureaucrats, endless fat brown carp perpetuating themselves in a pool; and not to Sadao Akaishi, who was *yakuza* and had therefore tainted the ancestor's memory, as well as the honor of all other descendants. It belonged to that part of the family that was still samurai, still had honor despite the taint of *yakuza*.

Six steps to the door. Another three to the desk, three more to the window again. Noguchi stopped and looked out, counting money in his head. So much for a ticket to Washington, so much for the minimum of expenses. So much left over to offer the *gai-jin*. Sadao Akaishi would never back away from the sword at Masayuu Noguchi's word. More likely, knowing the sword to be found, he would only send four more *ko-buns* to make sure of the job being done right. The *gai-jin* would have to take his chances. But if . . . *if* he outran Akaishi to Virginia Beach, it might be possible to divert him before he could catch up with the government man Ohmori.

Noguchi turned back to the desk, turned out his pockets and assured himself of keys, credit cards, spare glasses, the passport that he kept by habit in his wallet. Would possession of *Ko-getsu-nami* erase the shame that Sadao Akaishi's mere existence brought on the Noguchi family? Did he, Noguchi, in this day and age, really believe that? Yes. Noguchi stuffed keys and wallet back into his pockets. He wanted to be remembered as the man who brought honor, who brought the sword of Akinji Kobayasu, back into the family. It all depended on what sort of man this *gai-jin* was.

"You ever stop to think maybe this Hull bastard couldn't find his own ass?" Jem Shale took a last drag on his cigarette and flipped the butt into a bucket of water. There were buckets of water all over Ben Shale's camp, and Ben Shale enforced their use. One stray spark when a batch was cooking in the lab could be enough to blow them all as far as Roanoke. Jem lit another, shielding it with his hand from the breeze that always blew on the mountain. His expression was truculent. "If Hull was gonna find that goddamn sword, I reckon he would've by now. Maybe you're barkin' up the wrong tree, Ota."

Ota gave him the look he would have accorded a dog

that performs some not very clever trick. Ota valued intelligence, and Jem was stupid. "He *has* found it by now," Ota said. "He has been here too long. If he had not found it, he would have gone home. He is waiting for you to go away."

"Maybe he don't wanna go home." Jem grinned, his eyes sly. "Maybe he's dippin' into some good stuff. That's a nice little piece if you saw her fixed up. I saw him dancin' with her once. Livin' in her house an' all."

"He has a job," Ota said. "He is police. He is not the sort of man to leave that for a woman who lives in a place where he does not belong."

"Seems you know an awful lot." Jem was scornful. "For a man what ain't never seen him."

"I know my adversaries. That is as important as knowing your friends." Ota smiled benignly at him, and saw with satisfaction that his smile made Jem Shale twitch. "That is why I am here and you have learned to be afraid of me, because you did not take the trouble to know your adversaries and learn whether or not it would be wise to cheat them."

"I ain't afraid of you." Jem stood up. One of these days he was gonna put a knife in that slanty-eyed little shit, whether his old man liked it or not. "If they got the sword, why the hell don't we just go an' get it?"

"They have been to the police. The police did not give them much credit, but if there is another killing, they will. And then they will find you and your primitive operation on this mountain. Since you were fools enough to kill the woman's husband, you will just have to wait until this man makes a move. The sword is worth a great deal of money to him. It will begin to eat at him that he cannot have the money, and then he will try to get away from this place with it."

"It might be a damn sight easier if you just bought it from him," Jem said. "Ain't that how you folks do business? Can't hardly go in a store now without seein' cameras an' TVs an' shit knows what all."

"The only thing we need to buy is you," Ota said. "You saw to that for us. Now you will get us the sword." Ota had a file on Philip Hull half an inch thick. *Yakuza*, after all, was a business; research was properly done for new ventures. Hull's file showed two visits to Japan, friends among the respectable Japanese in California, and some trouble gone to on his last visit to Japan to return to the widow in question letters taken by an American soldier on Iwo Jima. Not a man who could be bought. Nor was it fitting for Sadao Akaishi to pay for his ancestor's sword. The hunt for *Ko-getsu-nami* was a duel, a matter of honor for both sides. That was not a principle worth explaining to Jem Shale. Shale was a ferret, useful for loosing down a hole when the quarry was inside, but incapable of understanding the rules of the hunt. And expendable, if need be, when the hunt was over.

"Well, I got business to tend to, back home," Jem said. He had two partners in Humboldt County and they were probably ripping him off for his last dime.

Ota chuckled, a sound that Jem had never heard him make before. It raised the hair on the back of his neck.

"When you have finished here," Ota informed him genially, "you will have learned a useful lesson—how to deal with associates who have decided to cheat you." He laughed. The laughter was a low, grinding sound that sounded to Jem Shale like the mills of hell.

"They're out there. Don't they sleep?" Hull twitched the eighth-inch opening in the living room curtains back into place. "They've been there a solid week. They know, damn it."

"They've been there since March," Mary Rose said. Being watched, she had discovered, was an experience of sustained terror that grew every day you knew there were eyes looking at you. She tucked her feet under her on the sofa and tried to grade an end-of-term paper on the implications of biotechnology in beef cattle. She was cold. The eyes seemed to make her cold. Maybe she was just tired. Tired of her life being hammered apart by men and put back together with holes in it that a cold wind could blow through. First Steven, and now Philip Hull. Damn them both. She wondered if Philip felt that way about her. He had gotten that fine-drawn look back again. "How could they know?"

Hull had flattened himself against the wall beside the window and was looking out. It seemed to be a compulsion. He had never strayed far from the window since he had talked to the man at the Japanese embassy two days ago. "Gut feeling," he said. He was still looking out. "I can't justify it. Except the same reasoning I'd use: the damned thing must have turned up by now or we'd be out of places to look. They'll wait for us to try to move it, but if we don't do it soon, they're gonna get impatient."

Mary Rose put the paper down. "I can't grade this. I can't even read it with them out there. Do you suppose the State Police would give us an escort?"

Hull snorted. "After they've talked to Sawyer? Maybe we could get the National Guard to lend us a tank too."

"Philip, I resent being treated like a moron!" Mary Rose snapped at him, and Hull looked over his shoulder at her, startled.

"Sorry. That wasn't my intention." He sounded stiff, like somebody else. Mary Rose narrowed her eyes at him balefully. They could work this up to a pretty good fight, if they tried.

"Well, what *are* we going to do?" she inquired.

"Fuck if I know." He dropped into a chair, staring with not much interest at a spot on the far wall.

"Philip, what's the *matter* with you?"

Hull straightened up. "Nerves," he said shortly. "You've never seen me before a bust or you'd recognize the symptoms." He gave her a half smile. "I think I'll make some coffee. I may not be very pleasant company, but you can regard it as educational."

Mary Rose's eyes rested in interested appraisal on Hull's back and shoulders as he fidgeted with the kettle on the other side of the kitchen partition. *The hell with your 'education,'* she thought. *Anyone who could live with a man who bricked things up in the walls could stand you.*

He came back with two mugs of coffee, put them on the coffee table, and reached out an arm to flick the radio on.

Mary Rose's oldies station was playing "St. James Infirmary Blues."

"Just in case they stuck another bug somewhere." He sat down beside her and leaned his head close to hers. His eyes were still as watchful as a cat's.

"I went down to the St. James Infirmary, saw my baby lyin' there . . ."

"I'm going to make a run for it," he said flatly. "I'll take the thing and try to outrun 'em."

"Are you crazy?"

"Somebody's gonna get killed if I wait much longer."

"I suppose it doesn't count if they kill you between here and Virginia Beach?"

"They won't. I'll take Steven's car. It'll improve the odds a little."

"Stock car racing's very big here," Mary Rose said. "You know how it got started? Bootleggers used to race each other on the back roads. They kept in practice running from revenue agents. The Shales know the mountains. You don't."

Hull's eyes met hers. "If I don't try it, they'll be in the house in another couple of days. And if they think we've already found the thing, they won't have any reason not to just blow us both away."

"But it isn't here."

"Why don't you go out on the porch and tell 'em that?" Hull suggested. He leaned his forehead against hers and closed his eyes. "Just shut up. I'll probably make it."

Mary Rose thought about the mountain roads, winding, secretive, half of them with no names if you got off the main highway. More people than the Shales lived up there. "Moonshine's an old professsion," she said thoughtfully. Hull was silent, perfectly still, not relaxed, but as if he rested in some precarious balance, all his muscles taut. Mary Rose sat back and looked at him. "How long have we got? How long will they wait for us to come out with it?"

"Shit, I don't know," Hull muttered. "Till Akaishi's *ko-bun* gets impatient. A week, maybe. What are you getting at?"

"Moonshine," Mary Rose said. "Don't think it's died out. To a lot of people here, running a little whiskey over the mountains at night is just a way of doing the government one in the eye. A lot of people up on the mountains don't take kindly to too much government. But whiskey's one thing, and dope's another. There are a lot who'd tell you they'd scorn to deal in drugs. Don't think I'm trying to turn them into folk heroes, because I'm not. They're nearly as dangerous as the drug runners. But there's bad blood between them and the drug people. The mountains are a very private place, and drugs draw too much attention. The moonshiners are used to dealing with ABC agents. That's an old and honorable war. But drugs bring in the DEA, and SWAT teams, and grand jury investigations. And a murder would bring worse."

"Don't tell me they've never shot a revenue agent," Hull said. "Folk heroes that they are."

"I imagine they have," Mary Rose said. "Although mostly they just lie low. The ABC men bust up the still, and a week or two later they've got another one going somewhere. They kill each other once in a while too, but the murder of an outsider would put everyone on the mountain at risk. They might help us."

"Uh-huh," Hull said. " 'They' who? You know any?" He could just see Mary Rose consorting with moonshiners. Mary Rose was about the most legal woman he'd ever met.

"Of course I do. Why do you think I brought it up?"

Hull stared at her. "How the hell?"

"I told you I grew up here. You have to live here to understand how people like me know people like Zeke Halloran."

"Zeke Halloran's a moonshiner?"

"The particular moonshiner I had in mind. He's up on Blue Mountain somewhere too, so he may know these Shales. My granddaddy used to like corn whiskey, especially on a Sunday night when you can't get anything else, and he bought it from Zeke Halloran until he got to be a judge and decided it didn't set a good example. And, believe it or not, I went to school with Zeke's son. Tom was the only Halloran who ever went to college." She grinned at him. "Virginia Tech, class of '79."

"The modern moonshiner," Hull said. "What did he take, business administration?"

"He was a chemistry major. And so far as I know, he went back up the mountain and put it to good use. I could probably get hold of him if you want me to."

Hull shook his head. "Christ. Yeah, get hold of him."

Tom Halloran had a sort of hangdog look about him that Mary Rose recognized from their college days. It had no significance other than a lifelong habit of keeping a low profile. Certainly it betokened no malleability on his part.

Tom shoved Shirley Simkins's dog out of one of the ratty chairs on Shirley's front porch and sat down. "Ol' Shirl ain't much of a housekeeper," he commented.

Shirley's tortoiselike visage poked through a window. "You ain't somebody I give a lot o' thought to keepin' house *fer*." His head snapped back in again with a triumphant cackle.

Mary Rose giggled. Tom Halloran pulled off a yellow John Deere cap, smoothed blue-black hair back from his forehead, and resettled the cap with the bill well down over his eyes. "What the hell are you up to, Mary Rose?"

Mary Rose considered that. "Well . . . it's complicated. Do you know anyone named Jem Shale?"

Tom's eyebrows shot up under the cap. "Shit, yeah. Squint-eyed little bastard t'other side o' the mountain. Him an' his daddy. Been there about two years, came from over on Six O'Clock Knob. I heard Jem was in California."

"Unfortunately, not just now."

"Look, will you just be kind enough to tell me what the hell you're doin', messin' around with the Shales? I know you, Mary Rose, you ain't the type."

Mary Rose started explaining. Halloran put his feet on Shirley's dog, which had gone to sleep again on the porch floor, and listened.

When she got to how they had found the sword, Shirley poked his head out the window again to add a corroborative grunt. "Them Shales ain't been back here since, neither. Know they'll get their fool selves shot."

Mary Rose flicked an eye at Tom Halloran. If the Shales figured out the sword was here, they'd be back soon enough. Formidable as he was, Shirley wasn't a match for them. "We're going to need help to get it out of here," she said.

"Reckon you are," Tom said. He considered. He liked Mary Rose; enough to have come over when Shirley said she was asking for him. And he didn't like the idea of the Shales running around knocking people off like they thought they were goddamn New York gangsters. That would just set the cops to snooping up Blue Mountain, and it had been Tom's experience that when the county cops got to barking after one case, everybody else in their path had better lie low too, since the sheriff's boys generally knew a still when they fell over one. That still left the matter of Mary Rose's cop, however. Tom Halloran considered further, and announced, "I got to meet him."

Mary Rose sighed. "Tom, I promise you, he isn't interested in anything but getting to the coast with that sword."

"*Be* that as it may, I ain't gonna stick my neck out 'less I meet him. You bring him up to visit, we'll talk about it."

"For Pete's sake." The trail that Tom Halloran had told them to take twisted along a ledge that would have done admirably for goats. Sylvester snorted as loose rock turned under his front hooves. "Tell me again why we're doing this," Hull requested.

"He doesn't like your profession," Mary Rose said. "You're the natural enemy."

Hull made an aggravated noise in his throat. The trail flattened out and dipped into a steep-sided hollow. Where the floor of the hollow widened, there was a willow, old and gnarled, ancient of its kind, with trailing fronds brushing the windblown grass. Hull didn't see anyone until they were almost on it. Then he discovered Tom Halloran sitting on a rock.

Behind him the mountain was silent, watchful. Hull had a sensation of being kept track of. He wondered how far anyone would get up the Hallorans' side of Blue Mountain without being noticed. He decided probably not very far.

Hull slid down off Sylvester's back and nodded at Tom Halloran as Mary Rose introduced them. They shook hands, and then, formalities concluded, hooked their thumbs into their belt loops and stared at each other suspiciously.

"Suppose you tell me how you got Mary Rose mixed up in this," Halloran suggested.

Hull rocked back on his heels a little. "I didn't get Mary Rose into anything. Mary Rose's husband, my late buddy, the damn fool, brought the sword out here and proceeded to stuff it up old Shirley's chimney."

"He do that a lot?"

"A fair amount," Hull said. "It was some kind of compulsion. You'd be surprised what we found."

"Not as surprised as you'll be, Hull, if you find anything up here you don't need to."

"If you mean whatever you're up to on this mountain," Hull said, "I don't give a rat's ass. Mary Rose says you don't deal drugs."

"Supposin' she was wrong."

Hull gave him a long look, yellow eyes narrowed reflectively. "Then you'd probably be sorry you ever let me up here. You know I'm a cop, Halloran, don't be stupid. If she was wrong, do us both a favor, let me back off now."

"Nah." Halloran pulled his cap off, ran both hands through his hair, jammed it down over his eyes again. "I just wondered what you'd say."

"Now you know," Hull said.

Mary Rose leaned against her mare's shoulder, arms folded, while they stared at each other, taking stock. Carmen threw her head up and blew down her nose, ears pricked down the hollow. Before Mary Rose could speak, Philip Hull and Tom Halloran were facing down the hollow, bodies tensed into identical stance, each with his hands curled around the dark outline of a gun. The hollow was silent, then Mary Rose heard the brief *chirrup* of a redbird. It didn't sound particularly outdone. Carmen lowered her head again and began to crop grass, mouthing it determinedly past her bit. Hull and Tom Halloran lowered their guns and looked at each other.

"Probably a fox," Halloran said.

"Probably." Hull stuck the gun back in his boot. "Probably goddamn leprechauns. I'll probably shoot my goddamn foot off next time if I don't get less jumpy."

Halloran nodded. He seemed to have made up his mind. He sat back down on his rock and stuck a piece of grass in his mouth. Hull sat down next to him and they contemplated the emptiness of the hollow for a while. Just good ol' boys together, Mary Rose thought with disgust. There was nothing like having made a fool of yourself with a gun to encourage male camaraderie. She decided that probably wasn't a useful remark to make, so she kept her mouth shut.

"Them Shales know where you're headed?" Halloran asked.

Hull shook his head. "Not that I know of. I pulled one bug off the telephone. I think it was all they had."

"Then all we got to do is lose 'em on the mountain," Halloran said. He grinned and pulled the bill of his cap lower over his eyes. "I reckon we can do that for you."

9.
Blue Mountain Back Road

Brown heels, tan linen suit . . . Mary Rose stared at her suitcase, with a yellow silk dress in one hand and a half-slip in the other. Thinking about the *yakuza* out there, she felt like an idiot, but when they got to Virginia Beach, she would have to wear *something*.

"What the hell are you doing?" Hull inquired behind her.

"Trying to decide if I need a raincoat," Mary Rose said truthfully.

"Oh, for— You aren't going." Hull snapped the bedroom light off. "And don't stand in front of a lighted window putting clothes in a suitcase if you're trying to be subtle."

Mary Rose tossed the dress into the suitcase. By the murky light from the hall outside her door, Hull's face was sharp-angled and risky-looking, like an unpredictable horse. Nerves, Mary Rose thought. His nerves, hers, tightly strung as a rubber band. "I'm not staying here," she said with finality.

"Look." Hull came into the room, put his hands on her shoulders. "Your friend Halloran may just do the trick, but this isn't a nature walk. I don't want to be worrying about whether you're all right. I don't want *any* distractions."

"That's a pure comfort," Mary Rose said. "And after you

give them the slip, they can come back here to ask *me* where you've gone. You're not leaving me *here*."

"Oh, hell." Hull took his hands off her shoulders and put them to either side of his forehead. "I didn't think of that." He threw his hands in the air. "All right, you can go. Christ! I need a drink."

He stalked down the hall to the kitchen.

Mary Rose followed him. "Are you always this obnoxious when you're working?"

"Yes."

He poured a tumbler half full of Virginia Gentleman and went and sat in the living room with it. Mary Rose followed and sat on the opposite end of the sofa. She crossed her arms and looked at him out of the corner of her eye.

"Yeah, all right," Hull said. "I'm acting like a pig. I'm sorry." He held out his hand and she scooted down the sofa to sit next to him, feet primly side by side in front of her. "If you must know," he said, "I'm scared to death you're going to get hurt and it's going to be my fault."

Mary Rose looked at him. "So am I," she said firmly.

Hull gave a hoot of laughter. He put an arm around her and pulled her head down onto his chest. "Nah, we'll make it." He didn't know why he thought so. Something about Mary Rose made him feel alternately armor-plated, invincible, and as if he were caught in one of those dreams in which one has unaccountably left the house naked and only discovered it in the middle of a large crowd of strangers. Mary Rose moved a little against his chest. He bent his head toward her and then stopped. Things were already too goddamned complicated. He cocked his head to look at her face. Her eyes were closed. He didn't think she was asleep.

Hull sighed. He imagined he had complicated Mary Rose's life as much as she had his. He reached out, turned off the light and turned on the radio, and they sat there without moving.

He woke her at four A.M. She had finallly gone to sleep, her head on his chest, and he knew if he woke her and sent her to bed, she'd never get to sleep again. So he closed his eyes too, and dozed, listening to the radio till it went off the air. He woke with a jolt to dead silence, and shook Mary Rose awake. He wanted to get them out of there in the dark, before the campus filled up with unidentifiable cars. The security cops were relentless in their pursuit of malefactors who left their cars overnight where they shouldn't be, and possessed a device with which they locked the wheels of any student car caught parking in the sacred confines of the faculty-staff lot. The Shales would still be out there, but at night they'd be on foot, and Hull wanted the head start that would afford him.

Mary Rose sat up, yawned, and looked at him in horror. "Did I sleep on you all night?"

"Pretty much," Hull said. He flexed his right arm and rubbed the shoulder muscles. "I think it's gone to sleep."

"You should have waked me."

"Nah," Hull said, "I went to sleep too." He stood up, feeling automatically to make sure his gun was still there. "It's time to hit the road. Is your stuff ready?"

Mary Rose nodded. "I just have to feed the mice—enough to last them a few days. Godzilla went home yesterday, thank God."

"Well, do it in the dark," Hull called after her. "I don't want to give them any more warning than we can help."

"In the—" Mary Rose started to argue with him, changed her mind. If she opened the cage doors in the dark, there'd be mice all over. She got the sack of feed and just poured it through the top of each cage. What the hell.

When she got back to the living room, Hull was pacing. He had marked out an apparently obstacle-free path in the unlit room and was traveling back and forth along it with the single-minded tenacity of a lab rat. "Say something when you come through a door in the dark," he said.

"Sorry."

"I knew a guy once who got blown away doing that," Hull muttered. He stopped pacing and began pulling on his jacket. "I don't want two of us going up to Shirley's. They'd spot you. Give me an hour and then get in the car and drive like hell and meet me where the road from

Shirley's comes down on that road with the old barn. That may work better than my coming back here. They won't expect you to run for it by yourself."

"All right. Are you sure you can find Shirley's in the dark?"

"Yes, dammit." One hand brushed her cheek. "You worry more than anybody I ever met." He went down the hall and took the screen out of the back bedroom window. Halfway through the window he stuck his head back in. "Don't take any more stuff than you can get in that little suitcase. I don't want you going back and forth to the car like it was a damn moving van—you'll have Shales curled up in the trunk."

She watched him go, his dark jacket and pants melting into the thicket of forsythia that grew along her back fence. In a moment she couldn't see him at all, or hear anything but the little breeze that blew over the meadow behind the row of faculty houses. It smelled wet and dark, with something indefinably unnerving in it. She wondered where the Shales were, if Philip had given them the slip, and what Shirley would do if they followed Philip up Shirley's mountain.

Hull ran, bent over from the waist, losing himself in tall, wet meadow grass. He couldn't hear anything behind him. At the pasture fence he lay down and rolled under it, then sprinted for the woods, a dark shadow brushing the white rails of the fence.

The blackness of the woods was unnaturally quiet. The wild things whose province it was had stilled themselves into immobility at his coming. As he passed, they would begin to move again, hesitantly at first, then, reassured, about their normal nocturnal business, while ahead of him the deeper woods fell silent, so that he traveled always in an envelope of stillness and of waiting.

Hull moved as quickly as he could along the path they had taken on horseback. There was a nearly full moon still up, enough for a man with good night vision to see by, but the trees seemed to soak up its light, and their dark shapes were somehow altered by the night so that twice he almost lost the path. Shirley was waiting for him; would, in fact, have brought the sword down to him, or given it to Tom Halloran, but Hull had refused, prompted by the compulsion—which he did not wish to examine too closely—that no one should handle the Moonshine Blade but himself. Stumbling up Shirley's mountain, he wondered how close he was coming to losing his grip on reality. The blade had become a living thing for him, an entity in itself, possibly a spirit to be placated.

The trail dropped down onto the old logging road that led to Shirley's cabin. Hull, with the way clear before him now, moved along at a trot. Below him, where the mountain brushed the edge of the college pasture, the wood flattened itself into stillness again.

Shirley's cabin was dark, except for the dim blue glow of the television. Shirley and his dog were watching *Miami Vice* on a VCR. Shirley heaved himself out of his chair. His top half was adorned with an ancient sweater, unraveling from the bottom. He jerked a thumb at the TV screen. "Don't get no decent reception up here but one channel, so Jim, he tapes me stuff off the TV at Delilah's. They got cable down there. I read in *TV Guide* where that guy Johnson wears eight-hundred-dollar suits on that show, but it looks like a goddamn T-shirt to me. I got your sword here. You have any trouble comin' up the mountain?"

"No."

Shirley pushed a button on the VCR so that the detectives on the screen were frozen in motion, jelled suddenly in the midst of gunfire. He rummaged in a battered foot locker. "I kep' it like you said, an' didn't touch the blade none, but I tell you I'll be glad to be shut of it. There's somethin' about this thing gives me the willies. Maybe it's bein' so old an' all. You reckon it ever killed anybody?"

"I reckon," Hull said. Shirley put the sword in his hands, and Hull pulled off the wrappings. He slid it out of the scabbard and looked at the blade in a thin bar of moonlight by the window. The waves washed along its length, endless broken reflections of the moon. *Ko-getsu-nami*, Moon on the Water . . . It felt alive. If it had come when he called it, he would not have been surprised.

Shirley watched him as Hull turned the blade in his hands. "Glad to've helped out," he commented.

"Yeah, thanks."

"Happy to do a favor for a friend. Gets mighty dull up here, nothin' to do but watch the TV, an' that ol' chair of mine just ain't up to my weight no more. Kinda sags on one side, you know. Sure could use me a new one."

Hull caught on. "Well, we appreciate it, Shirley. We might just take a look at chairs in Virginia Beach for you."

"Pretty good stores in Virginia Beach," Shirley said. "Don't get down there much myself."

"We'll check 'em out for you." If he got to the coast, he'd *owe* the old devil a chair.

Shirley's dog pricked up its ears and made a surly gurgle at the back of its throat. Hull spun around, but Shirley was at the window ahead of him. A shotgun had materialized in the old man's hand. "You reckon anyone's on your tail?"

"Shit, I hope not." Hull slid the sword back in its sheath and wrapped it up again in a hurry.

"Well, you get outta here an' leave 'em to me," Shirley said.

Hull hesitated.

"Go on—git!"

Hull dived out the door and ran for the cover of the woods. The sky was beginning to be gray-streaked, and the moon was fading in it. The dying night was silent except for the growling of Shirley's dog. Hull dodged among the trees, following the logging road down to where Mary Rose was waiting. The sensation of someone at his back came suddenly when the road made a dip, out of sight of Shirley's cabin. Hull looked over his shoulder but he couldn't see anything. He ran.

A loose stone slid under Hull's boot and he skidded, stumbling. A hand clutched his shoulder and they fell together, rolling into the road. Hull dropped the sword and twisted furiously as hands tried to close around his throat. The other man was not as heavy as Hull, but he was strong. He must have bypassed Shirley's cabin and waited by the road. In the graying light Hull could see pale hair and eyes. He thought it was Jem Shale.

They fought in murderous silence, Hull because he didn't want the old man in the cabin to be responsible for a murder, Jem Shale because he thought he could take Hull but not Shirley Simkins too. Hull saw the dull gleam of a knife in Jem's hand. He staggered to his feet and twisted out of the way as Jem came after him. The sword was still on the ground. Hull thought about the gun in his boot. If he killed Jem Shale with it, there'd be hell to pay: cops and coroners and investigations, and all the while the *yakuza* agent would know where the sword was. He dodged Jem again and dived for the sword.

Ko-getsu-nami slid from its sheath with a faint whisper. The sharkskin wrappings on the hilt felt cool but sentient, like living skin. Jem Shale's eyes widened. He took a step backward and Hull advanced on him. *Christ, don't let me overdo it*, Hull thought. *Ko-getsu-nami* was made to kill with.

Jem fumbled under his jacket. Jem had a gun, Hull knew. He'd use it if he had to and risk the noise. Hull leaped, the sword whistled in a low arc and bit through Jem's boot at the ankle. Jem dropped, mouth open, as his leg gave way under him.

Hull brought his own gun up, knowing he wouldn't have to fire it now. "Drop the knife."

The knife fell in the road with a thud while Jem stared at the blood welling up out of his boot.

"Put your hands behind you."

Jem turned his eyes to Hull. Panic glowed in them.

"Put your hands behind you before you bleed to death!"

Jem jerked them behind him. Hull prodded his gun into Jem's chest while he extracted the gun from Jem's jacket, made sure it was on safety and stuck it in his pocket.

Hull touched Jem's boot gingerly. He hoped he hadn't cut his foot off. He pulled the boot free while Jem turned pale and fell over. A deep gash had gone damn near down to the bone, but not through it, which had been entirely possible if Hull had misjudged his blow. With relief, Hull made a tourniquet out of the cloth that had been wrapped around the sword. Then he cupped his hands around his mouth.

"Hey, Shirl!"

He was gratified to hear a frantic barking and the bang of Shirley's front door. The light was almost full dawn. He couldn't leave Mary Rose sitting out there much longer. Hull grinned malevolently at Jem Shale. "You better let old Shirley stitch that foot for you. I don't think you're gonna make it to the emergency room." At the top of the hill he could see Shirley Simkins lumbering down the road. Hull wiped the Moonshine Blade on his jacket and ran.

Steven's car was parked at the foot of the logging road, in the shadow of an old tobacco barn. Hull came down the slope at a dead run, and flung himself into the driver's seat, pushing Mary Rose over. "Here." He put the sword and scabbard in her lap and let the clutch out.

"Philip!"

"Huh?" Hull maneuvered the car down the narrow county road. He hoped to hell they didn't meet anything coming the other way.

"There's blood all over your hands!"

He looked down. Against his dark pants and jacket it didn't show, but his hands were smeared to the wrists with it.

"What happened?"

"I met Jem Shale."

Mary Rose looked at the sword in her lap. There was a crimson splotch on the knee of her jeans. "Oh, my God."

"Relax, I didn't do anything permanent to him, but I hope old Shirley stitches his foot up with a carpet needle." The empty scabbard had fallen off her lap to the floor. "Try to wipe the rest of the blood off and put the thing away before *you* get cut."

Mary Rose, who was the kind of woman who would have a handkerchief in her jeans, pulled one out of her back pocket and wiped the blade with it gingerly. "Is Shirley all right?"

"Shirley's fine," Hull said. "Let's worry about us. Did anyone follow you?"

"I couldn't tell. But if they saw me pick you up, they'll know."

"Yeah." Hull cocked an eye at the rearview mirror. Farther up the mountain sunlight flashed on something metallic. "How far to your friend Halloran?"

"About five miles." Mary Rose clutched the side of the passenger seat as the car careened around a bend. "The first turn's right up here. Slow down or you'll overshoot."

"Where?"

"There. On the left."

Hull wrenched the wheel around and the Chevy slid into the turn. He saw the other car again, through a break in the trees. A light-colored Mustang. He couldn't tell whether they had guessed he was headed for Shirley's or followed Mary Rose, but it didn't make much difference.

They jolted over a narrow bridge and a pickup coming down a side road slammed its brakes on. A straight stretch opened out, and Hull pushed the accelerator to the floor. Behind them the pickup's driver stuck his arm out the window in a furious gesture.

The trees slid by at a sickening pace, and Mary Rose gritted her teeth. She didn't know whether she was more afraid of Hull's driving or the car behind them. "Take the next right turn, road 624. You'll see another tobacco barn just before you come to it."

Hull nodded. The old tobacco barns were ubiquitous; windowless log structures two stories high with a single low door at the bottom. There was less tobacco grown in the mountains now, and the barns were derelict ghosts, unfit for any other use and too sturdily built to tear down. The barn loomed ahead of him, its base shrouded in the early morning mist which was already beginning to burn off. Hull slowed down just long enough to make the turn, and hit the accelerator again.

Mary Rose gasped and managed not to shriek at him to slow down. Her right foot was braced against the floorboard as if her worst recurring nightmare had somehow taken residence in her conscious mind. She would dream sometimes that she was driving on a road like this one and the brakes would not work. She would push down her foot on the pedal as hard as she could and somehow the car would stop by sheer force of will.

Narrow roads switchbacked down the mountain, dropping into the valley of which the college occupied one end. The car shot across the top of an escarpment of stone and stunted pine trees, and Mary Rose could see it unpleasantly clearly from their height: red brick buildings as small as Monopoly houses, centered with the extravagant white lacework of the Administration Building.

"Are they still on our trail?" Hull asked her. He kept his eyes on the road, driving within a fraction of the edge of his control over the car, of the point at which, due to the principles of physics and the dynamics of its engineering, it would cease to obey him and simply slam into the mountain.

Mary Rose twisted around to look through the rear window. She could see nothing but the weaving road. She narrowed her eyes and searched the distance where occasional breaks in the trees showed the way they had come. Another flash of light, a glimpse of something pale. A white car spun into a curve above the valley and skidded toward the guard rail. She had time to see it right itself before the Chevy lurched again and the trees closed around them. Then the trees thinned again and the Chevy dropped down the last turn onto the Route 11 highway.

"How far?" Hull said.

"About half a mile," Mary Rose said.

Hull nodded. He let the Chevy out and hoped they didn't meet a state cop with a ticket quota. They were doing nearly ninety. He wanted as much lead as he could get. The highway narrowed, climbed a hill, and dipped suddenly into a curve on the other side. On the shoulder was a medium size tractor-trailer rig with its back doors open and a ramp down. Hull hit the brakes and the Chevy ran onto the shoulder in a spray of gravel. A tall figure in a yellow cap waved, pointing into the darkness of the truck. Hull hit the gas again, and ran the Chevy up the ramp. The doors closed behind them with a solid thunk. In a moment the truck gave a lurch and the clatter of its idling diesel engine picked up speed.

Mary Rose let her breath out. An answering sigh echoed from the darkness to her left. It was black as pitch in the truck. Hull flipped on the Chevy's interior light and inspected her.

"You look like a zombie," he said. "You still with us?"

Mary Rose leaned her head against the back of the seat and nodded. "I don't want any more adventures. This one's going to last me."

"Yeah, I bet." Hull turned the light off again. "Battery," he murmured. He put his arm around her, and she rested her face against the warmth of his shoulder. They'd be in this truck quite a while. She wondered what might happen in the meantime. She put her hand against his chest and felt the thud of his heart. *We'll see*, she thought.

"You two all right back there?" a voice inquired, and they sprang apart. The voice was loud and disembodied and its echo reverberated against the roof.

"Yeah, thanks," Hull said. He wondered irritably who the hell would put in a radio to talk to his cargo. The answer came to him after a moment: someone whose cargo was ordinarily a load of moonshine and a man with a shotgun.

"Thought you'd like to know," the voice went on—Hull realized it was Tom Halloran—"there's a white Mustang sittin' on our tail, madder'n spit. He keeps givin' me the finger 'cause he can't get past."

Hull chuckled and leaned back but he didn't put his arm around Mary Rose again.

Mary Rose stared into the darkness. It was black as the inside of a billy goat.

"Philip?"

"Yeah?"

"If we don't get some light in here, I'm going to go crazy."

Hull got out, felt his way to the trunk, and in a moment a yellow glow lit the darkness. He got back in the Chevy and put the trouble light on the seat between them. Outside there was a furious honking, an insistent staccato sound above the rumble of the truck's engine. A sharp bark of laughter came from the men up front in the cab: Tom Halloran and his father Zeke.

"There they go," Tom's voice said. "They finally got a chance to pass, the damn fools. Merrick's gonna keep his eye on 'em, so y'all just sit back and relax. It's a long drive to the coast."

Merrick was another Halloran, a brother or a cousin, Mary Rose wasn't sure which. Like the Shales, the Hallorans were a sprawling clan with a strictly family business. Merrick was muscular and stocky, with the gently pigheaded expression of a young bull. He drove on the NASCAR circuit when he wasn't making illegal liquor. Merrick would tail the Shales at an unobtrusive distance and report their activities as long as the range of his CB held out.

Hull's expression was delighted, eyebrows raised, mouth twitched into a grin. "Cookie," he said, "I think we did it."

Two months ago Mary Rose would have taken violent exception to being addressed as "Cookie" by anyone. Right now she didn't mind. She sat in the warm, dim safety of the Chevy and the truck, enjoying the thought of the Shales haring off southward while the truck turned east. She felt a little lighter than usual, not quite tethered to the ground. Nobody had got killed, and if Jem Shale had nearly got his foot cut off by Philip Hull, she found that didn't trouble her. Jem Shale had tried to shoot her. Jem Shale had probably also killed Steven, but she didn't want Jem's death on Philip's hands, whatever Philip might think about it. Another few miles and the tractor-trailer rig would turn east, up into the foothills of the Blue Ridge Mountains. On the other side of the Blue Ridge was the flat country of the Piedmont and, east of Richmond, the even flatter lowlands of the Tidewater. A five-hour drive, maybe. The satisfaction of having given the Shales the slip began to grow. She knew Hull was looking at her. She could see him out of the corner of her eye. If she looked back, straight into that amber gaze, it would catch and hold her, and everything else would be more or less inevitable.

*   *   *

"What do you mean you have 'lost them'?" Hidehiko Ota sat on the edge of his cot in the loathsome quarters allotted to him by the Shales and spat into the radio. He was in a fury.

"I mean they got ahead of us, that's what I mean." The Shale who was speaking seemed to be explaining something of great simplicity to the feeble of mind. "We got behind some goddamn truck an' by the time we could pass him, they was gone."

"What took you so long to pass?" Ota's words were clipped, carefully enunciated and dangerous.

Ben Shale grabbed the microphone from his nephew. "Goddamn highway curves all over the place," he said. "Asshole," he added under his breath.

"Then how did the Cullen woman and Hull pass the truck?" Ota snapped.

"Hell, I don' know, but they musta."

The first lesson Ota had learned from the *yakuza* was to investigate the unexpected. By the seemingly innocent coincidence does the enemy show his hand. "What sort of vehicle was this truck?"

"Big tractor-trailer," Ben said. "Can't get round them things on a curve no way."

"Go back!" Ota screamed into the radio. "Go back!"

". . . *turnin' around. I'm gonna repeat, they are turnin' around* . . ."

"Y'all hear that back there?" Zeke Halloran asked.

"I heard it," Hull said grimly.

"Well, hang on. We ain't outta gas yet." Zeke put the heel of his hand on the horn and leaned on it. A terrified Volkswagen in the right lane slammed on its brakes. The tractor-trailer slid over into the right lane and with a hellish grinding of gears lurched onto a side road. A white Mustang going the other way topped a rise, hit its brakes with a screech, and looked for a place to turn. There was none, and it had a bus on its tail. The Mustang accelerated again.

"They jus' went by," Zeke reported. "Ain't gonna take 'em long to turn around."

Hull opened the door of the Chevy, preparatory to dragging Mary Rose out bodily if he had to. "You better let me out. You'll never outrun them in a truck."

"I can sure as hell inconvenience 'em some," Zeke said.

The truck bounced onto a frontage road and swung hard left. Hull fell out the Chevy's open door and rolled into the wall of the trailer. He stood up, cursing, and staggered as the truck began to climb.

"Halloran, what the hell are you doing?"

"Gonna buy you a little time, son."

The truck kept climbing, and Hull could tell from their momentum that they were on a switchback road. It executed a final turn and thudded to a stop.

"All right, son," Zeke said. "Fire that thing up an' get ready. You're about halfway up Blue Mountain. When the ramp comes down, you back out an' pull up on the road. Tom's goin' with you."

The rear doors were open by the time Hull had the Chevy started. Blinking in the sun, he backed the Chevy down the ramp and headed its nose up the mountain. Tom Halloran shoved the ramp up, bolted the trailer doors, and sprinted for the car. Mary Rose climbed into the backseat to make room for him. Through the rear window she could see Zeke Halloran backing the truck out onto the road again. He had pulled partly off it onto a dirt trail that ended in a padlocked gate about ten yards from the road. Now he backed out again, wedging the truck sideways across the road. He locked the cab, stuck the keys in his pocket, and ran for the cover of the trees as the sound of the Mustang's engine came vengefully up the road behind them. On the other side of the truck Hull put the Chevy into gear as Tom Halloran dropped into the seat beside him.

"There's a gravel road on the right about half a mile up," Tom said. "Take that."

Hull nodded. "How long do you think that truck's going to stop them?"

"Till they jimmy the lock, I reckon, or figure out how to get around it."

"Your dad gonna be okay?"

"Hell, yeah. He'll lie low till they either get past or give up."

"You mind telling me where we're going?"

"Yeah, I mind. And you can just forget how you got there."

"I told you, Halloran, I don't care if you're making illegal hooch. That's not my department."

"I got a natural reluctance to let the wolf in the door, especially when he says he ain't hungry," Tom Halloran said. "But I don't see that we got much choice."

"I'm glad to hear it," Hull said.

In the backseat Mary Rose watched the trees whirl around them as Hull put the Chevy into another turn. The road was by now little more than a gravel track up the mountain, between banks thick with mountain laurel and hedgerows overgrown with honeysuckle. They skirted a high meadow and then the trees closed around them again. She looked back down the meadow and saw the white Mustang at the lower end.

"Philip, they're coming!"

"Shit!" The unfamiliar road doubled back on itself and Hull had to slow down.

Tom Halloran twisted around in his seat to look out the back window. The Mustang was closing on them. "The way they're drivin', I'd say they been up this road before, probably just to snoop. Their place is on the other side of the mountain, they got no business here."

"Well, they do now," Hull said.

Halloran glared out the back window. The Mustang was still closing, obscured by trees which now overhung the road on either side. As it came around a bend and got a clear view of them, a shot rang out. Mary Rose jumped, and Tom Halloran hit the floor. An arm reached over the backseat and shoved her down too. Philip Hull, not having any other choice, gritted his teeth and kept driving. There was another crack of gunfire and a bullet smashed the side mirror.

"Goddammit!" Hull said. "If they get a tire, we're sunk."

Tom Halloran pulled a gun from under his jacket and raised his head cautiously. The Mustang wove in and out of the trees on the winding road behind them. The Chevy's jolting made a steady aim almost impossible. Halloran fired and the Mustang kept coming.

The Shales were faced with the same problem, but Hull, sinking as low in the seat as he could, knew they were bound to get lucky eventually. He felt like a silhouetted target on the shooting range where his department had to qualify with a handgun every month. It was a highly unpleasant sensation. He checked the rearview mirror and saw Mary Rose lift her head. "Get down, goddammit!" he yelled. On top of everything else, he was going to get her shot. With sheer terror pushing him, he hit the accelerator and the Chevy slid dangerously around a hairpin curve.

Mary Rose looked at Tom Halloran. He was crouched beside the door, firing out the window, but the man on the passenger's side of the Mustang was keeping him pinned down. The Mustang hit a straight stretch and accelerated. In a minute they'd be in point-blank range.

Mary Rose scrabbled under Hull's seat and found the gun—Steven's gun.

"What the hell are you doing?" Hull yelled at her. "Get *down!*"

Carefully, Mary Rose pulled Steven's gun from its holster. It felt cold and unfamiliar in her hand. She knelt on the seat and rolled down the window. She looked at Tom and held the gun the way she had seen him and Philip do it, with both hands.

"Get *down!*" Hull screamed.

The Shales were concentrating on Tom. She'd have surprise on her side for maybe a count of five, she thought. No more. The Mustang came out from behind the trees, white against the green mountain. She took a deep breath, leaned out the window and aimed. A bullet whined past the Chevy on the other side. It was the most terrifying sound she had ever heard, like wasps. Mary Rose pointed the gun at the Mustang's left front tire and fired.

Another shot answered hers, Hull screamed "Get down!" again, and she pulled the trigger a second and third time.

With a squeal of tires, the Mustang suddenly slewed around and rammed into a tree.

Tom Halloran, hanging halfway out the window, took careful aim and put a bullet into what he hoped was the Mustang's gas tank. Philip Hull, cursing steadily under his breath, gunned the Chevy up the mountain, and it disappeared into the green thicket of the trees. And the Shales, smelling gasoline, dived out of the Mustang and lay flat, shielding their heads with their arms. After a while, when it didn't blow up, they went back and discovered that Tom Halloran had hit the gas tank.

Mary Rose felt cold, and for some reason her hands were shaking. Tom Halloran carefully detached them from the gun. "Honey, you can ride shotgun with me any time."

". . . goddamn *fool*," Hull said. He was so sick with terror, he thought he was going to throw up. What if they had shot her? He gripped the steering wheel with white-knuckled hands, turned left or right onto side roads when Tom Halloran told him to, and finally rolled the car to a stop when the road ended at the gates of an old cemetery. The windswept grass had been mowed and there was a bunch of plastic geraniums on one of the graves, but the stones were worn and leaning. There was no fence, only the surrounding woods.

Tom Halloran got out of the car and with apparent ease lifted four young pine trees out of the ground from beside the road. A dirt track lay revealed on the other side, and Halloran, grinning, waved them through. As the Chevy climbed the shoulder onto the Hallorans' private driveway, Hull could see a row of six-inch pipes sunk in the ground. He pulled up beyond it and waited while Tom Halloran tilted the trees back into their pipes. The pines were bushy and low branching. Even in winter they would screen the dirt road from unauthorized eyes.

Hull gave Halloran an appreciative look when he climbed back in the car. "You actually bury anybody back there?"

"Not that I know of," Halloran said. "But a graveyard's good cover. Lots of old ones up here, and folks tend to keep 'em up. It accounts for any traffic that might get noticed. We cut new pines every couple of weeks." He looked over his shoulder at Mary Rose. "You all right back there?"

"I'm fine." She looked carefully at her hands to see if they had quit shaking. She felt oddly detached and spacy, the way she had the time she'd had her wisdom teeth pulled and the dentist had given her codeine. "What's on the tombstones?" she asked him.

"Noells," Halloran said. "Lots of Noells around here. My sister made the stones, took a sculpture class in high school. Cassius Orville Noell, he's my favorite, died of diphtheria in ought six, left a wife an' eleven kids. You get so you almost believe in 'em."

"Thorough, aren't you?" Hull said.

"Like I told you, it's a business."

The Chevy jolted over another rut, and Hull wondered how much of its underpinnings were left. "I suppose it would be too businesslike to pave your road."

"We like to be inconspicuous," Halloran said comfortably. "That way we don't have to shoot any cops."

"You could put 'em in your graveyard," Hull said after a minute.

The road slanted steeply up the mountain and ended in another of the high hollows that had been inhabited by the first white men to come to the Blue Ridge. A weathered cabin with a steeply pitched roof slanting out to shade a wide porch stood at the end of the hollow. A pickup was parked in front of it, with two hounds lying in the truck's shadow. Hull had an impression of watchful movement behind the windows of the cabin.

Halloran got out and stretched. He leaned down to speak to Hull and Mary Rose through the Chevy's open door. "*I* don't know what we're gonna do with you, but we'll figure it out. For what it's worth, we can deal with those Shales easier up here, where nobody's gonna miss 'em."

To Mary Rose the peak of Blue Mountain and the hollow in its shadow looked misty and aloof, a piece of a world that she had always known about but had never inhabited. If one could measure distance as time, then it was two hundred years from the top of Blue Mountain to the house she had grown up in and the gates of Sarum College. Tom Halloran, with his Virginia Tech chemistry degree, was a time traveler, a man who could walk the treacherous ridges between his family and the modern world. One day, she thought, the journey might drive him mad.

The cabin door opened. An old woman and a young one and three men came out on the porch.

"Come on in," Tom Halloran said. "I think they'll be pleased to have the company."

10.
White Lightning

"Sawyer, have you got any idea what in the blue-eyed world is going on?" Sheriff Farley P. "John" Williams looked at Sawyer as if he didn't have much hope that he did.

"No, John." Sawyer glanced up from the contents of his morning In box. "What's eating you?"

"The phones are all haywire," the sheriff said. "Half the calls are ringing straight through to my private line. I just talked to a woman on 260 who called to tell me a big tractor-trailer rig passed her house doing about eighty miles an hour and nearly ran over her poodle. I told her to call the State Police."

Lieutenant Sawyer grinned. "Quick thinking."

"Well, I don't need this this morning. How am I supposed to get anything done? There it goes again." Through the wall they could hear the faint ringing of a telephone in the next office. "Serena!" the sheriff bellowed through Sawyer's open door. "The phone's ringing!"

The woman at the front desk cocked an ear. "I don't hear it."

"Well, take my word for it. That's why I ran for sheriff, so people would take my word for things, like the phone's ringing, or it's raining outside."

153

"I got it." Serena punched a button. "Sheriff's Department, dispatch."

"Some days nothing works, you know that?" The sheriff departed, a man with much to try him.

Sawyer went back to trying to decide what to cook for dinner. It was his turn, and he didn't think Rosalie was going to let him weasel out of it. Rosalie didn't get off work till six on Wednesdays, and by the time she had picked up the kids, it was seven and the kids had fought all the way home about who got to have two straws in the Coke she always bought them. Rosalie wouldn't ever trade on Wednesdays, and he didn't blame her. But he couldn't think of anything he felt like cooking except hamburgers, and the kids wouldn't eat those. Sawyer thought he probably had the only two children in the United States who wouldn't eat hamburgers. He was trying to decide whether that was proof of pigheadedness or just expensive taste when Serena's voice caught his ear over the static of the dispatch radio.

"Hey, hold on!" Sawyer shoved his chair back.

"Hold on for Lieutenant Sawyer." Serena punched a button on the radio and looked at him inquiringly.

"What's going on? Who's on Blue Mountain with a gun?"

"The lady on 260 called back," Serena said. "She got mad about her poodle and decided to go after that truck—saw it turn up Blue." Serena shook her head. "I guess she was gonna hit 'em with her umbrella. The Lord sure watches over some folks. The ABC boys broke up three stills on Blue Mountain this year already." Anyone who had been driving like a bat out of hell up there wasn't going to take kindly to being tailed by an old lady and her poodle.

"Now she's reporting gunfire?" Sawyer said. He had had Blue Mountain half in the back of his mind ever since that professor from the college and her boyfriend from California had been in. Word had been floating around for a while now that moonshine wasn't the only commodity being manufactured on Blue. Sawyer didn't put any faith in Hull's story about Jap gangsters, but if Hull nosed around and turned up rumors about drug manufacturers on Blue Mountain, Sawyer wouldn't put it past Hull to go up there and start a war if he thought the men who had trashed Mrs. Cullen's house were there. And if Hull was up there shooting people, that was going to be Sawyer's fault for not watching him. Hell.

"The poor old thing got about halfway up the mountain," Serena said, "and saw the tractor-trailer pulled off the road. She was going to get out of her car and give 'em what-for, when a black Chevy backed out of the back of the rig and went off up the mountain, and the tractor-trailer backed up and blocked the road. Then a white car came by and two men with guns got out and tried to move the truck, and she got scared and got down on the floor with the poodle and prayed, and when she got up her nerve to look out the window, the white car had got around the truck somehow and she heard shooting. That just did her in. She went home and took a Valium and she wants to know what the world's coming to."

"So do I," Sawyer growled. He looked at the dispatch radio. "All right. Have 'em call in to me if they find anything."

"Sure." Serena flipped the radio on again.

Sawyer sat back down at his desk and thought for a minute. He wasn't operating on much more than a hunch and the fact that he didn't like Philip Hull, but bootleggers didn't chase each other as a rule, and when the ABC boys were out hunting, they let him know. "Call her back and ask if that Chevy had California plates," he yelled at Serena. Then he picked up his own phone, looked up Mary Rose Cullen's number in the Sarum phone book, and dialed it. No answer.

Sawyer tried the college switchboard. "Well, where'd she go? . . . You can too tell me. This is Lieutenant Sawyer at the Sheriff's Department. . . . No, she hasn't been in an accident . . . If I knew where she was, I wouldn't be calling you . . . No, ma'am, nobody's *done* anything, I just want to get in touch with her." Sawyer drew irritated doodles on his note pad. Mrs. Cullen had taken personal leave. The switchboard didn't know any

more than that, but was plainly dying to. "What about her
houseguest, Mr. Hull? . . . No, *he* hasn't done anything
either. That I know of . . . Yeah, thanks. If she calls in,
just ask her to get in touch with me." He hung up the
phone, and his intercom buzzed.

"Are California plates blue and yellow?" Serena asked
him.

Sawyer sighed. "Get me a car. And call whoever you
sent up the mountain and tell 'em I'm comin' up."

Mary Rose looked down the long trestle table at which
the Hallorans, and their unexpected guests, had gathered
for supper. There were three of Tom's brothers she hadn't
met before: Asia, George, and Jim. She found herself
studying them with the eye of a geneticist, and then was
ashamed of it. She had never cared for researchers who
spent their sabbaticals in the isolated places of the world,
verbally pinning the inhabitants down on the pages of
notebooks, like bugs.

Mrs. Halloran, who was large and muscular, cleared
away the remains of meat loaf and corn pudding, and
shook her head at Mary Rose when she started to help.
"You rest. You've had a tryin' day." Mrs. Halloran stacked
the dishes neatly in stacks three deep and laid them along
her left arm. "I used to be a waitress," she said to Mary
Rose. "It comes in handy, in a family this size." She
went into the kitchen and came back with a fresh plate,
which she put in front of Merrick, who had appeared,
ravenous, as the rest of the family was finishing. Her face
was lit softly by five o'clock sunlight from the open window, and Mary Rose tried to decide what she had looked
like when she was younger. Like her daughter Noonie,
maybe, but more solid. Noonie was thin and pale, with
straight dark hair held off her forehead with a barrette.
Noonie had finished her supper in three bites and retreated to the sofa with a high school trigonometry book.

Tom Halloran gave his sister a look of pride mixed with
a certain ruefulness. "Noonie's our scholar. Better than I
ever was. She's gonna go to college next year."

"Makes two of 'em," Zeke Halloran said. "I didn't see the point in it at first, but I'm startin' to. Things change."

"Where do you want to go, Noonie?" Mary Rose asked.

Noonie looked up from her book. "Tech. Like Tom. I want to take geology."

Her mother made a rough noise of satisfaction. "And then she's gonna marry off the mountain," she said, "that's what. Merrick, ain't nobody gonna take that meat loaf away from you, you might slow down some."

"I'm hungry," Merrick said.

Mary Rose looked at Philip Hull, trying to guess his reaction to the Hallorans. He looked perfectly at home, with a can of beer in his hand and his chair tipped back like the rest of the Halloran men; as at home as he had looked holding forth on Middle Eastern politics with Lee Bowling. *You're a chameleon, that's what you are*, she thought.

"Bottom of the mountain's crawling with cops," Merrick said when he had finished his first slice of meat loaf and was looking around expectantly for more.

Hull's chair stayed tipped back, but his expression was suddenly alert.

"Just how many is 'crawling'?" Zeke asked.

"Well, a couple of cars," Merrick said. "County cops. But they been gettin' around. They been huntin' back and forth like a couple of dogs lookin' for possum, so I don't 'spect they got much."

"Oh," Mary Rose said, distressed. "Mr. Halloran, if we get you in trouble, I'm going to feel dreadful."

"Not like you'd feel if those Shales caught you," Zeke said.

"Merrick, you hush up an' eat." Mama Halloran put another slab of meat loaf on his plate. "You all are scarin' this child."

Tom Halloran looked at Mary Rose and gave a whoop of laughter. "This here innocent child shot out those Shales' front tire," he said. "I never saw anything like it."

Hull tipped his chair forward slowly. He looked down the table at seven assorted Hallorans. "Mary Rose is right.

If we're going to cause you trouble, you tell me, and I'll clear out with the sword."

"You just calm down, son," Zeke said. "I don't care if that sword belonged to Napoleon's granddaddy, it ain't worth tangling with copperheads like the Shales for till you're sure you can win. We have any luck, maybe the law'll get the Shales. They're givin' the mountain a bad name an' scarin' shit outta my customers."

"Don't worry about us," Tom said. "The ABC boys have been tryin' to find us for years, an' they know what they're lookin' for. The sheriff's boys let a guy who chopped up his wife's sweetie with a hand ax climb out the back window of the jail last year and they ain't seen him since. It's my personal opinion they couldn't find the sheriff's own ass with dogs an' a compass."

Lieutenant Sawyer's county car rolled to a stop in front of King's Country Market. It sat in the bend of a two-lane road on the lower slope of Blue Mountain, where a hand-lettered sign offered the traveling public GIFTS FOR ALL OCCASIONS and WHOLESALE MOTOR OIL. There was a Coke machine on the front porch. A brief afternoon thunderstorm had dampened the red dirt around it and left the air smelling of clay and wet leaves.

Sawyer got out, ambled up the steps, and leaned companionably on the counter just inside the door. Behind it a girl with frizzed blond hair was reading a copy of the *National Enquirer* headlined AMAZING DOG TALKS TO THE DEAD. She looked up reluctantly.

"Afternoon," Sawyer said. He picked out a Mars bar and put it on the counter.

"Fifty-two cents."

Sawyer rummaged in his pocket. "Got a report of gunfire around here this morning. You hear anything?"

The girl shook her head.

"Report came from right down the road," Sawyer said. "Don't see how you could have missed hearing it."

"I didn't hear nothing," the girl said. "I get pretty busy around here."

"I can see that."

Sawyer had been hearing much the same all day. Blue Mountain was wild country, high and isolated. Too many Blue Mountain folk had kin or connections with the numerous illegal doings that occurred on Blue. Those who hadn't were just leery of the rest, or distrustful of an authority that they encountered only in times of embarrassment or tragedy.

Sawyer peeled the wrapper off his candy bar. "You live around here?"

The girl nodded. "Up the holler a ways." She gestured at a gravel road that turned off the two-lane blacktop beside the store.

"Well, assuming that you *had* heard something—which I know you didn't—where do you think it coulda come from? Knowing the neighborhood as you do."

"I *didn't* hear nothing."

"I know you didn't. But *if* you were to hear gunfire—right now, for instance—who would you kinda think *maybe* it might be?"

"I dunno." She studied the photo of the Amazing Dog. "Right many people got guns. They shoot at cans an' stuff. No harm shootin' at cans."

Sawyer took a bite of his candy bar, chewed and swallowed. "How about shootin' at people who get found where they don't belong?"

The girl's impassive expression wavered for a moment, and her lip twitched. "I reckon it's been done," she said, "but I didn't hear it."

"Well, thanks," Sawyer said. He put another Mars bar and some more coins on the counter. He thought he'd just go home and make tuna salad. He didn't like it, but Rosalie and the kids did, and he wouldn't care if he ate enough candy bars. "I might be back through tomorrow," he said. "Just in case you remember anything." He paused with his hand on the screen door. "You know anybody named Shale?"

The girl's face became expressionless again. "Folks don't always tell me their names," she muttered.

"I guess they're pretty private around here. You ever see anybody Japanese?"

The girl stared at him and started to giggle. "Now, that I'd remember."

He might as well have asked her if she'd seen a Martian, Sawyer thought. *Damn that Hull, I told him so.*

The June twilight was warm and it hummed faintly, an unidentifiable insect noise that began as the sun set and would almost last the night. Mary Rose sat on the top step of the Hallorans' porch with her arms around her knees and wondered what Lee Bowling would do to her if she didn't get back before summer term started. Hull came out of the cabin and sat down beside her. Behind them there was a sense of unobtrusive activity. She imagined that some of the Hallorans' pursuits were of necessity nocturnal.

"I reckon we're here for a day or two," Hull said.

Mary Rose lifted an eyebrow at him. She had never heard him say "reckon" before. "You *are* a chameleon," she said.

"It's a professional habit," Hull said. "I need to be." All the same, he thought it was an accent insidiously easy to acquire. He looked across the clearing at the mountain laurel, misty as white smoke among the trees. "I never saw mountains this beautiful," he said quietly.

"No," Mary Rose said. "I don't think I could leave them."

The screen door banged behind them. Tom Halloran stood there thoughtfully, the John Deere cap pulled low over his eyes, shading them now not from the sun but from whoever might wish to look too closely into them. He considered Hull. "I got a few things to do," he said. "If y'all want to, you can come along."

Hull tilted his head, considering Halloran in his turn. He thought there was something about the invitation that was not to be refused; a mark of trust, an invitation into some other world, in its way as dangerous as that of the drug merchants, but also with the innocence of anachronism, of the morning of the land. *I'm losing my marbles,* he thought. *These guys make illegal hooch. If I don't watch it, I'm gonna start thinking old Zeke is Daniel Boone.* But he stood up. "Yeah, we'd like to come along."

Halloran nodded and set off up the hollow with no further comment. Hull and Mary Rose followed. At the tree line he turned into some path that neither of them could see in the thickening twilight. The moon was up, and they followed the bobbing of his yellow John Deere cap across a ridge and down into a hollow on its farther side. A dirt road angled up it and appeared to just run out and stop, whatever it had gone to reclaimed decades ago by the mountain. Halloran pushed his way through another row of young pines, and as they followed him, Hull wiggled one experimentally.

"Quit it," Mary Rose hissed at him. "He'll make us go back if you get too noticing."

"Y'all wait here a minute," Halloran said.

Hull cocked his head and listened to the night. With no voices or traffic sounds to mask it, the air around them reverberated with a clacking, humming, screeching chorus that was almost deafening compared to the stillness of a western night. He had never realized bugs were so loud. "What the hell *is* that?" he whispered to Mary Rose.

"Cicadas," Mary Rose said. "You hardly ever see them. They only come out at night. They're about three inches long and they look like a giant fly. All the ones MacArthur catches are dark, but I saw one come out of its chrysalis once, and it was pale green, like celery."

Hull looked as if he could do without a three-inch bug of any color. "How do they make all that racket?"

"I don't know," Mary Rose said. "I expect they're courting. The males make all the noise."

Hull looked at her sideways. Tom Halloran had vanished, leaving them alone in the raucous darkness.

"Doesn't California have any bugs?" Mary Rose said.

"None that carry on like that. We've got tarantulas. Six inches across, with big hairy legs." He waggled his fingers in front of her face.

"Oh, spiders," Mary Rose said. "I don't even count spiders. You ought to see the stuff that walks around on the screen door on a July night."

Hull gave up. The only rejoinder he could think of was praying mantises, and a bug whose central nervous system seemed to be centered in its sex organs—since those kept on functioning even after its lady love had chewed its head off—wasn't a subject he wanted to get into.

"Come on." Tom Halloran appeared like solidified smoke out of the shadows. "Step careful across here so I don't have to set it again."

Hull peered down and saw the faint line of a string stretched between two saplings.

"The ABC boys got a habit of settling in when they find a still," Tom said, "till whoever owns it comes back. They're right patient. I've known 'em to wait two, three days. That's why we've got the markers, make sure nobody's in there."

"What if they were?" Hull asked.

"Then we let 'em sit," Tom said. "After a while they get bored, bust the still up an' go home. They're gonna bust it up anyway."

"How many times has that happened?"

"Just once," Tom said. "That I can remember. I recall Daddy swearin' a blue streak. They'd knocked holes in all his boilers an' bust the cooling boxes all to hell. They never found out whose they were, though. An' I trust your interest is purely academic?"

"Purely," Hull said. He stepped carefully over the string. In the moonlight he could see the squat, utilitarian shape of a weathered shed. It occurred to him that if there was an ABC agent inside, he, Philip Hull, was going to get some publicity that would net him a very short career in law enforcement. He also had a suspicion that the Hallorans might not be as patient and peaceful as advertised. He looked at Mary Rose, picking her way carefully over muddy ground behind Tom Halloran, her shirt and jeans zebra-striped with the moonlit silhouettes of trees. Something very weird had happened to Steven's widow since March. Or happened to him. He thought of the phone call he'd made to Washington, the one that Mary Rose didn't know about. Maybe he needed his head examined. Maybe if they did, they wouldn't find anything in there. Maybe he'd been keeping his brain someplace else, like the praying mantis.

Inside the shed Halloran lit a kerosene lantern and turned it to a dim glow. Hull looked around him with interest. The shed walls masked the insect chorus outside, and from somewhere within came a faint, low buzzing like a beehive. Tom Halloran lifted a board off the top of a wooden vat and the sound intensified. Hull sidled over to look.

"This is the mash," Tom said. He didn't seem to mind their knowing what was in the shed, as long as they couldn't say with any certainty where it was. "The yeast makes it hum like that."

The top of the mash was covered with a layer of snowy foam. Halloran picked up a stick and flipped a small snake out of it. "The critters'll drink it if they can find their way in," he said. "You don't cover it up, you get foxes, coons, God knows what all drownin' in it. Some folks'll drop a dead coon in on purpose to kinda discourage the mash hounds."

"The what?" Mary Rose peered into the vat.

"Old drunks who'll sniff out a still just to drink the mash," Tom said. "Frankly, I don't think anybody that desperate's gonna mind a coon or a rat or two. We kinda take pains to keep 'em out."

"Good God," Mary Rose said faintly.

Tom looked amused. "Honey, you don't know the half of it. This is a scientific operation, 'cause it gets us a better price when folks know there ain't any hog feed in the mash and the whiskey ain't been doctored with paint thinner, but I could tell you tales about what some folks do to their liquor that'd curl your hair right up."

"Well, you already have," Mary Rose said.

"F'rinstance," Halloran said, settling the lid back on the vat, "mash turns quicker in hot weather. In winter it can take a right long time. Some folks'll drop a sack of manure or a car battery or a can o' lye in there to heat it up."

"Tom," Mary Rose demanded, "do you drink this stuff yourself?"

"Yup. Proof o' the quality o' the product," Halloran

said. "Lots o' folks in the white liquor business, they stick to Jack Daniel's, 'cause they know what's in their own. Now, we run a class operation. My daddy tells me your old granddaddy was a pretty fair judge of corn whiskey. You wouldn't ever sell him a jug that was doctored with wood alcohol or lye, or cleared up with Clorox, not more than once. Move a fair, honest product an' old Judge McCaskey wouldn't take notice of you unless he had to. But I heard he sent a couple of boys up the river for a right long time when he found out their stuff was givin' customers the blind staggers. My daddy says he tracked 'em down and turned 'em in himself. He musta been a character."

Mary Rose giggled suddenly. Honestly, the things you found out.

"You aren't even embarrassed, are you?" Hull whispered in her ear. He sounded amused.

"Well, you never know," Mary Rose said. "My grandmother had a yard man who worked for her for twenty years, and one day when he was getting old, he decided he was going to die and he wanted to get right with the Lord, and he told her, 'Miss Anna, my name's not really Will Jackson, it's George Ramfleet, and I'm wanted for murder in Tennessee.' You just never know."

"Well, who'd he murder?"

"I don't know," Mary Rose said. "I think my mother said he'd cut up his wife's lover in a bar. He was black, and the other man was black, and things being what they were then, they'd probably stopped looking for him years ago. I expect it set my grandmother back some, though."

"What did she do?"

"Well, I don't think she did anything. What *would* she do? He was old and sick, and it's not as if he was a homicidal maniac or anything."

"With stuff like that in the family tree, I'm surprised you're worried about a little thing like the *yakuza*."

"The *yakuza*," Mary Rose said firmly, "are after *me*. Besides, I'm not related to the yard man. Everybody I know has some kind of story like that."

Hull stuck his hands in his pockets and stood beside her

watching as Tom Halloran lifted the lid off a second vat of mash. "This is the damnedest place," he murmured.

The mash in the second vat was clear on top and the color of dark beer. Halloran trailed his fingers through it and stuck them in his mouth. "This'll run in a couple of days," he said. He motioned to Hull. "Here, taste it."

Hull poked a finger in the mash and licked it. It was sweetly sour and felt sticky on his finger.

"It's sweet when it starts out," Tom said. "You know it's ready to run when it loses that sticky feel and gets a bite to it."

"What happens then?"

"You pour the still beer off into the cooker. You *can* ferment the mash and cook it in the same pot, but that's a good way to scorch the grain, and scorched whiskey tastes like hell. And if you do scorch it, you can't mash back for another run."

"Huh?"

"You put in more sugar an' meal an' malt an' water, into the grain left from the first run, and ferment it again. The first run is sweet mash whiskey. The next is sour mash. We do maybe six, eight runs. Fourth run whiskey's about the best."

"Um." Hull could tell you how to cook dope—it was his business to know. But he had never stopped to wonder how whiskey was made. Since he didn't do dope, and did drink whiskey, he was curious.

"You pour off the mash into the cooker," Halloran said. He indicated an 800-gallon pot with a heavy cap. It sat on cinderblocks over a scorched pit with a propane burner in it. A pipe ran from the pot's cap to an oak barrel beside it, and from the barrel to a wooden box waterproofed with tar inside. Inside the box was a heavy copper coil which ended in a spigot that protruded, jug high, from the bottom third of the box.

"The alcohol will vaporize at about 173 degrees," Tom said. "Then it goes through the doubling keg. Heat builds up in the doubler, and it drops any meal residue, and more water. When it goes through the worm in the cooling box"—he indicated the copper coil—"it condenses back to a liquid, an' there's your whiskey. We got a nice little spring here to fill the cooler."

Hull saw that a pipe ran through the wall of the shed, its open mouth hanging across the top of the cooling box.

"But it's easy enough to sink a well shaft too. I know a guy who can witch water out of the ground just about any place you need it."

"Witch it?"

"They really can," Mary Rose said. "They take a forked stick, and the thing drops down where there's water. I watched a man sink a well one time, and he let me hold onto the stick. When it got to the right spot, it felt like there was a lead weight on the end."

Hull gave her a long look.

"Well, I don't know why it works," she said defensively, "but I'll swear it did. There was water there too."

Yeah, and I'm the King of Siam, Hull thought, but he didn't say it. Something about Tom Halloran's still, with its copper pots and coils, made him feel as if he'd stepped back about a century and anything was possible. "I never knew there was so much business in whiskey," he said.

"Hell, whiskey's always been a business," Tom Halloran said. He settled the lid back on the second mash vat. "They went and raised the 'sin' tax on legal booze again. That, an' times been hard. Times get hard, folks go to makin' whiskey. I read in the paper where the ABC boys think white liquor production's up about thirty percent. We keep track."

He rummaged in a corner of the shed, under a pile of empty sugar sacks, and produced two plastic gallon jugs full of a liquid so clear that it might have been water. "From the last run," he said. "Mountain hospitality."

Tom hefted a jug in each hand and strode back down the still path to the screen of trees that masked it from the old dead-end road up the hollow. They returned to the Halloran cabin in the next hollow by the same circuitous trail by which they had come; although Hull suspected that the two roads connected somewhere.

By the time they got to the Hallorans', the moon was full up and looked to Hull unaccountably large, like a melon, its black and silver shadows punctuated by the lazy green-gold lights of fireflies. The fireflies drifted through the trees, winking in and out above the stream, where moving water broke the moon into rippled pieces.

The Halloran boys had dragged into the open an assortment of rockers and cane-back chairs, and the ancient recliner that Mama Halloran favored. They escorted Mary Rose with grave ceremony to an overstuffed and musty armchair, upholstered in red horsehair.

Hull perched himself beside her on the arm, and when Tom Halloran poured him a juice glass full of Halloran corn whiskey, he accepted it solemnly.

Prodded by his mother, Tom's brother Asia brought out his guitar and fiddled with the tuning pegs while his audience offered suggestions. Once he blushed and said, "That ain't decent," with a glance under his lashes at Mary Rose.

Hull took a swallow from his glass. The whiskey was smooth on the tongue and raw going down. He choked and eyed the liquor with respect.

Mary Rose looked up at him, a smile fluttering around the corners of her mouth. "Watch it," she whispered. "White lightning's about a hundred proof."

Hull took a more gingerly sip and stared down at her, puzzled. He felt bemused, as if he were wrestling with some conundrum.

Asia Halloran was singing. His voice was a clear, beautiful tenor, and the song was old, older than whatever distant ancestor had brought it to the mountains.

"My true-love she sought my voice,
came running to her window,
crying, Oh, my love, I would be with you,
but locks and bolts do hinder!

"I stood a moment all in amaze,
considering my surrender.
My passion flew, my sword I drew,
I burst the door asunder."

Behind the action of the narrative, the notes were sad, with uncompromising knowledge of tragedy to come. Hull found them as achingly lovely as the mountain laurel.

"I took my sword in my right hand,
my true-love in the other,
said, if any man loves you better than I,
one man must slay another.

"Her uncle and another man
straight after me did follow.
I slew them both, I left them there,
in their own heart's blood to wallow."

Mary Rose had curled her feet under her in the red horsehair chair. The long fingers of both her hands were laced around a glass of Tom Halloran's liquor, and Hull saw that the glass was nearly empty. Hull took another sip from his own and then a long swallow, and could almost swear that he could taste the sorrowful beauty of the laurel in it.

Moonshine was potent stuff, he thought, not sure whether he meant the clear, white whiskey in his glass, or the watery light along a sword blade that he had followed here out of greed and misery. Or Mary Rose by moonlight. He looked down at the woman in the chair beside him. Moonshine, all of it, beautiful and dangerous as hell.

"We'll join right hands and swear our love
to bind us both forever.
Till fatal death doth spend our breath
We'll live our days together."

"That's a goddamn dirge, Asia," Zeke Halloran said. "Ain't you got somethin' with pep?"

"Sure." Asia ran his fingers over the strings.

"Somethin' old," Mrs. Halloran said. "I like to hear the words. Seems like all this new music, you can't understand the words."

"Preacher says it's Satan's music," Asia said. "Maybe you don't wanta hear 'em."

"Horseshit," Zeke said. "He can't understand 'em either."

Asia chuckled. His fingers flew along the guitar strings.

> *"When I was a young man growin' up,*
> *I thought I'd never marry,*
> *till I met up with a red-haired girl,*
> *and her name was Devilish Mary!"*

Hull slipped an arm around Mary Rose's shoulder and felt less maudlin as Asia Halloran picked his guitar and listed the dreadful things that had happened to the man who courted Devilish Mary. He chuckled and Mary Rose lifted her face, silvered and shadowed under the moon, to his. Hull's amber eyes glowed recklessly, not quite drunken. His mouth came down on hers. The Hallorans looked at them interestedly.

11.
Dreamscape With Owls

Hull shook a blanket out and spread it in the shadow of the Chevy, on the opposite side from the Hallorans' cabin. The cicadas had toned down some, and only an occasional firefly drifted silently through the warm dark shadows, blinking on and off.

Mary Rose clutched the two pillows with which Mama Halloran had provided her, along with blankets and sleeping bags. "There's room inside," she ventured. "Mrs. Halloran was going to put us in the front room, by the sofa."

Hull took the pillows out of her hands. "If you think I'm going to sleep with a houseful of Hallorans, you can think again. There isn't enough room for all of *them*, and they probably all snore." He unzipped a sleeping bag, spread it flat on the blanket, and laid the other one on top of it, while Mary Rose watched him uncertainly.

Hull knelt on the sleeping bags, looking up at her. "Besides," he said, "it's about time, isn't it?" His eyes caught hers and held them. His face had lost its usual half-mocking, half-piratical expression, and looked naked somehow, stripped of some outer skin. He stood up and put his hands on her shoulders. He bent his head and his lips touched hers, gentle and exploring.

She clung to him for a moment, and then he stepped

back to brace himself against the car and turned her around so that she leaned back against him. She lifted her face to his, and he put his hands on her breasts.

"You ever neck like this in high school?" he whispered.

Mary Rose giggled softly and nodded.

"I feel like I'm back there now," he said. "Awkward, wondering what the hell to do next." He wrapped his arms around her waist. The intensity of his desire seemed to frighten him.

The insect chorus hummed above them. Mary Rose tilted her head back in his embrace to look up at the stars flung against the sky. There was no time to feel guilty that Steven hadn't made her feel this way. This was something new entirely, and having given way before it, it was like traversing a river from which there was no way out save at the other end beyond the rapids—no going back.

The grip around her waist loosened and his hands found the buttons of her shirt. No going back. The shirt slid from her shoulders.

He undid the hooks of her bra, slipped it down her arms and held the shirt for her to put back on. (Who knew what Hallorans might be traveling in the night?) His hands caressed bare nipples.

Mary Rose arched her spine and flung her head back triumphantly. Hull knelt, pulling her down into the shadow of the car. He drew the top blanket over them and she lay for a moment motionless, listening to his beating heart.

Hull sat up and began to pull off his own clothes, leaving her propped on one elbow, watching him. He could see the moon in her eyes. He stripped his shirt off, and his jeans, and tucked the gun and holster into one boot. He reached for Mary Rose and found bare legs beneath the blanket. Bright eyes invited him to do what he wanted to about that.

Suddenly he was sixteen again, in "love" for the first time, trying to seduce his science teacher's daughter at a picnic. They had ended up in a ravine in the tangle of trees and underbrush behind the park's outdoor theater, and he had managed to get his hands down the front of her pants and hadn't known quite what he ought to do

after that. As it turned out, she knew, and things had gone
fairly well, but he found out later that there had been
poison oak in the ravine.

Hull chuckled ruefully and buried his face in Mary
Rose's shoulder.

"What are you laughing at?" she asked suspiciously.

"My past sins," he whispered in her ear. He pulled her
closer, feeling her body like a streak of electricity down
the length of his, and her long-fingered hands caressed the
muscles of his back. "I want you enough that it's killing
me," he said.

Mary Rose wrapped her arms around his back. She had
known it would come to this, if she ever ceased to watch
her step with Philip Hull. He lay on top of her now, his
hair hanging in his face, his breath coming faster. Whatever it was she had been looking for with Steven, she
found tonight.

Afterward he leaned on his elbows above her, trying to
catch his breath. "I'm sorry," he gasped. "I didn't come
up here meaning to do that." Then he smiled, embarrassed at the blatancy of the lie. "Yeah, I did." His fingers
traced the outlines of her face. "Yeah, I guess I did, at
that."

Mary Rose folded her arms behind her head and watched
the night move around them. The leaves fluttered in a
poplar tree above them and an owl floated by on silent,
smoky wings. Her arms felt like lead, but her heart hammered recklessly against her ribs, as if it clamored to get
out; to leave her and to go to him.

Hull flipped over on his back, sighing, and pulled the
covers over them enough to be decent. He rested his head
on the pillow by hers. "What was that thing that flew by?"

"An owl, a big one."

"I've never seen one up close."

"It's probably hunting." They lay in silence, ostensibly
waiting to see if the owl came back.

"I keep thinking about the money," Hull said finally.
"For a while there I kept wondering if I could keep the
thing, but . . ." He shook his head. "I don't know, I must
have been nuts, it'd be like keeping a bomb."

"They wouldn't ever give up, would they? The *yakuza* people?" she asked.

"Nope. Anyway, the money's been looking better lately, which is where I started; only not quite." He turned his head on the pillow and smiled at her. His face had lost the tight-strung look it had worn since she had known him. It seemed to be a new face altogether. "I thought Japan first—you'd like Japan. And afterward I'll take you to England. And down the river on your steamboat, if you still want to go."

"You left out the carnival in Rio," she told him.

"Absolutely," he said. "We absolutely have to go to Rio. I don't know much about Rio, but there's a poem of Kipling's, I read it when I was a kid,

> *Great steamers, white and gold,*
> *Go rolling down to Rio*
> *(Roll down—roll down to Rio!)*
> *And I'd like to roll to Rio*
> *Some day before I'm old.*

I don't know, it made an impression on me."

"That's from the *Just So Stories*," Mary Rose said. "I remember that." Odd, to think of him as a child. "What did you want to be?" she asked idly. "When you were that age?"

"As far as I can remember," Hull said, "a garbageman. How about you?"

"Oh, I was very feminine, I wanted to be a princess." Mary Rose grimaced. "That wore off." It had worn off during the time she had lived with a man who had told her that if she wanted to get her doctorate, that was all right as long as she didn't make more money than he did. Since even then she'd wanted to teach, it hadn't been a subject that was likely to come up, but it had been enough. She didn't think she'd tell Philip about that. She wondered how many women he didn't think he'd tell her about. "Do you remember this?" she said after a minute.

"There runs a road by Merrow Down—
A grassy track today it is—
An hour out of Guilford town,
Above the river Wey it is.
Here, when they heard the horse-bells ring,
The ancient Britons dressed and rode
To watch the dark Phoenicians bring
Their goods along the Western road.

When I read that, it was the first time I decided I wanted to go to England. Maybe Kipling's an unhealthy influence."

"He had a feeling for things that endure," Hull said.

"So many years of . . . of habitation," Mary Rose said. "Of people on the same land. There are places like that here. Not as old, of course."

"Yeah, and fine old traditions," Hull said, laughing. "Your dark Phoenicians, for instance, peddling bootleg whiskey. Which they brew up with lye and dead raccoons."

Mary Rose gave a little hoot of amusement. "Not," she said primly, "in *my* family. But it's a revered tradition all the same."

"I think," Hull said judiciously, "that my problem is not that I don't understand women, it's that I don't understand Southerners."

"Southerners don't understand Southerners," Mary Rose told him. "And nobody is supposed to understand Southern women."

"Why not?"

"It gives us a good excuse for going to bed with people we shouldn't." She put her hand to her mouth suddenly. "Erase that. Forget I said that."

"No." He sat up and pulled her up too. "Look, I know what you're thinking."

"No, you don't."

"You're thinking all I've been wanting ever since I got here has been to get you in the sack. Am I right?"

"No, you're *not* right."

"And you think I've got a dangerous profession and I'm not much of a bet for the long run—"

"I *said* you're not right!"

"And you wonder if maybe you're addicted to that, because you took up with Steven too."

"Damn you, Philip, that comes too close."

"Would it help if I told you most of it's not true?"

"It depends on which parts are," she said. "You can tell me that."

"All right, I have a dangerous job."

"Uh-huh."

"That's all. If you worry about the rest of it, you haven't got all your oars in the water."

"It doesn't bother *you*, about Steven?"

"No. It did for a while, but it doesn't now."

"Why not?"

"Think about it," Hull said. "You'll figure it out."

Mary Rose looked at the half smile playing around the corners of his mouth, and the way his eyes rested on her. If all he'd wanted was to get her in the sack, he'd have felt guilty as hell. That being the case . . .

"Uh-huh," he said. "I think you got it." His fingers touched her cheek. He drew them down her neck to trace the hollows of her throat. "Since we do happen to be here . . ." he murmured after a moment, and bent forward. His lips still smiled as they brushed lightly against her neck. Mary Rose laid her face against his damp hair.

"Lie down?" he suggested.

Passion returned with swift, unexpected intensity. There was some old magic loose in the mountains, in white liquor and the smoky blossoms of the laurel, in the insect chorus and the silence of the owl, and in the feel of her body twisting under him in the shadow of Steven's car. *You weren't ever Steven's.* He was sure enough of that that he didn't need to say it. *I'm sorry, buddy.* His weight pinned her to the blankets; his breath came in ragged gasps. *Jesus God, what if I'd met you while he was still alive?*

The uncertainty of their first encounter was gone. She clung to him, pale legs wrapped around his hips, her head thrown back. Her hair was a black tangle on the blankets. He pushed himself into her and she opened her eyes wide. He had never made love to a woman who looked him in the eye while he did it.

Later, when Mary Rose lay still again beneath him, Hull leaned over her, his head bent to her shoulder, and knew he was drunker than white liquor could account for.

The moonlight flowed along the leaves of the poplar like rippling water. . . .

"Philip!" Mary Rose struggled to sit up with a shriek.

"Jesus! What is it?" He lunged for the gun he had left with his boots.

"The sword! Where's the sword?"

He sank down on the blankets again, breathing hard. "It is in the trunk of the car," he said distinctly. "Under the carpet. You just took ten years off my life."

"I'm sorry," she said contritely. "I didn't think of it until now."

"It's been there since ten minutes after we got here. Tom knows where it is."

"But anybody might have—"

"With Hallorans all over the place? I'd just as soon stick my hand in a tank of piranha. Besides . . ." He looked at her accusingly. "You mean you just now stopped to wonder where it was?"

"I had other things on my mind," Mary Rose said. She felt around on the blankets, collecting loose hairpins.

Hull grinned at her. "Such as?"

Mary Rose put the hairpins in a neat little pile by the Chevy's back wheel. She snuggled down into the bed and pulled the top blanket over her. "You're conceited enough," she said.

Hull continued to look at her. She burrowed deeper, until only the top of her head showed.

"I expect I am," he said triumphantly.

The lights in the emergency room ceiling were round, like saucers, and they hurt Jem's eyes. If he looked at them for too long, the room started to go around, swooping sickeningly. They'd given him a shot of something.

"Well, son, next time you try taking your foot off with a

hatchet, try to do it some closer to town." A cheerful doctor put the last stitch in Jem's foot, while Jem lay miserably on the narrow metal cot. "If it hadn't been for your friend tying it up like he did, I don't expect you'd have made it."

"He ain't my friend," Jem said venomously. Shirley Simkins had wrapped Jem's foot up in a torn bedsheet pulled painfully tight, stuck Jem in the back of his pickup, and driven to the nearest telephone. There he had called the Rescue Squad and gone home.

"Well, you can just praise the Lord he didn't let you bleed to death," the doctor said. He was young and had grown up in Sarum. He had a pretty good idea that if it *had* been a hatchet that had chopped up Jem Shale's foot, it hadn't been Jem wielding it. And also that Jem wasn't going to tell him any more than he already had. Next week the doctor might find himself treating the other guy, also piously claiming to have slipped with a hatchet.

"I suppose it's too much to expect that you've got any insurance?" The admitting nurse sighed at him over the top of her clipboard. When Jem didn't answer, she made a brisk notation on the form, indicating that of course he hadn't—people who chopped each other up with hatchets never did.

The doctor checked the next cot, where a small boy who had eaten his mother's birth control pills was disconsolately throwing them up in a basin. "That's right, son. You want them to all come up." He returned his attention to Jem. "You got anyone to come get you?"

Jem was silent.

"How about it, son? You got a ride home?"

"My pa, I reckon," Jem said. His head felt funny and his foot looked swollen and grotesque. He had never been injured before, and he was outraged.

"All right, you can wait for him here." The doctor left Jem staring morosely at his bandaged foot. The little boy threw up again, assisted by a frightened, exasperated father. On the other side an enormously fat woman had one hand stuck in a tin can.

The automatic doors whooshed open to admit a tall man

in a slouch hat. He glared at the admitting nurse. "You got my boy in here? Name's Shale."

The nurse looked up at Ben Shale, dust-covered and truculent. Silently she pointed a finger at Jem.

"Get up offa there." Ben grabbed his offspring and hauled him upright, and Jem howled when his foot hit the floor. "It'll hurt a damn sight worse if I stomp on it," Ben informed him. "Ain't you got any crutches?"

"You gotta rent 'em," Jem said sullenly.

Ben Shale pulled a twenty dollar bill out of his front pocket and put it on the counter. "If it's more'n that, you can whistle for it," he told the nurse. He propelled Jem through the doors.

"That sumbitch tried to kill me with a sword," Jem said. "I hope you got him."

"That Jap says if Hull had tried to kill you, he'd a done it," Ben growled. "Get in." He pushed Jem into the cab of a blue pickup and threw the crutches in the back.

"I'm gettin' *tired* o' that Jap," Jem said. "I'm gonna fix him." The codeine slurred his words but produced the single-mindedness of a belligerent drunk. "I ast if you got Hull. I'm gonna fix him too."

"Just shut up." Ben Shale put the pickup in gear. "I've had about all I can stand."

"Ain't nobody cut *you* with a sword," Jem announced. He looked at his father suspiciously. "You didn't get him, did you?"

"Just shut the fuck up," Ben muttered.

"You din' get him," Jem said. His head nodded in a thickening mist of codeine and post-terror exhaustion. He lifted it with an effort and studied the interior of the cab. "What you doin' with Sulie's truck?"

Ben Shale thought about stopping the truck right there and just clipping him one upside the ear, but he was just too tired.

Jem began to snore as the truck ground up the back roads of Blue Mountain. In a quiet, unpleasant fury, Ben Shale saw the white Mustang limping up the dirt road ahead of them. Hidehiko Ota was waiting for them in the camp, perched like a vengeful schoolmaster on a stool outside his cabin.

Ben Shale gunned the engine and Ota lifted his head and looked at him. *I oughta run right over the bastard*, Ben thought, furious because he was afraid to. He gunned the engine again. Ota didn't move. Ben slammed the pickup into neutral and jerked the key out. Ota smiled slightly.

Jem's brothers Roy and Emlen and their cousin Sulie climbed out of the Mustang. They gave it a look of loathing and glanced at Ben. "We got her runnin' but we gotta weld that gas tank," Roy said.

"Well, go do it," Ben said. "And keep that welder the hell away from the lab!"

"Do it yourself," Emlen said. "You want to make delivery on that next batch, you give me some lab time."

"You do it." Ben Shale pointed his finger at Roy and Sulie. "And watch your sparks."

"Fuck you!" Roy shouted at his brother's retreating back. They had spent the morning, nerves tight-stretched, straightening the front end of the Mustang enough to drive it and jury rigging a patch on the gas tank. They had jumped at every sound and cursed each other at every opportunity. That Emlen was the only one among them who could cook methamphetamine to the buyer's specifications goaded Roy into a fury. "What about him?" Roy jerked a thumb at Jem, snoring in the cab of the pickup.

"Shake him outta there," Ben said. "He can help."

"I'd like to—" Roy jerked the pickup door open. "I thought you said that Hull didn't know the mountain," he shouted over his shoulder at his father. "You're fulla shit, you know that?"

Ben Shale picked up a two-by-four that happened to be lying there handy. "You open your mouth one more time, I'm gonna put this in it."

"Well, goddammit, where'd Hull get a tractor-trailer rig?" Roy yelled. Jem fell out of the cab with a scream of pain, and Roy hauled him to his feet. "Don't *you* give me any shit."

Ben watched them lurch off toward the barn that housed

the welding equipment. Sulie slid behind the wheel of the Mustang again and it rattled across the yard after them. Hidehiko Ota materialized silently at Ben's side, and Ben spun around. "Don't do that if you know what's good for you," Ben said darkly. "Folks walk too quiet around here, sometimes they get a bullet in 'em."

Ota smiled. It gave his face the expression of a maleficent buddha. "I also wish to know where Hull acquired his truck," he informed Ben. "And the men who drove it."

"Well, you go on wishin'," Ben said. "I got a delivery to make." He had recognized the driver of the tractor-trailer rig, and he hadn't liked what he'd seen. He knew Zeke Halloran by sight and reputation.

"Your delivery will wait."

"Like hell it will. We ain't there, they don't buy. I've wasted enough time on you. Got my boy hurt, ain't gonna be no use for a coupla weeks."

"Your boy was very lucky," Ota said. "*Ko-getsu-nami* is a killing sword. It takes life when it is drawn, that is its purpose. Philip Hull has very foolishly used it as a toy. This is the modern world, Mr. Shale, I do not speak of supernatural will. But you may believe me when I tell you that the sword will have someone's life before the matter is settled." It was not an idle threat. Ota believed that implicitly. He studied the rubbish-strewn yard. "Also, my employer is getting restless. If I cannot give him the sword, I will at least have to give him the young man who has tried to cheat us and make us look foolish. We *never* look foolish, Mr. Shale."

"Goddamn you." Ben Shale's pale blue eyes were vicious. Ota's were dark, slitted, unreadable. The *yakuza* agent was a good eighteen inches shorter than Shale, and his polished shoes and subdued and correct business suit would have been funny on anyone else. On Ota they underscored the menace that Ben Shale recognized, although he did not realize the extent of its power. Emlen would need two days to cook the rest of the batch, with Roy and Sulie to pack it and load it in the light plane that was parked in a plowed field a mile away. Manufacturers sold their product uncut, because it was easier to move that way. The buyer would step on it four or five times, and sell it again. By the time it hit the street, it might have been stepped on ten times, cut with milk sugar or powdered chocolate, the quantity doubling each time, the value increasing accordingly. The users would snort it, or sometimes slam it, inject it. If they were hardcore users, they would grow thin, pale, paranoid, seeing demons in the street. If it was stronger than they bargained for, it might kill them. None of this was of interest to Ben Shale, save for making his delivery. The doomed, the evil, and the hopeless who bought his product were the province of men like Philip Hull.

"I gotta have two days," Ben said. "They ain't going anywhere without we know it. There ain't that many roads down offa Blue."

"And if they run for it?" Ota said.

"I got folks here'll tell me. Your boys ain't the only ones that's learned how to twist an arm. When they run for it, we'll get 'em."

"No."

"What in hell you mean, 'No'?"

"If they run, you will chase them again, shooting off guns like an actor in a television program, until every policeman in your state knows about it, and Philip Hull will outdrive you again." Ota clasped his hands behind his back and gazed at the treetops. He emitted a sound Ben Shale finally recognized as a laugh.

"You're walkin' on shaky ground, Ota."

Ota lowered his gaze and turned it on Ben Shale. "Find out where they have gone to earth," he said. "I will wait."

Ben Shale, looking at him long and hard, realized that he meant it.

"*Roy!*"

Roy Shale stuck his head out the barn door. He was wearing welder's goggles, which did nothing to disguise his temper. "What the hell you want now?"

"Get over here!"

"For—" Roy cut his curse short and flung the goggles on the ground. "You want that car fixed or not?" he yelled, stalking across the yard. He was thin and towheaded, like the rest of them, and his pinched features gave his face the quick, vicious intelligence of a weasel. He jerked a thumb at Ota. "I ain't his messenger boy."

"You ain't in charge either," Ben said. "You been gettin' too big for your britches. That was Zeke Halloran drivin' that rig. He's got a still somewhere the other side o' the mountain, an' you're gonna go find out where. Break a coupla arms if you have to, but find out. An' stay clear o' the cops."

"You wanta make delivery or not?" Roy said. "That car ain't goin' nowhere with a hole in her gas tank, an' Jem's about as high as a kite on that hospital dope. He gives me any more shit, I'm gonna fix his other foot."

"You give *me* any shit, I'm gonna fix *you*," Ben said. He picked up the two-by-four again. "I can still do it." He didn't like taking orders from Ota, but he wasn't going to admit that was what he was doing. Ben kept his offspring in line with a stick. If he let down his guard, he'd wake up one day and find Roy in charge.

Roy considered the odds. If it had been him, the Japs could have had Jem with his compliments, but Emlen had a soft spot for Jem. If Roy beat his old man, he'd still have Emlen to contend with, and Emlen had a mean streak of his own. Sulie didn't count. Sulie was up here making dope because the cops were on him for rape down in Lynchburg. Sulie wouldn't cross anyone; he might turn out to be expendable.

Ben advanced on him with the two-by-four. "You gonna do what I say or am I gonna knock your head in?"

Roy pulled a billed cap out of his back pocket and stuck it on his head. "I reckon you can try it after we make that delivery," he said. "I ain't got time for you now." He climbed in the pickup and revved up the engine. "Go weld that gas tank!" he yelled out the window.

The pickup bumped out of the yard and disappeared under the trees that overhung the road. Ben flung the two-by-four at a crow hopping among the garbage that spilled from a green plastic bag outside the four-room cabin Ben shared with the boys and Emlen's wife. She was a sallow, round-faced girl with an air of almost botanical inertness that was less stupidity than it was a shield against the Shales. She came out on the porch to see what the noise was, looked at Ben expressionlessly, and went back inside.

"You go do whatever the hell it is you do all day," Ben said to Ota, "an' stay outta my way." He picked up Roy's goggles and went into the barn. In a moment Ota heard the hiss of the welding torch.

"Maureen!" Emlen yelled from the lab. The woman came out of the cabin again and trudged across the yard to help him. Ota wondered fleetingly what monstrous offspring their union would produce.

In his own cabin he laid the cake of ink and his writing brushes on the table and sniffed the air with disgust. The laboratory smelled like human excrement. In Japan the drug manufacturers did not live in the same house as their stink. The Shales were Neanderthals. He thought, *Sadao, I have done much for you this time*.

At nightfall Roy Shale came back in the truck.

12.
Ill Met by Moonlight

Mary Rose awoke to the smell of coffee and bacon drifting on the morning air from Mama Halloran's kitchen, and found Hull sitting on the hood of the Chevy, watching her.

"Have you been watching me sleep?" she demanded.

"Yeah, I wanted to see if you snore."

Mary Rose gave him an outraged look and felt around under the blankets for her clothes.

"Don't worry, you don't," he said.

Mary Rose grinned at him in spite of herself. "I do when I'm drunk," she informed him, "so you'd better watch it." She took a deep breath of warm morning air. It smelled of honeysuckle. Somewhere up in the trees a cardinal was congratulating itself on its good looks. She wriggled into her underpants and jeans, keeping the blanket half over her, since Hull seemed disinclined to turn his back like a gentleman. She started to button her shirt and Hull jumped off the Chevy, found her bra and handed it to her. He took a quick look to see that there were no Hallorans lurking nearby, and kissed her on the nape of her neck.

"I never ply women with liquor," he told her. "It's been my experience that it just makes 'em go to sleep on me."

Mary Rose smiled at him sunnily. "Maybe that's just

your personality," she said. She peeled her shirt off, hooked her bra, and dived back into the shirt again before he could start something. They smiled at each other, thoroughly pleased with themselves.

"Damn," Hull said. "Couldn't we just go back to bed?"

A shadow fell across the ground beside them. "Council of war," Tom Halloran said. "You got half an hour to eat breakfast, then we gotta talk."

"Come on," Hull said. "I've been in the kitchen already. Mrs. H. has outdone herself. If I ate like that every day, I'd weigh four hundred pounds."

"Ma's showing off," Tom said. "We don't get much company."

Hull held out his hand and pulled Mary Rose to her feet.

"I want my toothbrush," Mary Rose said. "And I want to wash my face."

"Fine-haired, isn't she?" Hull said. He walked around the car, whistling, and got Mary Rose's suitcase out of the backseat.

Tom Halloran looked from one to the other of them, and Mary Rose blushed. "You can freshen up in the house," Tom said. "Glad you slept comfortable." He departed, shaking his head.

"Oh, Lord," Mary Rose said. She put her face in her hands.

"I don't know what you're so worked up about," Hull said. "Your pals at the college think this kind of thing's been going on since I got here."

Mary Rose chuckled ruefully. "Why don't you just take out an ad?" she said. "Or skywriting would be nice."

"I feel like it," Hull said. "Come and eat breakfast." He strolled across the clearing to the Hallorans' front porch, whistling again. After a moment Mary Rose recognized the tune: the song Asia Halloran had been playing last night, "Devilish Mary."

At the table the Hallorans, making the most of unexpected plenty, were tucking into bacon, eggs, fried potatoes, and biscuits. Noonie had her trigonometry book propped in front of her. Mary Rose stopped to look over her shoulder.

"We got two more days to go," Noonie said. "An' finals both days."

"How are you doing?"

"Okay, I guess."

"She makes A's," Tom said.

Mary Rose put a hand on Noonie's shoulder. "You come see me next year if you want a letter of recommendation for Tech."

Noonie smiled. It lit up her thin face.

"That's right nice of you," Zeke Halloran said.

"You hit them books, Noonie, you'll live to make monkeys outta all of us," Asia Halloran said. He pulled a chair up to the table and stacked biscuits on his plate.

"That's kind of you," Mrs. Halloran said. She poured Mary Rose a cup of coffee. "No, you sit down. That's a one-man kitchen in there, and I got my own system. But I take it kindly that you take an interest in Noonie. She's got a talent for school, better'n anyone in the family." She dropped her voice a little. "She's gonna do somethin' with it if it kills me."

"I'm sure she will," Mary Rose said, embarrassed. She had grown up with a lawyer father and grandfather, and a grandmother who had been the first woman doctor in the county. Education had been taken for granted. "I'm going to get Noonie into Tech with a scholarship if I have to blackmail someone," she whispered to Philip Hull.

"Y'all 'bout through?" Tom Halloran said. "We got a coupla problems."

Mary Rose applied herself to her eggs. The Hallorans ate in silence, stoking up for the day. When they were through, they went off on whatever unlawful pursuits they practiced during the day, and Noonie picked up her schoolbooks. She waved at Mary Rose as she started down the dirt track, her books under one arm and a biscuit in the other hand. She had nearly a mile to walk before she could catch the school bus.

"The way I see it," Tom Halloran said, sitting down on the porch steps, "is, we got to get you all, *and* that sword, outta here to the coast before those Shales get wise to where you are. The less truck you have with them, the better." He looked at Philip Hull as Hull opened his mouth to speak. "You can come back here after, an' shoot 'em if you still want to, but you're a bigger fool than I took you for if you go lookin' to take 'em on now."

"They killed my buddy," Hull said. In the light of last night's events, it had become even more important to him, and to Mary Rose—and whatever was going to happen between them now—that Steven be avenged.

"I don't wanta tromp on anyone's feelings," Tom said. He looked at Mary Rose. "I know you were married to him. But he'll be just as dead whether you get yourself shot by Shales or not. An' as I understand it, if you get this sword everyone's so hot to lay hands on to this guy in Virginia Beach, that Jap that's callin' the Shales' tune'll be outta the picture. Make the Shales a sight easier to deal with."

Hull sighed. "I *don't* want to go up there and shoot them. I'm a cop, dammit. But I want to get enough on 'em to make the cops around here pay some attention."

"Won't be any harder afterward," Tom said. "You wanta get Mary Rose hurt?"

"Of course not," Hull said testily. "I'm going to have to run for it. I said that all along. I'd like to leave Mary Rose here."

"Well, you aren't going to," Mary Rose said. Her mouth had that stubborn set to it again. "That thing that got Steven killed is half mine. We've been through this before."

Hull stared at the toes of his boots, exasperated. He didn't want to make the drive to the coast in pure terror all the way that Mary Rose was going to get killed. But to do her justice, he didn't see how he could ask her to sit up on the mountain not knowing what was happening, fearing the same thing for him. "All right," he said quietly.

"I'm not a suitcase, Philip," Mary Rose said. "You can't just park me someplace while you take all the risks."

"I said all right."

"Shut up," Tom Halloran said. "You won the argument." He thought they were going to have an interesting time together, if it lasted. "You come down off the mountain quiet as you can—Asia an' Merrick an I'll hang around an' give 'em something to chase if they need it."

Hull couldn't find any fault with that. The Shales knew Zeke's tractor-trailer rig now. He and Mary Rose would do better to just take the Chevy. He stood up. "I'm gonna check the car out. It got hell shaken out of it coming up here. Tom, do you think Merrick would go down to town and pick some stuff up for me? I don't want to leave till dark anyway."

"Sure. What kind of stuff?"

"I'll give you a list," Hull said. He walked over to the Chevy, pulled the trouble light out of the front seat, and eased himself under the car.

Tom Halloran glanced at Mary Rose. "You sure you know what you're doin'?"

"No." Mary Rose wrapped her arms around her knees, rested her chin on them and sighed.

Merrick came back about six o'clock with Hull's shopping list: ammunition for Hull's revolver and the automatic that Steven had kept under the driver's seat, fresh batteries for the radio and the little recorder, and a five-gallon gas can. From other bags he produced a billed cap which Hull adjusted at the angle the Hallorans wore theirs, and a blond wig which Mary Rose regarded with loathing.

"I won't wear that," she informed him. "I'll look like a diner waitress."

Hull looked up from the Chevy's rear end, to which he was affixing a Texas license plate. "That's the idea," he said. "Plenty of black Chevies on the road. It's a nice inconspicuous car, that's why Steven drove it."

"I'll be about as inconspicuous as a fire in that wig."

"Well, you won't look like you, which is the point. Merrick, where's the rest of the stuff?"

"Right here," Merrick said. He handed Hull a cardboard box. "I got a little leery about signin' my name for this stuff, with all the cops that been cruisin' around—I saw two cars fulla the sheriff's boys again—so I kind of borrowed it from a fella I know that sinks wells for folks."

Mary Rose peered into the box. "Philip, that's dynamite!"

"Don't worry, it doesn't go off without a detonator." Hull stowed the box in the Chevy's trunk.

"Well, what's it for?"

"It's just in case." Hull pulled a blanket over the box and packed the gas can in beside it.

"Just in case *what*?" Mary Rose said. "You think you might want to blow up a bridge?"

"I might want to block a road," Hull said. "You know, us on one side and them on the other?"

"Do you know what you're doing with that stuff?"

"Probably."

"Don't worry," Zeke Halloran said. "I sunk many a well with dynamite. This new stuff they got wouldn't go off if you hit it with a hammer, not without you got the blasting cap. I remember back a ways, the damned stuff 'ud go off if you looked squinch-eyed at it. Now the ABC boys carry it around to blow up folks' stills with. You hear a blast up in the mountains, someone's sinkin' him a well or blowin' up another man's livelihood."

"Uh-huh." Mary Rose looked at Hull. He was putting on the front license plate, the cap pulled down over his eyes. She was beginning to suspect he liked the way he looked in that cap. Blowing up a still with dynamite was one thing, but Mary Rose wouldn't take any bets that he could block a road with it. She wouldn't bet he couldn't either.

"Done." Hull tossed the tool kit in the trunk. "It'll be dark enough in half an hour. If I can get down the hill with no lights, I'm gonna do it."

"You can if I go with you," Tom said. "I'll come back up with Asia and the truck, once we know you got off okay."

"I appreciate it." They looked at each other awkwardly, not sure how to make their parting. The damnedest good-byes he'd ever said, Hull thought.

A quavering, furious, singsong howl erupted from under the front porch, where the Halloran hounds spent most of the day in the cool. A moment later the yard was full of barking dogs.

"Jesus!" Zeke Halloran sprinted for the cabin.

Hull spun around, trying to see into the twilit woods. He thought he caught a flicker of movement on the slope above them.

"Shales!" Merrick said. "It's gotta be!" He ran after Zeke.

"How do you know it's not cops?" Hull shouted after him, but he got his gun out.

"Like hell," Tom Halloran said. "They don't catch us at the still, they got nothin' on us. Somebody who knows how to get here is scareder of the Shales than he is of us."

A shot came from the woods above them in confirmation of that. Hull jerked the door of the Chevy open. "Get in!" he shouted at Mary Rose.

"No!" Tom yelled. "You can't get out, not with them comin' up! There's a car down on the road somewhere, that's what set the dogs off!" He grabbed Mary Rose by the arm. "Get in the house!"

Hull hesitated, torn between the sword and Mary Rose, who was halfway across the yard. Another shot rang out, erratic, but closer. He could see men now, running down the hill through the trees. The dogs had spooked the trespassers into firing before they had a clear aim, but they were nearly on him now. If he didn't get away from the car, they'd know what was in it. Hull heard the other car now, coming up the road with an angry whine. Tom and Mary Rose stumbled up the front steps. The hounds, their duty done, disappeared under the porch again as the long barrel of Zeke Halloran's shotgun slid through the window and Tom pulled Mary Rose through the door.

Hull sprinted across the yard after them while the white Mustang skidded around the last turn. A shot went past his ear and he flattened himself behind the low stone firepit that provided the only cover in the yard. The Mustang stopped with a squeal of brakes and two more men came running from the cover beyond the road, crouching by the car as a blast from Zeke's shotgun went over their heads. Someone swore, and the Mustang backed ten feet off the road, until it was out of Zeke's angle of fire, with the men following, bent over beside it. One was shorter than the Shales, but broader in the shoulders. He wore a suit, incongruous and oddly menacing in the circumstances, and his hands cradled a small snub-nosed gun of very probable efficiency. He lifted his head and Hull saw his face.

"So you're real," Hull breathed. "I'm gonna take you to Sawyer on a plate." He hadn't doubted the *yakuza* agent's existence since the note on Mary Rose's doorstep, but he felt vindicated. Sawyer wouldn't have given the note the time of day, but a warm body with an undoubtedly faked passport—let Sawyer put that on his fiddle and play it.

The *yakuza* man hadn't seen him yet. Hull wriggled around until he had the firepit between him and the car, as well as the men on the hill, and took careful aim.

A bullet spat up a splatter of red clay by Ota's feet, and he wrenched the Mustang's door open and crouched behind it.

The men on the hill had reached the bottom of the slope. They stopped just inside the woods, and a bullet ricocheted off the rocks in the firepit. Hull looked longingly for other cover, but there wasn't any. He saw movement at the cabin windows. Another shotgun, with Tom Halloran behind it. Hull tried to take aim on the men in the woods, but he was afraid to lift his head for fear the Hallorans would inadvertently blow it off. He was between them and the foot of the hill. He lay flat along the ground, painfully aware that the rest of his ammunition was in the Chevy, parked on the far side of a much too open clearing. A bullet from the trees nicked the heel of his boot and he jerked his feet back until he was curled nearly into a ball. The twilight was fading steadily, the moon beginning to glow above the trees, illuminating him unpleasantly, while the men in the woods were only shadows among other moving shadows made by the night wind in the leaves.

A crack of rifle fire told Hull another Halloran had joined the fray, but in another few minutes they were going to need a night scope to pick anything out of those shadows. Hull lay low and turned his attention and his dwindling ammunition to the men behind the white car, specifically the *yakuza* agent, but he couldn't really see them either, any more than the men by the car could get a clear shot at the house. What the hell were they trying to do? If the Shales had learned enough about the Hallorans to find their way here, they must know they couldn't take on the whole Halloran clan with five men. They'd have to get them all to get the sword, and as far as Hull could tell, they weren't really trying. Two possible explanations occurred to him and he fired a last desperate shot as he saw the *yakuza* agent lift his head and take careful aim with his pistol at the far window of the cabin. Hull's shot went wide by no more than an inch, but it was his last cartridge.

The noise of a pitched gun battle was hellish. It swallowed up all the other sounds of twilight. Maybe Sawyer would hear it, if he was still prowling around. And how long would it take him to find them? Too damn long, Hull thought grimly.

There was a sudden cessation of sound. For unknown reasons, the Shales held their fire. And the Hallorans ceased because they couldn't see anything to shoot at. The night was silent: not a bird, not an insect. The wild creatures of the mountain were frozen in stillness, cowering in their burrows and hidden dens before a sound they knew well: men with guns. The only movement was the whisper of the night wind. For Hull fear was an emotion embodied by a sensation of trying to run through knee-high water with a swift-footed enemy behind. It came on him in earnest now. He lifted his head enough to risk a glance over his shoulder at the cabin. Mary Rose was inside, guarded by a platoon of Hallorans. If he could make it in too, they could probably stand them off. He drew himself up into a crouch and a bullet whipped past his ear. He flattened himself again, cursing. Had the Shales been counting his shots? When he didn't fire back, they'd be certain. Hull pounded his fist in the dirt, cursing himself for not having stuck a handful of cartridges in his pocket. Nobody but a moron went out without some backup.

The Shales and the *yakuza* man began to fire again, a steady barrage against the windows of the cabin. Hull looked up and saw the two men from the woods coming at

him across the clearing, zigzagging as they ran, against
ragged fire from the cabin. Hull looked for a place to run
to, but there was nowhere that wasn't in the line of fire
from the car. He stood up to run anyway, but they were
on him. He lashed out savagely with the barrel of his gun,
but they had guns that worked, and one of them put a
bullet through his foot. Hull staggered, and they grabbed
him under the arms, dragging him toward the white car.
There was another crack of rifle fire and one of the Shales
stumbled now, hands clutching his chest. He ran, falling,
toward the car, and arms reached out and pulled him in.
Hull connected his fist with the second man's chin, but his
damaged foot gave way when he put his weight on it. Ben
Shale dodged out from behind the car, grabbed him by
the other arm, and dragged him, thrashing frantically,
toward it.

"*Philip!*"

Hull heard Mary Rose's terror-stricken voice from the
front porch and looked back. "Get *inside!*" he screamed at
her. The Shales and the *yakuza* would have taken which-
ever one of them they could lay their hands on first, and
they might still change their minds.

With the struggling Hull between him and the Hallorans,
Ota crouched beside the car and with deliberate marks-
manship put two bullets in the back tires of the Chevy,
and of Merrick's green Ford and the Hallorans' pickup,
which were parked beside it.

The white Mustang's trunk was open, and Hull, fighting
wildly, felt himself lifted bodily and thrown inside. The lid
came down with a bang that reverberated inside his skull.

Behind them Merrick ran out of the shelter of the side
of the cabin, which he had reached by the expedient of
climbing out a window, and aimed his rifle at the now
vanishing car. He lowered it again and swore. If he hit a
tire at that speed, they'd probably go into a tree again,
and this time they might blow up. If he missed, he stood a
good chance of hitting the trunk instead.

Hull writhed in pain as the Mustang lurched into a tight
turn and threw his injured foot against the trunk wall.
Something smooth and heavy rolled against him. He put

out a hand to stop it and recognized the cold, familiar geometry of a tear gas grenade. The Shales had come prepared to flush out their quarry if need be. Hull didn't know what it would do to him if it went off inside the trunk, and he cradled it to him desperately as the Mustang went into another turn and he passed out.

The Mustang twisted down the mountain with Sulie bleeding in the front seat. At the Sarum hospital's emergency entrance, Roy and Emlen got him out between them and half dragged, half carried him through the doors. The nurse saw them and took charge.

"What happened?" She pushed a button and they were surrounded by doctors, nurses, a stretcher, and an IV rack.

"Got in a fight outside Delilah's," Emlen muttered. "We didn't see who done it."

The nurse didn't bother to answer. Delilah's was apt to turn up one or two patients a month in the course of an average summer. "Stay here," she said, not looking up. "The police will want a statement." When it appeared that the man on the stretcher was stable, she gave her attention more fully to his companions and discovered that they had vanished in the commotion.

Roy and Emlen flung themselves into the Mustang and Emlen put it in gear.

"What did you tell them?" Ota asked.

"Didn't tell them nothing," Roy muttered. "Think we're stupid?" He lapsed into silence, trying to figure how to get Sulie out of there before the Lynchburg cops took notice of him. The Sarum police would file some kind of report. Roy had no idea who they might share it with, but he figured if it could inconvenience him, they'd probably show it to everybody from the DEA on down. Roy turned and glared at Emlen. "This is your fault. Fucking dogs heard the car before we got close enough."

"Shut up," Ben Shale said. "What did the doctor say?"

"He ain't gonna die."

"Then I ain't gonna worry about him now," Ben said. If it hadn't been for his sister Mercy, Ben figured he'd just as soon have shot Sulie himself by now. Sulie had a mean streak that he never put to any good use but cussedness, and it made him unreliable in a business operation. But Mercy was cussed enough herself to sic the cops on him if anything happened to her boy that she thought was Ben's fault.

"We shoulda hung around long enough to make sure he told 'em what we told 'em," Emlen said.

Ben snorted. "An' have that bastard wake up an' start poundin' on the trunk?"

The white Mustang headed up Blue Mountain again. Hull groaned, tried to wake up, and slipped back into darkness. He came to as they dragged him from the car and tied him to a chair in the dilapidated barn; passed out again; and recovered consciousness unpleasantly when Ota held an open bottle of ammonia under his nose.

"Mr. Hull." Ota produced a camp stool and sat on it, according Hull a look of immense satisfaction.

The barn was almost empty, a cavernous space that loomed above Hull, appearing to expand and contract before his blurred gaze. He tried to focus his eyes on Ota.

"You are particularly stubborn," Ota said. "I haven't time for that."

"Maybe you're just particularly stupid," Hull said. "You mighta got the sword if you hadn't killed my buddy." He closed his eyes again, trying to still the sensation that the barn was moving like a bellows above him. His head ached, probably from carbon monoxide in the trunk. His foot had gone numb. He looked down and saw that someone had taken his boot off and tied a bandage around it. Apparently they didn't want him to bleed to death. He twisted his hands behind him, trying to work them loose from the cord that bound them to the chair. The cord bit into his wrists and didn't budge. His muscles were already beginning to cramp from the unaccustomed position. His ankles were bound to the chair legs in similar fashion. He shifted his foot a little and feeling returned abruptly in the form of searing pain. The barn expanded again, wavered, and closed in. It seemed to be in rhythm to his own breath.

"Where is the sword, Mr. Hull?"

Hull's eyes slitted open. "Fuck you."

Ota stood up. "You misunderstand me, Mr. Hull. I am offering to buy Ko-getsu-nami. I will give you your life for it. When you have sat in that chair a little longer, you will find that a reasonable arrangement."

Ota picked up the camp stool on which he had been sitting, and Hull heard the barn door creak shut behind him. Hull tried to focus his eyes on the barn. The floor was wood, bare, and grimy with years of dirt. Welding torches and a pair of acetylene tanks stood in one corner, amid nameless rubbish. A battered tool bench held an anvil and a vise, and an electric fan that someone had taken apart and given up on. A horseshoe that had been nailed over a window had slipped and hung upside down, with the luck running out of it. Hull hoped grimly that it wasn't his.

His head slumped forward on his chest. If he slept, maybe he wouldn't hurt so much. Ota would be back soon enough.

Ota set his camp stool down outside the barn door and sat on it, calmly waiting. He had learned long ago exactly how long it took the muscles of a man who was tied to a chair to cramp beyond bearing. Mr. Hull would produce the sword. And if he did not, there was always the woman. Ko-getsu-nami was only a thing to her—a thing worth money, but with no spirit; she would see no honor in it. She would give the sword or anything else she had to get the man back, Ota thought. She was stupid, ignorant as the Shales were. Yet Ota was aware that Philip Hull was not. That was the piece of the soul that they possessed in common, the dark kinship that bound natural enemies together.

Mary Rose ran to Steven's car and flung herself at the trunk. Frantically she wrestled with the latch. The Hallorans grouped themselves around her.

"Hold on, now," Tom said.

Mary Rose dragged the heavy box and the gas can out of

the trunk and pulled up the carpet. "I'm going to give it to them," she said. "What good is it to me?"

"Honey, you can't do that." Zeke Halloran put a hand on her shoulder.

"I can and I will. I don't care what Philip thinks."

"It ain't that," Zeke said. "You give it to 'em, what're they gonna do? Turn you and your friend loose to get 'em hauled in for kidnapping? That's serious business."

"Ohhh." Mary Rose slumped against the car.

"Zeke, you're scarin' her to death." Mama Halloran put a protective arm around Mary Rose. "There's been about enough o' that today."

"Best be said." Zeke's gruff voice was gentler than usual. "Look at it this way—they ain't got the sword, he's still alive."

Mary Rose pulled the Moonshine Blade out from under the carpet and turned it over in her hands. "What will they do?"

"Try to make him tell 'em where it is," Zeke said. He thought he'd better not elaborate on how. From the look on Mary Rose's face, she already had a pretty good idea. "Then they'll send someone for it. Probably with a note from Philip to say to hand it over peaceable. They know we outnumber 'em."

"What if he won't tell?"

"I 'spect they're hopin' *you* will."

"Well, what do we do?" Mary Rose felt out of her depth. She felt inclined to let these tall, dangerous men, gathered around her so solicitously, decide, although they seemed to have varying opinions themselves.

"Turn the cops on 'em—we ain't got no choice."

"Go in there ourselves an' take 'em apart."

"Wait till they send somebody an' hang on to him to bargain with."

"Ben Shale wouldn't ransom his own grandmother."

"They see the cops comin', whatta you think? They'll kill him an' scram."

"Shit, we shoulda cleaned 'em out a long time ago. They been bad for business since they showed up. I say we do it."

Mary Rose stood looking numbly at the sword while they argued. Tom Halloran was right, it would have to be them—her and the Hallorans—because nothing else would work, and because she couldn't leave Philip in the Shales' hands until they hurt him badly enough to break down. Anyone would break down eventually, Mary Rose suspected, but Philip would stand it longer than most people, and be hurt worse. But she couldn't ask the Hallorans to do that. They would have to decide it for themselves.

It appeared that they had. Other opinions died down and Tom Halloran came over and stood in front of her. "We're goin'."

Mary Rose looked at him, relieved. "I'm grateful."

"We got to scout 'em out first," Tom said, "but Pa's got a pretty good idea where to look—he hasn't lived on Blue since before the Flood for nothin'. An' Asia says there's a plane sittin' in a field up by Copper Hollow. He saw it the other day. We figure it's the Shales'. Nobody hides a plane that's not figurin' on doin' something right illegal with it, and folks here don't fly whiskey. If they're fixing to make a delivery, they're gonna be kinda occupied tonight. So we're goin'."

"Not just you," Mary Rose said.

"Now, wait a minute. This is gonna be tricky."

"Don't argue with me, Tom."

Zeke looked at her consideringly. "I reckon it would help if you went."

Mrs. Halloran put her hands on her hips. "Zeke, I don't like that at all. She don't know what she's up against."

"It's my fight," Mary Rose said.

Noonie put an arm around her mother. She looked at Mary Rose with sympathy. "She's got a right, Ma. I'd go if it was me."

Mrs. Halloran sighed. "I 'spect I'd let you." Halloran girls learned to fight like men because they hadn't any choice. "Mary Rose is different."

Mary Rose thought about that. "I don't think so," she said.

"All right, she's goin'," Zeke said. "Enough o' this. Asia, you cut up Copper Hollow an' see what you see."

Merrick looked at the cars. "Have to find us about six new tires first," he said with disgust.

Mary Rose tugged at the box of dynamite and looked up at Tom. "Help me get this in the house where there's some light."

"What you got in mind?"

"Methamphetamine's very volatile while they're making it," Mary Rose said as they lifted the box. "Philip says when they go out on a drug bust, if it's—what did he call it? Crank, if it's crank, they always have the fire department stand by. He says he's seen a whole house go up from one spark."

Tom looked down at her as they lugged the box up the porch steps. "You used to be such a prissy little thing. How the hell did you take up with a bandit like Hull?"

"He's not a bandit," Mary Rose said. "He's a police officer."

Tom gave a snort of half-admiring amusement. "He's got all the instincts." He saw the threadbare look on her face and relented. "All right, we'll get him back for you."

13.
The Dreadful Hollow

"Mr. Hull."

Hull's eyes snapped open, and pain returned along with consciousness. His arm and calf muscles were screaming and the small of his back felt as if someone had laid a red hot poker along it. Ota appeared to find that promising.

"Now we will consider your position." Ota spoke in Japanese, whether because he found it restful or because he intended to keep his dealings private from the Shales, Hull wasn't sure. Hull studied the *yakuza* agent's face, trying to concentrate on something besides pain and the growing fear, every time he looked at his bandaged foot, that he was going to limp for the rest of his life. Ota's face was broad and flat and, except for an unpleasant intelligence in the eyes, unremarkable. Hull had long since passed the stage where all men of another race looked alike to him, but Hidehiko Ota's face was unmemorable even to the careful eye; a good soldier's face.

"You have studied in Japan, Mr. Hull." Ota appeared to thumb through some mental file.

"*Hai*," Hull said guardedly. "I have been there twice." The effort of conversing in Japanese became another distraction, a mental anesthetic.

"Ah? Very good. Then you understand karma. Karma is what must be. For instance, it is my karma to find *Ko-*

getsu-nami. And it is your karma to be tied to that chair. But there are always possibilities within each karma. Yours are for you to decide."

"Maybe you ought to think about your own," Hull said. "For instance, it may be your karma to be arrested for manufacturing illegal drugs if the police get here while your friends are still operating. That would diminish your usefulness to your employer, I imagine."

"Possibly. If the police should do such a thing." Ota put his hands on his knees and smiled blandly. "However, since you have already been to the police and they did not believe you, I do not understand why they should appear now."

"We didn't have any proof then. We do now. I expect you are in this country illegally, Mr. Ota. Or at least the name on your passport is someone else's. You have kidnapped a citizen of this country. That is not allowed."

"I agree. But it would be difficult to prove, if I was not to be found and the . . . victim was no longer capable of speech." He got up from his camp stool and selected a two-foot length of thin iron pipe from among the rubbish in the corner. He reseated himself and prodded Hull's injured foot with it lightly. Hull's mouth opened in a gasp of pain. "It would be simpler, Mr. Hull, and more pleasant for you, if you simply produced *Ko-getsu-nami.*"

"Go to hell," Hull said, when he could speak.

"You are not acquainted with the man whom I serve," Ota said thoughtfully. "He has, I assure you, Mr. Hull, sent many more people to hell than you would dream of."

"Sadao Akaishi," Hull said.

Ota's eyes narrowed. "You are well informed."

Hull gritted his teeth, trying to stop Ota's face from wavering in front of his eyes. He was well informed enough to know that he lived only so long as Sadao Akaishi did not have the sword. Once the blade was in Ota's hands, Hull would be evidence to be disposed of, a track to be covered, if not by Ota, by the Shales. Maybe Mary Rose too.

"It is unfortunate that we should be adversaries," Ota said. "Karma is very strange. These men here, with whom I must ally myself, know nothing of *Ko-getsu-nami* or of what it means; of duty—honor. You do, I think. That is very ironic, eh?"

"I know enough to know that to give the sword of Akinji Kobayasu to *yakuza* is defilement," Hull said. "If that is what you mean."

Ota's eyes snapped dangerously, and Hull stared stubbornly back at him. Oddly enough, he did mean it. The question of money and of his own life aside, there was something inherently evil in the idea of Sadao Akaishi possessing *Ko-getsu-nami*.

"I am growing tired of this." Ota prodded Hull's foot again. "Where is the sword?"

"Ahhhh!" This time the pain was excruciating. Hull could feel the sweat running down into his eyes.

"If not you," Ota suggested, "there is always the woman."

Hull shook his head. "She doesn't know where it is," he muttered in English. Japanese was too much trouble.

Ota raised his eyebrows. "I find that hard to believe."

"We don't get along so well."

"You are partners. Also, from what these men have seen, lovers."

"It didn't work out," Hull said. "She wants her share and then she'll split. I'm just making sure she doesn't get my share." He tried to shake the sweat out of his eyes. The pain was beginning to make him sick.

"In that case," Ota said, "*you* had better tell me. There are more painful things than a broken foot."

Hull shook his head again.

"If I grow too impatient," Ota said, "I may call in the Shales to convince you. I am only a soldier, Mr. Hull. I do what I must. But I think *they* would enjoy it. It will be worse than this."

He lashed out with the length of pipe again and Hull choked back a scream. He tried to fix his mind on cold, clear water, on the white outlines of the mountain laurel, on anything that would fight down the nausea in his throat. As long as he didn't tell Ota anything, Ota couldn't kill him. He forced himself to remember that, and wondered how long it might be before he didn't care.

*   *   *

Steven Cullen's black Chevy moved quietly down the mountain, running without lights, with Merrick at the wheel. In the passenger's seat beside him, Mary Rose sat with her hands clenched in her lap, nails digging into her palms. Tom Halloran was in the backseat, and behind them was the Hallorans' pickup, with Zeke and Asia in the cab and Zeke's two older sons, George and Jim, in the back. George and Jim never seemed to say much, but they had a competent look about them. Mary Rose hoped that it extended—as they had assured her it did—to knowing what to do with dynamite. Philip's box of dynamite was in the truck with them, repackaged by Mary Rose into less powerful doses, just enough to be sure of setting off a reaction with the volatile methamphetamine.

The Chevy swung around a narrow turn and headed up a road that Mary Rose could barely discern even in the moonlight.

"You got a right good bootleggin' car here," Merrick informed her. "Not much to look at, and it handles real sweet. I like all them cutoff switches, got me a mind to wire up my Ford that way." He looked cheerful and anticipatory as he pulled the Chevy up on the grass beside the road, along a wire fence.

"You sit tight," Tom told Mary Rose. "We're goin' in the back door."

He got out and approached the fence gingerly. He held his hand just above the wire for a moment, then waved at the truck which had pulled up behind them. Zeke got out and lifted two six-foot poles and a short coil of insulated wire out of the truck bed.

"Wire's hot," Merrick explained to Mary Rose. "See them insulators on the posts?"

Mary Rose saw that the top wire ran along white knobs nailed to the fence posts. "What are they going to do?"

"Fix us a little gate," Merrick said. "Don't want to break the circuit, they may have an alarm. Asia says it looks like that plane's gettin' ready to take off, an' if they've got a delivery to make, they'll be jumpy an' keepin' an eye on things. Asia says they've got some dope in the plane already. He caught a copperhead an' turned it loose in there while he was at it."

Zeke uncoiled the wire, which had an insulated clip on each end, and attached the clips to the fence wire six feet apart. The insulated bridge trailed on the ground between them. Zeke produced a pair of wire cutters, also insulated, from his back pocket and cut the fence between the clips. Then he and Tom took the two poles, which were trimmed to a point at the bottom, and set them in the soft ground at either end of the gap. They fastened each end of the bridge wire to the post tops with U-shaped staples.

"Neat as a pin," Merrick said as Tom got back in the car. He drove the Chevy under the wire into the field beyond, the pickup following.

"How did you know the wire was going to be hot?" Mary Rose asked.

"Mostly they are," Tom said. "It kinda discourages strangers. Farmers use a hot fence to keep the stock from leanin' on it; you use 'em down at the college, I expect, but those don't have much of a bite to 'em. They get real unpleasant if you set the current a little higher."

The Chevy jolted across the open field and onto a gravel road that ran along the other side, this one with no fence beside it.

"Told you that wasn't a stock fence," Tom said. "This one was hotter'n hell too, like he'd wired it into somebody's house current."

A half mile farther up the road Merrick stopped the Chevy and waited while Zeke pulled the truck off as close under the trees as he could get it. "Near enough," Merrick said. "They got their doings about a mile straight up here. If they ask, you came up through Copper Hollow an' you don't know why they ain't seen you."

Mary Rose nodded. The point of the detour had been to make sure the Shales didn't see the truck. She slid over into the driver's seat as Tom and Merrick got out.

The four men in the truck got out too. Jim and George took what they wanted from the dynamite and put it in their jacket pockets.

"Got enough here to blow them Shales to Kingdom Come," George said with satisfaction.

"Blow 'em straight down to the devil more likely," Jim said, "and long overdue, if you ask me."

"You just make sure you don't blow one of us while you're at it," Zeke said. "And you wait for Mary Rose's signal. Y'all be careful."

"You gonna be all right, honey?" Tom leaned in the window of the car.

"I'll be fine," Mary Rose said.

"You give us ten minutes, then turn the lights on and drive slow." Tom disappeared into the trees, leaving Mary Rose in silence.

She looked at her watch, fidgeted, staring nervously into the night, and looked at her watch again. One minute. She took a deep breath and tried to make herself relax. Bereft of the Hallorans and their encouraging air of cheerful, competent menace, her fears returned redoubled into nightmare proportions. The country road where she waited was an alien landscape, terrifying in the moonlight, and her mind conjured up hallucinatory visions of Philip dead or dying in it. A verse that unaccountably terrified her as a schoolgirl came back to her: *I hate the dreadful hollow behind the little wood.*

The sword was under the backseat, in a compartment where Steven had hidden God knew what. If she needed to, she would give it to them, and hope they would let Philip go. It would be no satisfaction to Steven's ghost if Philip died.

Not Philip too. Mary Rose put her head in her hands and managed to shut her nightmares out. After a while she looked at her watch again. The seconds blinked over with infinitesimal speed.

Ten minutes. Mary Rose turned the key in the ignition and flipped the Chevy's lights on.

Lieutenant Sawyer climbed in his car and slammed the door, with a look of exasperation at the uncommunicative trio lounging in a row of chairs in front of the Amoco station. They couldn't deny having heard more gunfire, but they didn't reckon they knew where it came from, since sound bounced around right funny in the mountains. And they couldn't recall anybody named Shale. Hadn't seen any strange cars either.

The whole damn county could be invaded by green men from Pluto, and there were some folks who'd swear they hadn't seen a thing, if a cop asked them about it, Sawyer thought, sighing. Blue Mountain had always been no man's land. But nobody had been carrying on like the boys at the OK Corral until now, either. He was beginning to have a suspicion that Hull was at least half right. And he'd probably got himself in the middle of whatever was going on up there, him and that damnfool teacher. If you asked Lieutenant Sawyer, the sheriff ought to take care of whatever was going on up on Blue besides whiskey-making, before someone like the DEA moved in and did it, and local law enforcement ended up looking like a bunch of country hicks with their pants down. The sheriff *hadn't* asked him, but Lieutenant Sawyer had volunteered his opinion anyway, and got a snort and a pop-eyed look for his pains, along with excerpts from Sheriff John's election speech about having his finger on the pulse of Sarum County. There hadn't been any calls for assistance, and the sheriff didn't need any lunatic from California, which in the sheriff's opinion was populated entirely by lunatics, to teach him his business. What it boiled down to was, he didn't have the money or the men. Sarum was a rural county and the taxes were minimal. The sheriff had his hands full just keeping up with what he could prove, but he didn't like admitting it, even to Sawyer, who knew it anyway.

Shit. Sawyer turned his car aimlessly up another road. He wished he knew what he was looking for. He hoped it wasn't a couple of bodies.

The Shales' gravel road ended in a quarter of a mile. Or rather, it rounded a sharp bend and became a dirt track. As Mary Rose approached the turn, she saw headlights flash on ahead of her and slammed on the brakes. A car pulled out of the trees, blocking her way, and someone on foot yanked her door open. Mary Rose crouched on the seat, looking up at one of the thin, pale-eyed men who had broken into her house the night that Philip came.

"Now how in hell did you get up here?" He looked angry and maliciously interested.

"I made the Hallorans tell me," she said.

"An' how did *they* know where to go?"

"I don't know, but they did," Mary Rose snapped. "I've got what you want, so you just let me alone and take me to that man that's with you."

"You come up Copper Hollow?"

Mary Rose nodded.

Emlen Shale grabbed her by the arm. "I didn't see no car."

Another man got out of the car ahead. "Maybe that's 'cause you're stupid." Roy Shale shoved Emlen aside. "If she gets that fucking Jap outta here, I don't care if she flew." He looked at Mary Rose. "Funny thing, we was just about to come an' get *you*, so you better have that sword with you. Where is it?"

Mary Rose shook her head stubbornly. "I won't give it to you. I'll give it to the man who has Philip. You take me to him."

"Like hell."

"*You're* stupid," Emlen informed his brother. "Nobody but Ota knows which damn sword it is."

"I'm *sick* o' that fucking Jap," Roy said. He yanked Mary Rose out of the car. She fought him frantically as she felt his hands on her, under her sweater and down the sides of her jeans, but he didn't seem interested in anything but whether she had a gun. "Goddammit, hold still."

Mary Rose gritted her teeth and let him search her.

"All right, get in the car," Roy said. He figured he'd settle with her later. They owed her and Hull for Jem and Sulie and a hell of a lot of wasted time. "Start drivin'," Roy said. He looked in the glove compartment for good measure, and pocketed the ammunition that he found there. Emlen backed the other car out of the way, and in the rearview mirror Mary Rose saw it pull onto the road again behind her. She drove as slowly as she dared. Tom Halloran had said that ten minutes would be enough, but what if it hadn't been? Her hands began to ache and she realized that they were clenched around the steering wheel. The road wound up through trees and through an open gate that the man in the car behind her got out to shut.

At the top of the mountain the road leveled off and ended in an open yard surrounded on three sides by a pair of weathered cabins, a barn, and a long cinderblock building. Her headlights illuminated an older man and a woman with a round, goblin face.

"Stop here," Roy Shale said. "You get out." Mary Rose hesitated, and he shoved her at the door. "Out."

She pushed the key into the pocket of her jeans and climbed out. The older man looked at her with a snort of malevolent amusement. "You're gonna come in mighty handy," he said. "Roy, you go get Ota."

Roy walked away toward the barn, and Emlen, who had driven the car behind her, got out and went in the opposite direction, toward the cinderblock building.

"Maureen, you watch her," Ben said. He followed Emlen into what Mary Rose thought must be the lab. The air in the yard had a putrid smell. The woman remained, staring at the visitor with blank, disinterested hostility.

Mary Rose looked at her curiously. Maureen Shale wore a pair of cheap, too tight, jeans and a dingy sweater. Her round, unappealing face was not so much reserved as shielded. Mary Rose thought she had never seen anyone so well hidden.

Maureen heard steps behind her and turned to see Ota striding across the yard. "You better have what he wants," she said.

Ota glanced at Maureen. "You go away." Maureen went up the steps into one of the cabins without answering.

Ota was almost the same height as Mary Rose, and she looked into black, efficient eyes and saw in them the intelligence that had directed the hunt they had run from for so long. He terrified her.

"Where is *Ko-getsu-nami*?"

Mary Rose looked past him, trying to shield her thoughts

from eyes that she felt could read them. Ota had come
from the barn. Was that where Philip was? And *was* that
cinderblock building the lab? She had to be certain, she
couldn't afford to be wrong. "I'll give you the sword for
Philip Hull," she said. She backed away a step. "That's
why you took him, isn't it? Where is he?"

"Give me *Ko-getsu-nami*. Then we will discuss Mr.
Hull."

Tom Halloran was right. She looked at Ota and knew he
wasn't going to let them go, sword or no sword. If she
stalled too long, he'd start taking the car apart. "Where is
Philip?" she said frantically.

Ota made a low chuckle in his throat as a scream came
from the barn.

"Philip!" Mary Rose shrieked.

Philip Hull glared at Roy Shale. His sodden hair dripped
sweat into his face and his chest ran with blood where Roy
had dragged a nicked-edged hunting knife across it. Hull's
breath came in choking gasps and the pain in his chest and
feet had left him writhing. He knew Shale was deriving
great satisfaction in making him scream, but he didn't give
a shit. He wasn't going to tell the bastard the time of day,
but he wasn't above screaming. In its way, it helped to
dull the pain. And if he was lucky, the Hallorans might
hear him. Or Sawyer. If anybody had managed to track
him this far. Hull spat blood out of his mouth—he had
bitten his tongue—and retched. Roy waited for his shoulders to stop heaving, and came at him with the knife
again.

Mary Rose leaned on the hood of the car, shaking.

"Mr. Hull has declined to cooperate," Ota said conver-
sationally.

Mary Rose wrapped her arms around her stomach and
bent over the car, trying not to be sick.

"No doubt you feel differently," Ota went on. Philip
screamed again. "I left someone with him to, ah, continue
persuasion. One was all that was available, since they are
occupied tonight with their own business, but there is

very little that two men can do to a subject that one cannot."

"Business?" Mary Rose grasped at that, but when she looked at Ota, her face was puzzled, a woman with only her lover on her mind.

Ota shrugged. "Their business is not your concern, or mine. You will give me *Ko-getsu-nami* before the man in there finishes with your Mr. Hull. Otherwise, I assure you, he will not be worth having back. And I will have the sword anyway." Ota's expression was contemptuous. "Do not be a fool, woman. The others are close enough to call on if I need them." His face said plainly that he saw no reason to think that he would.

Mary Rose turned her head slowly to look directly at the cinderblock box that stood at right angles to the barn. Lights glowed in the high, narrow windows. The other Shale men had gone in there. If they were cooking drugs tonight, it had to be the lab. She looked back at Ota and then deliberately turned her face toward the lab again, hoping desperately that the Hallorans could see her from wherever they had positioned themselves in the dark woods beyond.

"Their business is not your concern!" Ota snapped. "Where is the sword?"

Mary Rose bit her lip. Where was Tom Halloran? She moved slowly toward the car door, placating Ota. Had the Shales found them, or the Shales' dogs? Surely there must be dogs—dogs were a better alarm than wire fences. But surely if they had been caught, there would be a commotion. Philip screamed again, and Mary Rose reached desperately for the door latch.

There was a sound like a great breath being sucked in, and a deafening roar, and the interior of the cinderblock lab went up in flames. The door burst open and flew upward as if thrown by an angry hand. Smoke and a hellish orange light poured through the opening and through a jagged hole in the roof. As Ota spun around, Mary Rose grabbed Steven's gun from under the driver's seat of the Chevy. She fired once, wildly, and ran without waiting to see if she'd hit him.

A figure stumbled from the lab with its hair on fire. The door of the Shales' cabin banged open and Emlen's wife ran down the steps with her hands to her mouth, screaming.

Between the lab and the barn was a smoldering pile of cinderblock rubble with metal rods sticking out from it like arms. Mary Rose could hear Ota behind her, choking on the smoke and a stench so thick that it was like walking through something solid. The barn door burst open and a man looked out into the nightmare glow that lit the yard. He ran cursing toward the burning lab.

"Shale! Come back!" Ota barked.

Roy Shale stopped and turned around in a fury. As Mary Rose fled past him, he grabbed Ota by the shoulders. "Goddamn you and your goddamn sword!" he shouted. "This is your fault!" He flung Ota from him and stumbled toward the lab.

There was another explosion and flame shot out of the lab windows. Mary Rose ran through the open barn door, tugged it closed behind her, and dropped the bolt. She saw Hull as she turned. His face was wet with sweat and he was frantically trying to pull his wrists free of the chair. "Oh, my God," Mary Rose whispered.

Hull's face was imprinted with pain and there was blood in the corners of his mouth. He was shirtless and shoeless, his chest and feet caked with blood. Mary Rose pulled a pocketknife out of her jeans and hacked at the cords around his wrists with it.

"I thought I was going to burn to death," he whispered.

Mary Rose tried not to touch his feet as she cut the cords around his ankles. "Can you walk?" The look in his eyes terrified her.

"I'll have to," he said thickly. He slumped forward and flexed his hands with gritted teeth. "Give me that." Clumsily he took the gun that she had tucked under her arm. "You'll shoot yourself."

He stood up as she pulled the cords loose from his feet, but his legs gave way under him. Mary Rose pulled at him urgently, and he dragged himself, with the gun in one hand, across the barn floor. On the other side, behind the workbench, there was a back entrance. Ota was slamming something heavy into the main door. It would give way in a moment.

"Hurry!" Mary Rose tugged at Hull. She wasn't sure he was entirely conscious. But when Ota burst through the shattered door, Hull turned, sitting, and fired at him from the floor.

Ota dived back behind splintered wood, and Hull managed, barely, to get to his feet. His legs felt rubbery, almost useless. No one ahead hindered their way as they stumbled through a cleared space into the trees behind the barn. The yard was lit by the burning lab, an infernal landscape of rubble and flame. They cut across the end of it toward the car. Pain jolted through Hull's legs with every step. Ota's gun cracked behind them. Hull turned to fire back, stumbled and fell. He dragged himself to his feet again and Mary Rose put her shoulder under his arm, her own arms around his waist. The car was a hundred feet away.

Behind them Ota crouched beside the Shales' cabin and leveled his gun. A shot went past him from the other side of the yard and he dropped, rolling into the shadow of the cabin porch. He tried to take aim again from there, but the flames made moving, swaying shadows that walked along the ground, and he couldn't find his quarry in them. So Ota ran, bent low, keeping to the darkness of the porch, and across the yard Tom Halloran lowered his gun, cursing. He'd lost sight of Ota, couldn't tell if he had hit him or not, and the rest of Tom's clan were out there somewhere too. Now he didn't know who he was shooting at.

Hull fell again and Mary Rose pulled at him desperately. The flames from the lab rose and fell. When they flared up, she could see that he was leaving blood on the ground at every step. The car was fifty feet away, then ten. The yard was chaos. Running, shouting figures crossed and recrossed it and she couldn't see who any of them were. Maureen Shale kept on screaming, a high-pitched shriek that went on endlessly, like a whistle.

Mary Rose dragged the door of the Chevy open, Hull dropped into the seat, and Mary Rose slid behind the wheel and spun the car around. A shot slammed through the back window, and then there was no sound but the whine of the engine, going downhill too fast.

Hull slumped beside her. He tilted his head back and let out a long breath. He turned his face toward her, said something that made no sound, and smiled.

The road was steep, rutted dirt, and Mary Rose concentrated on keeping the car on it. In some places it was almost too narrow for the car to pass and overhung with a menacing limestone bank that had not seemed, on the way up, to lean so far into the road as it did now. Fighting panic, she slowed the Chevy to a crawl only because she had to. At the gate she flew out to open it and ran back to the car. She knew she was more afraid of what was behind her than she was of the road. But Ota couldn't outrun a car, and surely the Shales wouldn't give him theirs, not now. He had let loose the fires of hell on them.

Hull lifted a hand, the wrist rubbed raw, and touched her arm gently. "That fire," he said. "Was that you?"

"It was Jim and George Halloran," Mary Rose said. "And your dynamite."

He was silent, his battered face weary past exhaustion, and the eyes that rested on her face held a queer uncertainty. "I thought they'd blown it themselves," he said finally. "I've seen factories go up like that just from the dope. Roy Shale was going to leave me to cook in it." He closed his eyes and put his hand on her knee as if he wanted to assure himself that she was there. His fingers felt cold.

Unaccountably, Mary Rose felt her cheeks running with tears. She sniffed, and Hull opened his eyes.

"Are you all right?" he asked her.

"Are you?" She didn't think so. Even sitting motionless, he had a strange, flyaway look about him, not quite solid.

"I don't know," he said. "Parts of me hurt like hell."

The car jolted around the hairpin bend at the bottom of the dirt road, onto the gravel one that Tom Halloran had said would go through Copper Hollow.

Hull gave her another smile, forced maybe, crooked

and a little rueful. "Relax, I'll make it. Are you crying over me?"

"Yes. No. I don't know." Her emotions seemed to fluctuate as unreliably as quicksilver.

Hull's face still lay turned toward hers. "I love you," he said quietly. It had been all he could think of since she had come and got him out of the Shales' barn, an obsession that he had to tell her that.

Mary Rose looked straight ahead, tears flowing down her face.

"What is it?" he said. "Was that something you didn't want to hear?"

"Asia found you for us," she said. "Coming up here, I couldn't think straight, I was so afraid I was going to lose you. All I could think was, *Please not you, too.* No, not even that. Just, *not you.*" Mary Rose started to sob.

Hull leaned over and rested his head against her shoulder. "We'll be all right," he said.

He looked down the road and watched the trees slide by on either side of them, silvered and lovely. Magic. Bewitchment. He felt lightheaded, drugged, inexpressibly tired. He wanted to put his head in her lap and sleep. A pinpoint spark of light in the rearview mirror caught his eye. He stared at it curiously. Lovely, like a reflected star.

"Philip." Mary Rose sounded frightened. "Look behind us."

Some kind of alarm went off in his head. He twisted around to look out the rear window. It was starred and broken, refracting the headlights behind them into jagged shares of light.

14.
The Spirit in the Blade

"Did the Hallorans have another car up there?" Hull asked desperately.

"No." Mary Rose's hands clenched the wheel as she took the next curve in a spray of gravel. The Chevy plowed past the shadowy form of the Hallorans' pickup, still parked by the road. The car behind them was coming up fast. "Who is it?" Mary Rose whispered.

"Ota," Hull said grimly. "It's got to be."

"He must have got the keys to the Shales' car," Mary Rose said. "I didn't think they'd—"

"He must have hot wired it," Hull said. "It's not that hard. If I hadn't been half off my head, I'd have done something about that car." He picked Steven's gun up off the floor and began methodically pulling papers from the glove compartment. "Where's the ammunition?"

"The Shales took it," Mary Rose said.

"Oh, Jesus." Hull pulled the clip out and looked at it. Four shots left. "Did you call Sawyer before you left?"

"No," Mary Rose said between her teeth. She was driving fast enough to terrify her. The car went around a bend with a sickening lurch, just barely under control. "Tom said if they saw police, they'd kill you and run."

"They would have," Hull said. "But we better hope we can call in the cavalry now." And hope Sawyer was still

217

prowling around like the good, pigheaded cop he was. Hull flipped the radio on.

"Sawyer, are you out there?"

The radio answered him with a burst of static.

"Goddamnit, Sawyer, I know you're looking for me, where are you?"

The road forked and Mary Rose slammed on the brakes. Tom hadn't said anything about a turn.

"Just pick one," Hull said. The lights behind them glared through the shattered window.

Mary Rose swung the wheel hard right and hit the accelerator. The road was narrow and the trees arched overhead. The turns were fast and mostly blind, even in the high beam of the Chevy's lights.

"Sawyer, damn you!"

"Hull, is that you?" The radio sounded startled.

"What's left of me, after your fucking nonexistent Jap got through with me!" Hull yelled.

"Where are you?" Lieutenant Sawyer was businesslike now, alert and official.

"Where are we?" Hull said.

"On 2816," Mary Rose said. Rural county roads had numbers, rarely names. "Heading down, toward Copper Hollow. I hope," she added. "It forks. I took the right turn."

"You get that?" Hull said.

"Yeah. What's going on up there?"

"There's a car behind us. A white Mustang, probably. Ota's in it. The suspect has a gun," Hull added with a certain amount of sarcasm.

"Who's Ota?"

"That's the man who doesn't exist, you fucking asshole!" Hull screamed at him.

"All right, hang on, I'm coming up."

"Big of you," Hull growled. "I got a present for you, if you get here in time."

"Yeah?" Sawyer sounded wary.

"One crank lab, what's left of it." Hull left the radio switched on and turned to look behind them again. Ota wouldn't know the road any better than Mary Rose did.

With luck, they might stay ahead of him long enough for Sawyer to find them. Ota wasn't going to give up. He couldn't go back to Sadao Akaishi without the sword.

"Where did you leave it?" Hull said. "At the Hallorans'?"

"What?" The car bounced and jolted over a series of potholes and slithered around a hairpin curve.

"The sword! Where is it?"

"It's in the back," Mary Rose said. "Under the seat."

Hull twisted around and wriggled over the seat back to get at it, ignoring the pain of that procedure.

"Philip—"

He yelped and swore, and finally slid back into the seat with the sword in his hands. "You were going to give it to him, weren't you?" he said accusingly.

"I was if I had to," Mary Rose said. She kept her eyes on the road.

Hull put the scabbard across his lap. His face had a look of stubborn obsession. "The hell you are. Think again."

"I think you aren't right in the head about that thing, that's what I think," Mary Rose said grimly.

Hull let out a long breath. "Maybe I'm not," he said. *How nuts am I?* he wondered. The sword had begun to seem alive to him, something sentient, with a will of its own. Maybe he was going crazy, which under the circumstances didn't seem too farfetched an idea. Ota had beaten the shit out of him. He'd known that to do weird things to people's heads.

"Philip, I mean it," Mary Rose said. "You're beginning to scare me. What *is* it about that thing?"

"I dunno," Hull muttered. "Maybe the fucker's haunted." On this moonlit back road with Ota behind them, that didn't seem too farfetched either.

The car careened down the mountain, trees opening and closing above them. With some satisfaction Hull heard a crackle and squawk from the radio, which was Sawyer calling up some help. He reached under the seat, pulled out the red police light, and switched it on. He rolled down the window and leaned out to stick the heavy magnetized base to the Chevy's roof. It flashed ominously, bathing trees and road in bloodred light. They weren't going to lose Ota anyway, and it would give Sawyer something to spot. He wished to hell he had a siren.

The car spun around a curve with Mary Rose's hands clenched whitely on the wheel, fighting the Chevy out of a skid. She was twice as frightened, driving, as she had been as a passenger. She knew she didn't drive as well as Hull did, it was like being thrown into water when she couldn't swim, but there was no time to switch. And if there had been, he couldn't have kept his injured feet on the accelerator or the clutch for more than a few minutes.

"You're doing fine," Hull said, seeing her white, set face and her clenched jaw.

"I don't know where we are," she said between gritted teeth. "We've passed two more forks—I don't know where they went."

"Just keep going," Hull said, "as long as it goes somewhere." A battered county road sign flashed by. "2712. Sawyer, does that tell you anything?" He heard a fading chatter from the radio again, and static. "Shit, I think we've got the mountain between us and him. *Sawyer!*"

Lieutenant Sawyer heard Philip Hull's voice fading into a hiss of static. The deputy next to him had a county road map spread out on his lap and was trying to find road 2816 or 2712 with a flashlight. Sawyer grimaced. Half these county roads were goat tracks some overefficient engineer had stuck a number on. And a lot more were private easements that went over three or four people's land and didn't even have a number. The county was going to go to a 911 emergency service in a couple of years, and every road was going to have to have a name and sequential house numbers for that. The county engineers were tearing their hair out over these roads. In the meantime the only people who seemed to know where they were going were the rescue squads that had been navigating by the seat of their pants for years. Sawyer punched a button on the radio and picked up the mike.

"Blue Mountain Rescue Squad." The voice sounded hopeful. The squads were volunteer outfits, their trucks paid for with bake sales and pancake breakfasts and a good-natured annual door-to-door strong-arm campaign. They liked to get a little excitement for their money.

"This is Lieutenant Sawyer, Sheriff's Office. I'm proceeding east on 260 just past Plum Creek. I may need a truck."

"We're on our way."

"No you ain't," Sawyer said, "because I don't know where I'm going."

"We have right much trouble with that," the voice said sympathetically. "Residents up there take the road signs down themselves sometimes."

"Oh, fine."

"They're a local embarrassment, that's what they are," Deputy Hartman said, peering at his map.

"Blue Mountain Station, what I need from you right now is directions," Sawyer said. "Hartman, shut up and listen."

The rescue squad dispatcher gave them the benefit of his local knowledge. Sawyer backed the car up, turned it around, and switched the lights and the siren on. Maybe that would scare somebody off. He still didn't quite believe in Japanese gangsters, but if Hull had stuck his nose in somebody's drug lab, he was in enough trouble anyway.

"Sawyer! *Sawyer!* Dammit, he's gone." Hull fiddled with the radio but nothing came in. They were in a steep-sided pocket of the mountain; a canyon to a Californian, a hollow to Mary Rose. Whatever it was, it was hell on broadcast signals. Hull looked over his shoulder. Ota was still behind them.

Hull heard a sharp, terrified gasp from Mary Rose, and the car fishtailed around in the gravel as she slammed on the brakes. The momentum flung Hull against the door, and the jagged trunk of a fallen tree flashed by the window. The car came to rest at an angle, with its back bumper against the tree. The trunk was two feet thick, double branched and solid, and Hull could see an upraised tangle of roots and a gaping hole in the bank where the last rain had washed it loose. There was no way around it on either side of the road.

"Get out!" He threw his door open, jumped, and rolled behind it as the Mustang pulled up a hundred yards away. Mary Rose scrambled out on the other side and ducked into the narrow angle between the bumper and the fallen tree. Hull sat up slowly, wincing. He found that he was still holding the sword, and he pushed it under the car. He looked over his shoulder at the tree. It was thick and branchy, but he thought Mary Rose could get through it. He knew he couldn't run very far. The door of the Mustang eased open. Hull looked at Mary Rose and jerked his head at the tree. "Run! Get over that tree and run like hell."

Mary Rose shook her head.

"Run, damn it, I've only got four shots."

The whirling light on the Chevy's roof flashed sweeping beams of red across the road and its glow passed along the Mustang's windshield. A bright flash and the crack of a gunshot followed the light. Mary Rose curled herself into a ball between the Chevy and the tree, but she didn't move. In desperation Hull knelt, leveling his gun with both hands, and hoped for one clear shot. Somewhere down the mountain he could hear the faraway wail of a siren. Too far away.

"Hull!" Ota's voice snapped out of the revolving pattern of light. "Throw the sword out. And your gun!"

"Go to hell, Ota!" The *yakuza* agent would keep no bargains; he could hear that distant siren too. A shot answered him, spraying gravel against the doorframe. Hull fired back at Ota's face, momentarily illuminated above his car. The face vanished, reappeared in a fusillade of fire, and was gone again. Hull cursed steadily under his breath while the gunfire boomed and echoed in the hollow, counterpoint to the dismal howling of the siren.

Ota sprinted from the Mustang toward the trees beside the road, and Hull fired twice at the movement. Ota crouched low and disappeared into their shadowed shelter, and Hull cursed himself again.

Mary Rose watched him silently, in steadily mounting terror. Hull's face was alternately shadowed and incarnadined by the spinning light, his eyes dark, demonic, as she imagined Ota's must be. Ota was frightened of him, she realized, more frightened than he was of anything else except perhaps of abandoned honor, of facing Sadao Akaishi without the sword. In some fearful way, he and Philip were matched, reflections in a dreadful glass. And because Ota was afraid, Ota could not stop the battle.

The *yakuza* agent moved among the trees, a shadow passing over shadows. Hull's head throbbed and his legs were beginning to cramp again. One shot left. One shot. One shot. The knowledge reverberated in his skull. Crimson light flowed across the trees into darkness, welled up again and flowed away like blood. Hull shifted to keep himself out of Ota's line of fire and waited for Ota to show himself. His face dripped with sweat in the humid night, and the salt bit into his lacerated body.

Ota timed his movements for the darkness of the red light's sweep, but this time he miscalculated. The light caught him, suspended like a photographic negative, between the trees, and Hull fired.

Ota ducked backward, but he didn't fall. Hull's gun clicked uselessly on an empty clip as Ota fired back. The wailing siren faded in the distance. Hull gasped and fell beside the car, the gun spinning from his hand into the road.

"*Philip!*" Mary Rose screamed, and then put her hands to her mouth as she saw Hull's hand, shadowed by the Chevy's door, slide under the car and come to rest on the sword's hilt.

"Hull!" Ota shouted from the trees, but there was no reply.

"You—Mrs. Cullen! Throw out the sword!" This time a terror-stricken sobbing answered him. Ota moved cautiously nearer the road.

Slowly the blade slid from its scabbard, the faint sibilant whisper of its passage masked by the distant siren and the sound of weeping. From where he lay, Hull could see Ota's feet in the tall grass at the edge of the road.

Ota took another step, and then another. He kicked Hull's empty gun away with his foot. Behind the car nothing moved. He looked into the shadows. He could see one outflung hand, fingers curled into the palm, empty. He nodded with satisfaction and moved more swiftly toward the car, his gun still leveled, looking for the woman.

Mary Rose was aware of the faint gleam, red and then moonlit, of the waiting blade, and Hull's eyes, not closed but darkly watching. As Ota moved nearer, Hull's arm tensed. Mary Rose felt on the ground beside her and her hand closed around a stone. Ota came forward more quickly, searching for her. She ducked her head and flung the stone upward, over the fallen tree into the road beyond. It landed with a clatter of loose gravel, and Ota spun around, firing into the night.

Hull leapt: he came to his feet in a single movement fueled by terror and adrenaline. The sword made a soft hiss as it swept into an arc above his head. Ota turned back too late. Lit by the whirling light, the blade looked as if it already streamed with blood. Ota saw it above him and screamed, lifting his gun.

Ko-getsu-nami came down in one red stroke and the shot went wide. The scream ended in a dreadful cough, and blood welled up like a river. To her horror, Mary Rose saw that the blade had bitten through Ota's collarbone and sunk nearly through his chest. The body fell, taking the sword with it. Hull swayed on his feet and crumpled in the road.

Lieutenant Sawyer heard the scream over the radio and hit the accelerator.

"Jesus!" Deputy Hartman peered up the road ahead of them. "What was that?"

Sawyer didn't answer. Hull had left his radio on. If Sawyer's radio was picking it up in this hollow, they were nearly on him.

"I never heard nothin' like it," Hartman muttered. He cocked an ear at the radio. "I don't hear nothin' now, though."

"Hartman, just shut up!" Sawyer snapped. He spun the patrol car around a curve, and leaned forward over the wheel. A red glow flashed rhythmically through the trees ahead.

"Looks like police," Hartman said, interested.

Sawyer took the next curve too fast and stood on his brakes as the white Mustang loomed before them. Sawyer's car skidded to a halt behind it.

Dr. Cullen's Chevy was parked beyond the Mustang, and Sawyer's headlights illuminated a white-faced woman crouched in the road with her head between her knees. Sawyer pulled his gun and got out. "Cover me." He cut off the shrieking siren.

Mary Rose stood up as Sawyer approached. "You're a little late, Lieutenant," she said acidly.

"Where's Hull?" Sawyer put his gun away. "Oh, Christ!" His gaze traveled past her and he started to run.

Hidehiko Ota's body lay where it had fallen, and Sawyer bit down on the inside of his mouth as his stomach started to churn. Ota's torso was split from the shoulder to below the breastbone. Beside him Philip Hull sat in the road, methodically cleaning the blade of a four-foot sword on the cuff of his jeans. He didn't look up, and Sawyer didn't think he was more than about half conscious.

"What happened?"

"He needs a doctor," Mary Rose said.

"I take it you mean Mr. Hull." Sawyer looked at the dead man and swallowed hard. You couldn't have put Ota back together with string and glue.

Hull looked up and his eyes focused on Sawyer. "There's your *yakuza*." He pulled Ota's shirt away from what was left of his chest. Across the pale skin was tattooed the ancient straight shape of a Japanese sword rising from a bulbous clawed handle. "*Yakuza* all mark themselves. That's a *vajra* and *ken*. Very old, very symbolic." He looked down at the sword in his lap and rubbed it on his cuff again.

"Help me with him," Mary Rose said.

Sawyer looked at Hull's feet and chest. "Hartman! Get me the first-aid kit. And get somebody up here for him." He gestured at Ota. The coroner would have to do an autopsy for form's sake, but there wasn't much doubt about what had killed him. Sawyer's eyes rested on the sword. "He have a gun?"

Mary Rose pointed at Ota's. Steven's was back in its slot under the driver's seat. With luck, she wouldn't have to produce that.

Sawyer picked up the gun with a handkerchief and handed it to Hartman. The deputy's eyes widened when he saw the body. Behind them another sheriff's car came screaming up the road. Two more deputies got out, and one of them was promptly sick in the tall grass beside the Chevy.

"Get me a couple of blankets," Sawyer said. He put one of them over Ota, to everyone's relief, and spread the other one at the edge of the road. "Can you walk?" he asked Hull.

Hull lifted his head slowly.

"Come on." Sawyer put his hands under Hull's shoulders and helped him to his feet. Hull still had the sword.

"Give it to me," Mary Rose said quietly. Hull let go, and she put it in the back of the Chevy.

Sawyer sat Hull down on the blanket and opened the first-aid kit. Lights flashed red and blue, tinting the ground and the interested faces of Sawyer's deputies. Sawyer turned Hull so that the headlights fell on his chest, and began to clean it.

Hull yelped. "Goddamn you, Sawyer, leave me alone."

Sawyer grinned in spite of himself. He had always found there was nothing like a little antiseptic to snap a man back to reality. "You wanta tell me what happened?"

Hull told him, in a few not particularly well-chosen words.

Sawyer started on Hull's feet. "They worked you over pretty good," he said.

Hull glared at him.

"All right, I was wrong. One of these days they'll put that on my tombstone. You need a doctor for that bullet hole."

"Later."

Mary Rose knelt on the blanket beside him. "Philip, it'll get infected."

"There's an antibiotic in the first-aid kit," Sawyer said. "You allergic to penicillin?"

"No."

Mary Rose found the bottle and handed Hull a tablet.

"You got any water?" Sawyer said.

"I didn't bring my canteen," Hull said sourly. He made a face and managed to get the pill down.

Sawyer finished cleaning Hull's left foot and started on the right one. "You're lucky." He inspected the bullet hole. "It went clean through and missed all the bones."

Hull gritted his teeth. "*Shit!* You make a lousy nurse."

"I can give you a painkiller."

"No. It would probably knock me cold."

"That wouldn't hurt you," Mary Rose said.

Hull ignored her. Sawyer finished cleaning the wound and taped a dressing over it. "You're going to need something to put on your feet."

"He's going to the hospital," Mary Rose said.

"Well, to tell you the truth, it'd be a right lot of help if he went back up there with us," Sawyer said. "We got to mop up what's left in that lab, and I'm not so sure we can find it."

"In my suitcase," Hull said. "In the car. Slippers."

"Philip . . ."

Hull seemed to focus on her for the first time. He reached out and touched her cheek. "I'm all right. Just get me my slippers."

Mary Rose got up. "You aren't." But she got the slippers. She thought that he was past the point of exhaustion already, functioning on some precarious second wind which was fueled by sheer nerve. In this mood he'd grow more stubborn the more she argued with him.

"While we're on the subject," Sawyer said while Hull, wincing, inched his feet into the slippers, "you can tell me how *you* located the place." He looked thoughtfully at Mary Rose.

"A friend helped me," she muttered.

Sawyer sighed. "Let's be a little more specific," he suggested.

"They just found the Shales for me. They didn't have anything to do with the rest of it."

"Good. What's their name?"

"Smith."

"Smith?"

Mary Rose looked at him balefully. "Halloran."

Sawyer's eyes opened wide and then his lip started to twitch. He let out a hoot of laughter. "Hallorans!" He shook his head. "Mrs. Cullen, I got a new respect for you."

"But they didn't—"

"Oh, sure they didn't! That'd make it the first piece of devilment Zeke Halloran's boys haven't had a hand in in the last thirty years. Jesus—the Hallorans! I shoulda known!"

Hull looked at Mary Rose's troubled face. "They weren't even there," he said quietly.

Sawyer managed to stop laughing. "Mrs. Cullen, unless I fall over 'em, I'm not in any mood to look for your bootleggin' buddies." An ambulance pulled up behind the Sheriff's Department cars and two men got out with a stretcher. Sawyer looked at the blanket-covered body and his expression sobered considerably. "Whatever else went on up there is another matter. Let's go." He helped Hull to his feet.

Mary Rose looked at Philip dubiously. His account of the night had left out the dynamite as well as the Hallorans, but Sawyer wasn't an idiot.

Hull put an arm around Mary Rose and limped to the car. He fished the scabbard out from under the Chevy, put the sword in it, and switched off the light on the Chevy's roof. "You follow us," he told Sawyer.

"Yeah." Sawyer gave the light a telling look and Hull took it down and put it on the floor.

"Philip, what's going to happen when he gets up there?" Mary Rose whispered while they waited in the car for the ambulance and the patrol cars to get out of the way. A deputy was backing the Shales' white Mustang around. "I think that fire killed somebody."

"I don't know," Hull said, "but he isn't about to let loose of me until he gets everything down in triplicate. If I went to the hospital now, he'd send a deputy along to babysit me. We'll just have to play it by ear."

"I'm not very good at that."

Hull gave a rueful chuckle. "I'd say you've done okay so far. And Sawyer's feeling like an ass because he didn't believe us about Ota. That'll be good for something. It's all in the psychology." He leaned back and closed his eyes. He hoped so.

The ambulance headed back toward town, and the other cars pulled off the road, waiting. With the sirens turned off and the lights stilled, the hollow felt unpleasantly empty. Hull looked as if he were asleep. Mary Rose began to retrace their path back up Blue Mountain, slowing at each intersection in the ill-marked maze of country roads to make sure she was on the right one. The closer she got to the mountaintop, the more reluctant she felt to go back up there. Sawyer and his deputies were a comforting presence behind her.

When Mary Rose got to the spot where the Hallorans had parked their truck, it was gone. She looked down the empty road, worried. The devil had been up Blue Mountain tonight, and sometimes the devil wasn't picky who he came down with. "Where *are* they?" she said aloud.

"Around, I think," Hull said. He hadn't been asleep. "They couldn't have caught Ota, but I bet they tried. I thought I heard a car back there while Sawyer was playing doctor. It got pretty close before it took off again. They know we're all right."

"I'm worried about *them*," Mary Rose said. "That fire scares me. It's a good thing we had a rain."

"It scared *me*," Hull said. "I told Sawyer he'd better call the fire department. But I think it was more contained than it looked. It may have got the barn, but you'll notice there was a good wide stretch between the barn and the trees. You don't take chances when you're cooking that shit. The Hallorans are all right or their car wouldn't be gone."

Mary Rose decided to be comforted by his certainty. And the "gate" that Zeke and Tom had cut in the electric fence? Was that gone too, loose ends neatly tied? Maybe the Hallorans weren't worried about the devil.

The Chevy bumped up the last incline. Sawyer pulled in behind her and got out, gun in hand and highly suspicious. Life on the mountaintop seemed stilled into an unnatural dormancy: no insect sound, no yip of foxes, no movement around the faint glow among the cinderblocks. The barn was still standing.

"They're holed up," Sawyer said. "They heard us comin'."

"Or dead," one of the deputies said. "Fire got 'em, maybe."

"Maybe. I ain't gonna ask who put out the fire. You go in careful. Take the barn. Hartman, you cover me, I'm goin' in that cabin." He looked at Hull. "You get out of the way. You've done enough free-lance law enforcing."

Hull limped back to the Chevy with a grin at Sawyer. This wasn't the time to cross him. "Keep your head down," he advised Mary Rose. "Things are apt to get a little weird out there."

They sank low in their seats and waited to see what would happen. Sawyer ran up the cabin steps and flattened himself against the wall beside the door. Hartman sprinted up the steps and took up a position facing Sawyer. Sawyer kicked the door in and they jumped, crouching, guns pointing inward. There was no sound. Sawyer nodded and they went in warily.

Silence.

Hull let his gaze travel over the yard. Nothing moved but the shadows of the other two deputies outside the barn. One of them pushed the barn door open with some caution and slipped inside. Hull and Mary Rose could see the beam of his flashlight moving across the floor. The other deputy had disappeared around the back of the barn, and in a moment another flashlight beam crossed the first.

"Lieutenant!"

Sawyer and Hartman dived out of the cabin. A deputy met them halfway across the yard, his gun hanging from one hand. He was laughing. He said something to Sawyer, and Sawyer trotted across the yard toward the barn.

The deputy ambled in the opposite direction, toward the Chevy, still chortling. He leaned his head in the window. "Damnedest thing I ever saw," he said. "The lieutenant says you might as well come on."

Hull looked disinclined to move.

"The lieutenant just said bring you," the deputy informed him.

"Aw, for—" Hull got out, put his arm around Mary Rose again, and they followed the deputy across the yard. The light of a kerosene lantern sprang up inside the barn, spilling a wan glow out the door. Down the mountain the rumble of heavy engines announced that the fire department had arrived. Deputy Hartman came out of the barn, scratching his head, and went to deal with them.

Sawyer emerged behind him. He motioned to Hull. "All right, get in there."

Hull and Mary Rose stepped inside, and Hull's eyebrows shot up into his hair. In a corner of the barn, malevolent as a nest of weasels, were Roy Shale, Ben and Emlen, hair and clothing singed, tied to each other and then to a post. Deputy Hartman, bred in local chivalry, had untied Emlen's wife. She sat on the floor, feet straight in front of her, her hands in her lap. She didn't bother looking at Emlen.

"I'm not as amused about this as you might think," Sawyer said, but there was a glint in his eye all the same. "Who did this?"

"I honestly don't know," Hull said.

"Uh-huh. Mrs. Cullen?"

"I don't know," Mary Rose whispered. She knew, Hull knew, Sawyer knew. She wondered if he was going to force the issue.

"How'd the fire get started?"

"It's a crank lab," Hull said. "What do you expect?" He looked Sawyer in the eye. If Sawyer wanted to get an arson squad on it, he could probably prove something.

Sawyer thought it over. Sometimes you were better off with the obvious explanation. He thought these men had damn near killed Philip Hull. If Mrs. Cullen had got a little desperate, he wasn't sure he blamed her. "This all of them?" he asked Hull.

"There's one in the hospital in Sarum," Hull said. He hesitated. "I think there's one in the lab." Jem Shale wouldn't have been able to run very fast.

"These the men who broke into your house, Mrs. Cullen?"

Mary Rose nodded. "Him, and him." She pointed at Emlen and Ben. "And . . . and the one that's not here." She began to shake. Jem Shale was probably the man who had killed Steven, but to burn to death . . .

"All right, get 'em outta here." Sawyer put his hand over Mary Rose's. "Mrs. Cullen, I'm inclined to believe what you thought about your husband's death, now. But at this late date, unless we get a confession . . ." He shrugged. "They'll go up for a long time on kidnapping, and the evidence from that lab, if it's what you say it is, but . . . well, I'm sorry. Sometimes we just screw up, there's no good denyin' it."

Mary Rose sighed. "Well, that's honest of you, Lieutenant."

Sawyer looked embarrassed, and she thought: *He isn't going to ask about the Hallorans now*.

"Don't tromp around in that any more than you have to!" Sawyer yelled out the door at the fire department crew. "There's evidence in there!"

One of the crew came over to him. She pulled her helmet off and wiped her forehead with the back of her hand. "There's a body in there too," she said. "But somebody's put most of it out with chemical extinguishers."

"Yeah," Sawyer said noncommittally. He had seen the empty racks in the Shales' cabin where the extinguishers had been. "We got lucky."

15.
Conversation With the *Gai-Jin*

Hull picked up his boots and shirt from the barn floor, where they lay next to the overturned chair, and regarded them with disgust. The shirt was in ribbons, the right boot had a hole that went clear through it, and everything was sodden with blood. He dropped them again and found his empty holster. "Where's my gun?" he muttered. "They got it when they jumped me. I want my gun."

Mary Rose touched his arm and pointed. Guns and knives were scattered on the workbench among the oddments of the dismantled fan; a collection prudently removed from the Shales by the Hallorans, no doubt. Hull strolled over and collected his revolver before Sawyer decided to. He stuck it in his pocket. A deputy came back in, headed for the workbench. Hull gave him a bland smile as he passed.

Sawyer had vanished into the yard, and they followed him. Outside was a body under a canvas sheet, and a horrible smell of burned flesh. Mary Rose gagged.

"He's pretty unpleasant," Sawyer said. "I'm not sure anybody but his dentist would know him."

Hull lifted the sheet gingerly. Jem Shale had no face left, but Hull could see charred bandages around one foot. He looked down at his own foot and thought vaguely of theories of coincidence and probability.

"You holdin' up all right?" Sawyer looked at him dubiously.

Hull managed to focus his eyes on the lieutenant. "Yeah."

All in all, he was a lot better off than Jem Shale.

"You identify him?"

Hull did so, swaying on his feet a little. Mary Rose pulled him away from the body, and Sawyer followed them across the yard, keeping pace with Hull's halting steps. Sawyer's deputies had handcuffed the Shales to the back of the fire truck, the most immovable object present, and were sniffing through the premises like well-trained hounds. They had already produced a passport with Ota's likeness, which might very well have been fake, but most certainly indicated his origins.

Hull glanced at it and with an effort forebore to mention to Sawyer that he had told him so.

Sawyer was conscious of that, but he had done all the apologizing he intended to. "I'll tell you what," he offered. "The next time some loony out of California comes roaring in here with a tale about Jap gangsters, I promise to listen to him."

"I don't expect you'll get many more," Hull said. He opened the Chevy's door and extracted a clean shirt from his suitcase.

Sawyer looked him over, considering. "You want a job?" he said finally. "We don't get this much action as a rule, but it has its moments."

Hull chuckled and buttoned his shirt. "Thanks, but I'll pass." He picked up the sword from the backseat and looked at it with satisfaction, sliding the blade out of the scabbard and turning it so the moonlight flowed along it like water. "This'll hold me for a while."

"What's that?" Deputy Hartman peered over his shoulder.

Hull gave Mary Rose a sideways look. "A ticket to the carnival in Rio."

"The hell it is," Sawyer said. "That's a murder weapon."

"*Murder?*" Mary Rose stared at him indignantly. "That man was trying to *kill* us!"

"Damn it, Sawyer—"

"All right, all right!" Sawyer held up his hand. "The

weapon in a justifiable homicide. And I gotta impound it.
You oughta know that."

Hull clutched the sword. "Sawyer, have you got any
idea what this thing is worth and what I went through to
get it? Stupid cops, country hoods, Japanese crooks nobody believed in?"

Sawyer sighed, but he didn't give any ground. "I gotta
have it. You'll get it back."

"Yeah, next year sometime!" Hull kept a firm grip on
the sword.

"Hand it over, Hull."

"Sawyer, you bastard—"

"Now." Sawyer stared at him implacably.

Hull gave him the sword and watched furiously as Sawyer carried it—gingerly, remembering what Ota's body
had looked like—to his patrol car. He put it in the backseat
and locked the doors. Then he went off to consult with the
fire department crew, leaving Hull pounding his fists on
the roof of the Chevy in an exhausted fury.

Deputy Hartman decided he had other things to see to,
at least until Hull cooled down.

"I wish I'd known Sawyer would do that," Mary Rose
said wistfully.

"Well, you should have thought of it!" Hull snapped,
infuriated past the restraints of logic. He looked at her
sourly, aware that *he* should have thought of it. He decided he was too tired and mad to admit that. A certain
curiosity filtered through his fury. "*Why* do you wish
you'd known?"

Mary Rose walked around to the trunk and opened it.
Silently she pointed to the *katana* they had found the
night Hull arrived in Sarum. "I sent Tom back to the
house for it. It's the right length. I thought maybe I could
confuse Ota with it."

"Well, you're an idiot. That wouldn't have fooled Ota
for a minute. Just because they all look alike to you—"

Mary Rose glared at him. "They probably all look alike
to Sawyer too. However, since he's locked it in his car, it's
a little late to find out."

A slow grin spread over Hull's face. He grabbed Mary

Rose around the neck, kissed her gleefully, and deftly twitched a hairpin out of her bedraggled hair. "You're the only woman I know who uses hairpins," Hull said. "Sometimes God provides." He straightened it out and rebent it.

"What are you going to do?" Mary Rose asked.

Hull looked around. Sawyer and his minions were elsewhere, and the Shales, for what they were worth, were out of sight behind the fire truck, arguing over whose fault it was.

Hull took the sword out of the trunk and sidled over to Sawyer's car. He beckoned to Mary Rose. "Come stand in front of me." When she did, he eased the hairpin into the door lock.

"Philip, that's a police car!" It seemed somehow more heinous to pick the lock of a police car.

Hull stared at her. "Are you nuts? I think you're nuts." He turned the hairpin gently and the lock popped open.

"Where did you learn to do that?" She looked impressed.

"I don't think I'll tell you." Hull stripped the fittings off the *katana*, using the hairpin to poke the peg out of the handle. He dumped them in Mary Rose's hand and closed her fingers over them. "Don't drop anything."

He took another quick glance around, eased the jimmied door open, and extracted the Moonshine Blade. It only took a moment to pull the fittings off it and put them on the *katana*. As an afterthought he wiped the *katana* on his cuff. Maybe it would pick up some of the blood he had wiped off *Ko-getsu-nami*, for the benefit of the sheriff's forensics department, if he had one.

Mary Rose looked jumpily over her shoulder, but Sawyer was still nowhere in sight. *Ko-getsu-nami*'s scabbard was a tight fit on the *katana*, but it just made it. Hull put the *katana* in Sawyer's car and locked it in, and stuck *Ko-getsu-nami* in the *katana*'s empty scabbard.

"Come on." He climbed into the front seat of the Chevy, and Mary Rose followed him, still clutching her handful of fittings. Hull took them from her one by one and refitted his salvaged treasure. "Fittings don't matter. It's the blade that counts." He slipped the *tsuba* and its mountings over the tang and pushed home the elaborately wrapped handle. "These are nice, though."

"Philip," Mary Rose said thoughtfully, "what *was* that sword we just gave Sawyer? I mean, what's it worth?"

"Well, you could have picked a cheaper one," Hull said. "About three grand."

"Three thousand *dollars*?" Mary Rose was appalled.

"Relax. You'll get it back. Eventually."

Mary Rose considered the uses of three thousand in the hand. "You're mighty free and easy with my sword," she informed him.

"*You* were gonna give it to Sawyer," Hull said indignantly. "You were gonna give it to Ota. Hell, you were gonna give him this one."

"That was different," Mary Rose muttered.

"So's the price between 'em," Hull said. He lifted the backseat and stuck the Moonshine Blade in the compartment underneath.

"You two holdin' up all right?" Sawyer's genial face appeared at the open window and Mary Rose jumped. "I reckon we're about through here," Sawyer said. "You can head for the hospital now if you want to. No hard feelings, I trust?"

"I wouldn't say that," Hull said balefully. "Ah, hell, no, no hard feelings."

"I'll take good care o' your sword."

"You do that," Mary Rose muttered.

"Hearing shouldn't take more than a month or so to wind up." He looked at Hull. "I don't need to tell you not to go anywhere in the meantime," he added pointedly, but he wasn't very worried. Hull would stick like glue as long as the sheriff's office had his sword. Sawyer scratched his head. The thing didn't look like much to him, but he'd figured out tonight that it was of considerable importance to some people.

"I'll be here," Hull assured him.

"Can we go now?" Mary Rose asked.

"Yeah, scram. I'll be in touch."

Mary Rose put the key in the ignition. "If you don't find

what you need, Lieutenant, I heard about a plane in a
field down the ridge a way you might want to check out."

"You heard?"

"Uh-huh. Just heard." She turned the key. "Tell your
boys to be careful, though. There might be a snake in it."
She smiled sweetly at Sawyer and backed the car out of
the yard.

Mary Rose pulled the Chevy up outside the emergency
room doors. "Philip." She nudged him gently. "Philip.
You have to get that foot looked at. You'll get gangrene."

"Yeah, I know." Hull opened his eyes and yawned. "I
feel like I'm made outta lead."

"You can sleep on the way to Virginia Beach. I assume
we *are* going to Virginia Beach?"

Hull smiled. He turned his head and kissed her, carefully. All his muscles felt stiff. Tomorrow he was going to
feel like a truck had hit him. "We're going to Virginia
Beach," he said. "You go put some more gas in the car and
find a nice quiet spot and change the license plates again.
Sawyer's seen these."

Mary Rose did as she was told, selecting a pair of New
Mexico plates around a dark corner behind the gas station,
guiltily expecting Sawyer to leap out at her from the
bushes at any moment. But he didn't. She returned to the
hospital to find Hull perched on an examining table with
what seemed like an unnecessary number of nurses tut-
tutting over him.

A doctor with a harassed expression was giving a couple
of State Police troopers what-for. "Look, I don't care what
you want him for, you absolutely can't have him tonight.
He's got a gunshot wound to the chest and he's so doped
up he couldn't walk out of here if he wanted to."

Sulie, Mary Rose thought. Sawyer was losing no time.
She glanced at Hull. He seemed to be enjoying the
conversation.

"Look, ma'am," one of the troopers told the doctor, "*I*
don't want him. Hell, I don't even know what I don't want
him *for*. All I know is, the sheriff's office called and asked

us to kind of help out, seeing as they're shorthanded tonight."

"You can put a guard outside his room if you want to," the doctor said.

The trooper sighed. "Guess I'll have to. He say anything?"

The doctor relaxed, and grinned a little. "Nothing you want to hear. You can ask the kitchen to send you up some coffee and sandwiches."

The trooper brightened a little. "Well, that's kind of you, ma'am."

"We're hospitable." She turned to inspect Hull. "You look like a bear had been chewing on you." She looked at his foot. "A bear with a .38. You know I have to report gunshot wounds."

"It's reported," Hull said. "You can check with the sheriff's office." He handed her his identification.

"The sheriff's office is mighty busy tonight." She looked at his Fresno ID. "What are you—a consultant?"

"No, I just got in the way."

"Somebody did a decent job of cleaning this," she said, cleaning it again anyway while Hull winced. "Are you in pain?"

"Hell, yes." Hull wondered why doctors always asked that, as if they thought somebody with a hole in his foot might not be.

"Well, I'm going to give you a shot of antibiotic and something for the pain, and a prescription you can fill in the morning. When was your last tetanus shot?"

"Years ago."

"I'll give you a tetanus booster too." She scribbled instructions on his chart and handed it to a nurse. "Wait here. Have you got someone to drive you?"

"Me," Mary Rose said.

The doctor looked up. "Good. He shouldn't drive." She turned back to Hull. "Come back and let us look at you again in a couple of days. And you should rest till then. You're probably in worse shape than you think."

"I doubt it," Hull said. "I'd be dead."

The doctor chuckled and vanished, taking the nurses with her, and Mary Rose came and sat by him until a nurse reappeared with two syringes and a bottle with a couple of pills in it.

"You can take one of these now," the nurse said, handing him a pill and a cup of water after she had emptied the syringes into his forearm and his backside respectively, while Mary Rose modestly looked the other way. "And you can take another in six hours if you need it. Get this filled in the morning." She handed him the prescription.

Hull stood up. "Let's get out of here before Sawyer decides to put a guard on *me*." He signed everything the nurse at the admitting desk handed him, and they went out to the car.

"Are you really all right?" Mary Rose said.

"As opposed to what?" he said sleepily. "I hope you know how to get to Virginia Beach." He got in the car and closed his eyes.

It was almost dawn when they crossed the Blue Ridge Parkway and started down the picturesque switchbacks of U.S. 60. They should get to Virginia Beach by ten, Mary Rose thought. She'd find a pay phone in Farmville and wake up Philip, and he could wake up Mr. Ohmori. Mary Rose took another sip of the coffee she had bought at Sarum's only all-night gas station, where they apparently brewed it up with motor oil, and thought longingly of a seat on a nice bus. It was going to be a long drive.

She bought more coffee in Lynchburg and, tired of drinking it stone cold, more coffee and a thermos at a truck stop outside Appomattox. At the truck stop she took her suitcase out, locked all the doors—on the theory that if anyone was after them they would have to wake up Philip to get in the car and would probably find him surly enough to give them pause—and went in the ladies' room. What she saw in the mirror under the gruesome glare of the fluorescent lights did little to reassure her that any hotel in Virginia Beach she might want to stay at would even let them through the door, so she washed her face, combed her hair back into a severely academic bun, and put on a blue plaid shirt and a khaki skirt. She couldn't bear to put the jeans she had been wearing back in the suitcase, so she wadded them up and stuck them in her straw purse. Buoyed by new respectability, she bought a box of cartridges for Philip's gun on the way out, trying not to look as demented as she felt. The cashier didn't seem to care if she was, and sold her the cartridges, and Mary Rose got back in the car and pulled out onto the highway again, giggling at the notion that she had just bought Philip his first present from her; cartridges were a hell of a love offering. After a minute she decided that she probably wasn't entirely lucid, and drank some more coffee.

In Farmville she poked Hull awake, gave him her MCI card and a few quarters in case it didn't work or he got fed up with trying to figure out which code to punch in next, and waited while he got Mr. Ohmori out of bed. She hoped Ohmori was sound asleep, and went and got some more coffee.

She was sipping it when Hull came back to the car. "He's on his way," he said with satisfaction. "Cash in hand, the devious old bastard. He made me tell him eveything that happened, and he 'trusts I have not injured the sword.' If I didn't want the money so bad, I'd like to use it on him. Where are we anyway?"

"We're in Farmville," Mary Rose said.

"Superman's home town," Hull murmured, settling himself in the front seat.

"That was Smallville," Mary Rose said. "Go back to sleep."

In Virginia Beach, she pulled up at the Ramada Inn on the beach on Atlantic Avenue, since that was where she had told Hull to tell Mr. Ohmori he could find them, and left Hull out cold again in the car while she went in to register. She registered them under their right names, since hers was on her credit card and Hull's was the one Ohmori would be inquiring for, and booked one room, giving the clerk a look that dared him to look at her funny. The clerk didn't bother. Unmarried couples of the opposite sex were practically the norm. He'd rented a room to two men in kilts and one in a dress the night before last.

She had to go out and look at the license plate since by

this time she couldn't remember what she had put on the car the night before. While she was at it, she poked Hull until he woke up. "We're here," she said. "Can you carry something, or should I get a bellboy?"

"I can carry something," he said. He looked at her closely. "How much coffee did you drink? You look like one of Ben Shale's customers."

"I wish I'd had some," Mary Rose said. "Coffee's not much good after a certain point."

"Come on," Hull said. "You need to get in bed." He picked up both suitcases. "I'm in better shape than you are."

Mary Rose wrote down the license number while the clerk at the desk gave Hull's slippers and bandaged feet a raised eyebrow.

"Alligators," Hull said. He gave the clerk a bland smile and escorted Mary Rose to the elevator.

In their room Mary Rose kicked her shoes off, stretched out on one of the double beds, got up again, looked out the window at the people baking themselves to a crisp on the beach, lay down again, got up, and started unpacking her suitcase.

"For Christ's sake," Hull said. "Put your nightgown on and go to sleep. Ohmori won't be here for a couple of hours at least. He doesn't carry a hundred and fifty grand around in his pajamas."

"Mmm." Mary Rose pulled a nightgown out of her suitcase. It was a deep wine color and reached the floor, but other than that there wasn't much to it. Hull gave a snort of amusement and she turned her back on him. He had seen her in her nightgown before now, but her choice in nightgowns generally ran to long sleeves and little flowers, in flannel or cotton, according to the season. She wondered if he knew she had packed this one with him in mind, even before their moonlit adventure under the influence of the Hallorans' white lightning. She supposed he must. He wasn't an idiot.

Mary Rose got into bed. She pulled the covers up to her chin.

Hull fiddled with the television.

"Whatever you both enjoy, that is what is normal," Dr. Ruth Westheimer informed him firmly.

"Jesus." He turned the television off.

Mary Rose buried her head under a pillow, but her shoulders shook.

Hull strolled over to the bed. He sat down on it and put his hand on her bare back. "How awake are you?" he said.

"Too damn awake," she said, her voice muffled by the pillow.

Hull's hands slid under the shoulder straps of her nightgown. "I could fix that," he said tentatively.

Mary Rose flipped over in the bed. Hull's hands tangled in her nightgown, pulling it down. She lay looking up at him. "I thought you were in pain."

"Severely," he assured her. Her nightgown was tangled around her ribcage, and he traced the curve of her breasts and the hollow between them with his fingertips, and listened to the blood pound in his head. It hadn't been the white lightning, after all, or even the laurel that had ensnared him, just Mary Rose. He stretched out beside her and cradled her with one hand while he tried to take his clothes off with the other. After a while he gave up and let Mary Rose unbutton his shirt. His chest was wrapped with bandages underneath it.

"You probably shouldn't do this," she whispered.

"Shut up. You're not my mother." He kissed her and stripped his jeans off, half laughing, half urgent.

Mary Rose pointed at his gun, now back in its familiar holster around his ankle. "Take it off," she said firmly. "I'm not a gangster's moll either."

Hull dropped the holster on the floor and settled back into bed, pulling her to him. "Do gangsters make love with their guns on?"

"I don't know any that well," Mary Rose said. "I suppose it depends on whether they're making love to other gangsters." She wriggled closer to him and tilted her head back to look at his face. There was a dark bruise on his temple and another beginning to show beside his mouth. He looked like a gangster himself. If Louise Evans and

Anne Ogilvie could see her now, they would think she had taken leave of her senses. Maybe she had.

She didn't think Philip had, though. His face, bent above hers, was reckless and hungry, but his body possessed an underlying and watchful intensity that was not for her. She thought that he knew how many inches it was from his hand to the gun, how many feet from the bed to the door. Making love to him was like making love to a bomb. She wondered if he just didn't trust Mr. Ohmori, or if it would always be like this.

What if it would? Would it make a difference to her? Philip wouldn't be Philip if he sold insurance. He had come a little too close to the truth when he had said that that was what had attracted her to Steven; but for Steven she had been a refuge, some place to hide from horror and old ghosts. She could look into Philip's eyes and know that that wasn't what Philip wanted from her.

"Hey, have you really got your mind on this?" Hull propped himself up on his elbows and grinned at her.

Mary Rose smiled up at him. "Yes, believe it or not, I do."

"Well, you look like someone who was trying to decide what color to paint the living room."

Mary Rose wrapped her arms around his neck. "I already decided."

She twisted her legs around him, and he thrust himself into her with a breathless gasp of laughter. Whatever she'd had on her mind, it seemed to be settled. They rolled together in a tangle of nightgown and bedclothes, and afterward lay spent, with their heads together on the pillow.

Hull put an arm around her. "Tell me about England again," he suggested.

"Do you know you can still walk on the top of Hadrian's Wall?" Mary Rose said. "In the right light they say you can almost see the Roman soldiers marching down it. I always imagine them as looking a lot like you."

Hull gave a hoot of laughter. "Nah. Like Charlton Heston in a nightshirt."

"Well, at any rate, they look sort of romantic and pig-headed and convinced they're right."

"I wish I could say I imagine Japanese geishas as looking a lot like you," Hull informed her, "but they don't."

"I shouldn't think so," Mary Rose said. "They don't have to get up in the morning and teach an eight o'clock class."

"Cheer up," Hull said. "I bet they can't knock up a cow singlehanded either."

Mary Rose bit him on the ear and gave him a satisfied look when he yelped in pain.

Hull grabbed her and tickled her, pinning her to the bed.

"Quit it!" she gasped. "I hate that."

He stopped. His hands traveled over her gently instead, and then with increasing insistency. "I've got a better idea," he murmured.

There was a knock at the door.

"Oh, shit!" Hull sat up, grabbing for his clothes. "The son of a bitch is early. Just a minute!" he yelled at the door.

"It is all right," a voice, English-speaking but unmistakably Japanese, said from the other side of the door. "I will wait."

Mary Rose snatched her clothes out of the suitcase again and wriggled into her skirt and blouse. She stuck her bare feet in a pair of sandals and began pulling the bed back together. Hull grinned and helped her. He didn't give a damn if Ohmori knew how they'd been passing the time, but he knew for certain it would bother Mary Rose.

Mary Rose twitched the bedspread into place and ran a comb through her hair. Hull stuck his gun in his pocket, kicked the holster under the bed, and went to unlock the door.

A tall, middle-aged Japanese man in a rumpled gray business suit stood in the hall. He had a heavy, square face and eyes that drooped a little at the corners. "I am sorry if I have disturbed you," he said.

"It's all right," Hull said. "We drove all night. I was just going to catch some sleep." He opened the door and ushered the visitor in. "Mr. Ohmori, I presume?"

"No, I am sorry. My name is Masayuu Noguchi."

Hull gave an aggravated groan and sat down on the edge of the bed. "Does Ohmori know you're here?"

"No." Noguchi smiled. "If he did, I doubt that he would let me within three miles of you. Do you know who I am?"

"Yeah, I know who you are," Hull said. "And if Ohmori doesn't know you're here, how the hell did you find us?"

"His office," Noguchi said. "I have been in Virginia Beach for several days. Every day I call the embassy in Washington and ask for Mr. Ohmori. He is always busy, as I know he will be, so I say that I will call back later and do not leave my name. The embassy gets many calls. A call with no name will not even be passed on to him. This morning when I call, they say that he is out of town. So then I give my name and tell them that it is an emergency. Also, I tell them that I am calling from Tokyo. The secretary has put through a call from Mr. Ohmori to me some days ago, so she knows who I am. She tells me that if it is an emergency, perhaps I can reach him through you, here at this hotel."

"Ohmori called you? What for?"

"To ask me to help him acquire my ancestor's sword for my government," Noguchi said. "I declined."

"You can't outbid him," Hull said.

"No, I know that," Noguchi said. "My family has only modest means." He studied Hull intently. "I can only try to persuade you by other methods."

"Christ, not again," Hull muttered, standing up. He pulled the gun out of his pocket and aimed it at the other man. "Noguchi, get out of here. I've had it with your family, and I've got the scars to prove it. You mess with me now, and I'll send you back to Tokyo in a box."

"You are mistaken, Mr. Hull," Noguchi said quietly. "We are not *yakuza*. That is why this sword matters so much to us."

Hull let his breath out slowly. He sat back down on the bed, but he kept the gun in his lap. "It mattered a lot to your relatives too," he said, pointing at his bandaged feet. "So I'm just a little nervous. Sit down and put your hands in your lap."

Noguchi sat.

"Mary Rose." Hull spoke without turning his head. "Sit by that phone. If anything starts to go down, dial 0 and yell like hell."

Mary Rose sat down on the other bed and put her hand on the telephone that sat on the nightstand between them, but she thought Hull was beginning to believe that Noguchi was telling the truth. He wouldn't have let him stay if he hadn't.

"I'm listening," Hull said.

"You know what *Ko-getsu-nami* is," Noguchi said. "You must, or you would not have offered to sell it to my government. The government only repatriates national treasures."

"Akinji Kobayasu's sword," Hull said. "And a Munechika blade. They don't get much better than that. I might as well tell you I got a hundred and fifty thousand out of Ohmori."

"Whatever Ohmori offered, it is more than I can pay," Noguchi said. "I already know that. *Ko-getsu-nami* is more than money to my family, Mr. Hull. It is honor. It is restoration of honor. You know that Sadao Akaishi is my kinsman." Noguchi's face was immobile, very carefully masking what Hull thought was utter distress at having to mention Akaishi's name aloud. "Do you know what *that* means to my family? To me, as head of my family?"

"Yeah," Hull said. "I know." To a man like Noguchi it would mean shame of the most unbearable sort. He put the gun back in his pocket, looking embarrassed.

"*Ko-getsu-nami* is redemption, Mr. Hull. To possess again the sword of our ancestor is counterbalance to the taint that Sadao Akaishi has brought upon us. In the eyes of the world, and in our own souls."

"If your government has it, then Sadao Akaishi doesn't," Hull said. "And you can't tell me that wouldn't be ten times worse. If it wasn't for us, Akaishi *would* have it."

Noguchi nodded. "I know. I am grateful."

"I don't want you to be grateful," Hull said uncomfortably. "Try realistic. I nearly got killed for the thing."

"That is why I hope that you may be persuaded," Noguchi said. "Why did you not offer the sword to an American collector? They would pay more than my government could offer, and there are some who would be willing to fight Akaishi for it."

"Because it ought to go back to Japan," Hull said. It was as simple as that. He had never considered an American collector. He thought Noguchi knew it.

"Ah. For my government, that is very comforting. For us . . ." Noguchi spread his hands out, eloquent of emptiness. "For us it is only marginally better than the sword never having been discovered at all. It is my family's, Mr. Hull. It is *family* honor. My government's possession of *Ko-getsu-nami* restores us nothing."

Mary Rose watched them thoughtfully. Philip was troubled, she could see that, and thought that he was mainly troubled because he wasn't going to let Noguchi win and felt sorry for him.

"Which is more important to you, Mr. Noguchi," Hull said after a moment, "possession or ownership? If the government owns the sword but leaves it in the keeping of your house, would that satisfy you?"

"The government would never agree."

"Well, I'll try to help you convince them," Hull said, "but that's all I'm going to do. I'm sorry."

Noguchi sighed. He stood up, his face breaking from its enforced calm. "It was too much to expect. I see that now. I had hoped . . . because you had visited our country, studied it . . . But it was too much to expect that you would think like a Japanese."

"I'm afraid it was," Hull said grimly. "I can't afford to." He didn't know any Japanese who would hand Noguchi the sword either.

Noguchi hesitated, his eyes uncertain and distressed.

"The offer still stands," Hull said. "I'll try to convince Ohmori for you." Damn the man, anyway.

A light tap at the door drew their attention. "That's

Ohmori," Hull said. "You can stick around if you want to."
He opened the door.

The man outside was of medium height, slim and long-boned. He had an odd air of muscular grace such as a race horse carries, and a face that declined to give its age. He might have been anywhere from thirty to fifty. He ignored Hull's hand and came swiftly into the room, and as his eye lit on Noguchi, a gun came out of his pocket.

Mary Rose gasped and reached for the telephone.

"*No!*" The gun was leveled against Hull's chest, and she dropped the phone. "Hang it up." His voice was thickly accented, but clear enough. Mary Rose put the receiver back in its cradle.

The man looked at Noguchi. "How unfortunate to find you here," he said, but he shrugged and turned away as if Noguchi didn't matter much.

Hull stared at the barrel of the gun. Whoever the hell this was, it wasn't Mr. Ohmori of the Japanese embassy. He wondered if this was another of Sadao Akaishi's *ko-buns*, and if it was, what he was going to do about it. Noguchi was staring at the man as Hull had once seen someone with a loathing of snakes stare through a glass window at a python.

"Where is the sword?" Speaking in Japanese, their visitor's voice took on an even more unpleasant timbre.

"Put that goddamn thing down," Hull said. "I haven't got it."

"Then you will get it."

Hull noted that there was a silencer on the gun. Jesus. If this was one of Akaishi's men, then he wouldn't be inclined to leave any of the three of them alive. Hull was standing by the foot of the bed nearest the door, Mary Rose was behind him on the other bed, and Noguchi stood beside the chair from which he had just risen, between the bed and the door. Hull could see Noguchi but not Mary Rose. The man with the gun could see all three of them, but he was keeping his attention on Hull. Hull twisted his head slightly, trying to catch Mary Rose's eye.

"Turn around!"

Hull jerked his head back.

"This is not a game." The man with the gun kept it leveled on Hull: "I will kill you. Do you want that sword badly enough to die for it?"

He'd kill them anyway; Mary Rose knew that as well as Hull did. Philip had been trying to tell her something or he wouldn't have turned toward her. What did he want her to do? She knew Philip had a gun, if he could just get at it. Someone had to do something. It was either her or Noguchi, and Noguchi appeared to be frozen in his tracks. Hull and the gunman were speaking in Japanese. Mary Rose felt as if she would choke. The air felt thick, like fear made solid.

There was a heavy glass ashtray on the nightstand. Mary Rose snatched it up with both hands, heaved it at the gunman in one desperate motion, and dropped to the floor between the two beds.

She had given Hull one chance, and there wouldn't be a second. The gunman's attention wavered for a split second, and Hull flung himself to the carpet and rolled, one hand already in his pocket. The ashtray bounced on the carpet with a thud. The gunman spun toward Hull, and Hull came up behind the far bed with his gun in his hand. He aimed it to fire, and froze.

Behind the gunman Masayuu Noguchi jumped with an anguished howl across the intervening space. In the second in which Hull looked frantically for an angle at which the bullet wouldn't go through the gunman and into Noguchi, he saw Noguchi leap in the air, arms spread, one foot rising in a kick that connected at the base of the stranger's skull. The gunman dropped, and the gun that fell from his hand clattered against the heavy ashtray and lay spinning on the carpet.

There was utter silence in the room. Hull and Mary Rose watched as the gun spun in slowing circles and stopped. The man on the floor didn't move.

Hull let his breath out slowly. He picked up the gun and gave it to Mary Rose, and crouched on the floor with his own gun in hand in case their visitor came to. "That was nice," he said appreciatively to Noguchi, "but you damn near got shot." He bent cautiously over the man on the floor, and then his eyes widened. "He's dead," Hull said. "His neck's broken."

16.
The Devil to Pay

Noguchi nodded. He stood where he had landed, arms at his sides, his face pale.

"Did you know you were going to kill him?" Hull demanded.

Noguchi nodded again. *"Hai."*

"Jesus Christ," Hull muttered. Ohmori was going to love finding a dead body in the room.

"That is Sadao Akaishi," Noguchi said. His voice was almost a whisper, but it snapped Hull's head around.

"That?" Hull stared at the body on the floor, in a fleeting moment of terror that it was going to come alive again. "How the hell did he get here?"

"That I do not know," Noguchi said, "but believe me, I recognize him. He knew me too."

"He didn't know you well enough, that's for sure." Hull shuddered mentally, thinking of all the things that could have gone wrong. "Where did you learn karate like that?"

"In Japan it is not considered particularly respectable," Noguchi said. "It is not . . . good manners, to know karate. But it is highly effective. A discipline in which one can immerse oneself. It burns energy. Gives hatred a direction, perhaps. I do not think I can explain why I learned it."

"Never mind," Hull said. "I understand." Thank God

for Noguchi's obsession. He sat down on the edge of the bed, and the three of them looked at the body of Sadao Akaishi. Finally Hull said, "We gotta do something with him."

"Call the police?" Mary Rose said.

"We can't." Hull looked at Noguchi. "If Sadao Akaishi's family finds out who killed their boss, Mr. Noguchi here isn't even going to make it from his plane to the university."

Mary Rose looked horrified.

Hull ran his hands through his hair and contemplated their difficulty. His nerves had toned down enough to be practical. "Has he got any buddies outside, do you think?" he asked Noguchi.

"I doubt it. They would be here," Noguchi said. "If he has men with him, he uses them, he does not come himself. But occasionally he goes alone, when circumstances warrant it."

"Why come alone now?" Hull asked.

"Pride. Honor. To send a *ko-bun* for his ancestor's sword once, that is acceptable. But since you are here, the *ko-bun* has failed, and this is a personal matter. To send another employee would make him look foolish."

Hull thought Noguchi was embarrassed to know so much about his late relative. If you were related to a snake, Hull supposed you kept track of him.

"He'll have a car," Hull said. "We'll have to get rid of it." He felt in Akaishi's pockets and found a key. Then he lifted the body under the arms until he had it in a sitting position. "Come on," he said to Noguchi. "You take the other side." Hull got his shoulder under the corpse's right arm and together they got him to a standing position. The head lolled forward horribly.

"Where's my hat?" Hull said.

Mary Rose got the red-billed cap out of the suitcase and reluctantly put it on Akaishi's head. She said, "What are you going to do with him?"

"I'll decide after I get him out of here."

"What about Mr. Ohmori?"

"Stall him."

They lurched to the doorway, and Hull paused to look

up and down the hall. "He's drunk," he informed Noguchi. "So are we, but not as drunk as he is. We're going to sing a little."

Mary Rose watched the macabre trio weave down the hall, singing, for reasons she could only guess at, "Oh, Susannah." Maybe it was the only American song Noguchi knew.

When they were out of sight, she went back in the room and looked out the window. After a minute she saw them come out and stagger toward the Chevy. Hull and Noguchi put Sadao Akaishi in the backseat and Hull got in. Noguchi prowled down the row of cars until he found the one that matched Sadao Akaishi's key and got in that. No one seemed to take any notice of them.

Mary Rose closed the curtains and leaned against the window with her hands to her forehead. *I've just helped Philip and a Japanese English professor hide a dead gangster in my car*, she thought. *I must have gone completely crazy.* She stood there a minute, waiting to hear screams or sirens or large, indignant policemen pounding on her door, but nothing happened. When she looked out again, the cars were gone. *My God.* She bolted the door and put the chain on it.

What was she going to do with Mr. Ohmori? Mary Rose lay down on the bed and stared at the ceiling. The sword was still under the backseat of the Chevy, on Philip's theory that the Chevy, which didn't look like much, was less likely to be broken into than their hotel room, and you couldn't carry a four-foot sword into the dining room. Maybe Mr. Ohmori would be late.

Hull turned off Atlantic Avenue onto a cross street and zigzagged through several miles until he found what was, if not the worst section of Virginia Beach, certainly well into the low-rent district. He pulled up outside a dingy apartment house and Noguchi pulled Sadao Akaishi's rented Buick in behind him.

Hull motioned Noguchi into the Chevy and they pulled out again. "If we're lucky, someone'll steal it," Hull said. "Did you leave anything in it?"

"No." Noguchi looked at him curiously. "Are you really a policeman?"

"Yeah." Hull scanned their surroundings, looking for some place suitably deserted. "And I'm not gonna worry about that technicality right now, except to keep my hands off anything that might take a print." If they found Noguchi's fingerprints in the Buick, it wouldn't matter much, but Hull's were on file in California and his name might occur to someone; Sawyer, for instance, who was no dope.

Mary Rose turned on her side. What was Philip going to do with a body in broad daylight? What would happen if someone saw him doing it? Half-formed visions of herself and Philip trying to explain the unexplainable to the Virginia Beach police drifted through her mind. Her thoughts became vaguer, the imagined conversations garbled, as she fought off sleep. She had been awake for thirty hours. She ought to sit up, but she knew she wasn't going to; she felt wiped clean of initiative or decision. She wrapped her arms around the pillow and closed her eyes.

A knock on the door, growing steadily louder, woke her. Philip wasn't back. Mary Rose sat up groggily and pushed her hair out of her face.

"Who is it?"

A voice in the hall announced that he was Akira Ohmori, in charge of a department with a title she couldn't quite hear, at the Japanese embassy. Acquisitions, no doubt, Mary Rose thought wryly. Assuming he really was Mr. Ohmori and not yet another interested party, God knew who. She left the chain on the door and eased it open an inch. "I'd like to see some identification," she said firmly.

Mr. Ohmori passed her his driver's license and passport. The pictures matched his face, so she took the chain off the door. He came in and looked about him with interest.

Mr. Ohmori was a round little man, well groomed. He wore an expensive suit, had an inquisitive eye and the air of a man on the alert for difficulties. He reminded Mary

Rose of a robin in black and white. "And where is Mr. Hull?" he inquired.

"He had to step out," Mary Rose said. "He ought to be back any minute." *What am I going to do with him?* "Would you like some coffee?"

"Thank you. That would be delightful." Mr. Ohmori sat down and put his hands on his knees, regarding her expectantly.

Mary Rose called room service, asked for coffee, and wondered what to do next. Mr. Ohmori appeared to be prepared to wait for Philip, whom he plainly assumed to be in charge of the proceedings. *I'm terribly sorry, Mr. Hull has gone out to dispose of a body. It won't take him long. Won't you have tea while you wait?* "I hope you had a pleasant drive," Mary Rose said, and decided she must be losing her grip.

"Most pleasant," Mr. Ohmori said. "I do like this time of year. Not so beautiful as spring, of course, but lovely. Lovely. I trust your own drive was uneventful."

"Quite uneventful," Mary Rose said dryly, "if you don't count anything that happened before midnight."

The coffee arrived and Mr. Ohmori took a cup thoughtfully. "I'm delighted to hear that," he murmured.

"Mr. Ohmori," Mary Rose said, aggravated, "in the past few months I have been shot at, had my house broken into, and Mr. Hull has nearly been killed."

"Most difficult for you. I understand," Mr. Ohmori said. "But since you left your college? You have had no further trouble?"

Mary Rose looked at Ohmori suspiciously. She put a packet of sugar, which she didn't like, and a dollop of cream in her coffee. "What kind of trouble were you expecting?" she asked, stirring.

"Nothing of concern," Ohmori said. He smiled reassuringly. "We did hear that someone with, er, an interest in the matter was in the country. On the West Coast," he added hastily.

Mary Rose stared at him in furious surmise. "Do you mean *yakuza*?"

Mr. Ohmori clicked his tongue and looked uncomfortable. "We prefer not to use that term."

"Well, this isn't Looking Glass Land," Mary Rose said. "You won't make them go away. You *knew*," she added accusingly. "You *knew* that Akaishi person was coming here, and you didn't even warn us!"

"Akaishi?" Mr. Ohmori choked as if he had found a very small *yakuza* swimming in his coffee. "He is here?"

"Not now," Mary Rose said enigmatically. "Have one of these little cookies they brought, Mr. Ohmori. They're very good."

Philip Hull and Masayuu Noguchi sat on a bench on the public beach with a sack of potato chips and two cold beers. A sea gull *awked* at them from a distance and Hull flipped it a potato chip.

"What will happen when they find him?" Noguchi said. They had found a good ditch, suitably overgrown with blackberry vines, and Sadao Akaishi was at rest at the bottom of it.

"God knows," Hull said. "I have a strong suspicion your embassy will shut up everybody within shutting distance, if they can. What I want to know is how he found *us*."

Noguchi smiled faintly. "The same way I did, I expect. The embassy should possibly retrain its secretarial staff. How he got here so quickly, though, I don't know that. I have always thought of him as a devil," he said somberly, turning the beer bottle in his hands. "Perhaps he was."

"He had to have been in the country already," Hull said. "Given that, he just had a good information system."

"I don't understand."

Hull grimaced and took a drink of his beer. "Reports get written. When his *ko-bun* bought it, a report got made and probably sent on to the feds. Maybe the DEA on account of the drug angle. Somebody has a hold on somebody with access. It happens. Not so fast usually." He flipped the sea gull another potato chip. "Those people are very efficient. I don't ever want to mess with them again."

Noguchi watched the Atlantic tide come in for a moment. "I am very grateful, Mr. Hull," he said quietly.

Hull smiled. "*You're* grateful? I didn't know who I was about to tangle with. He probably would have killed us both. I'm getting past the stage where I'm willing to die for money." He stretched and picked up the empty potato chip bag. "I've gotten older the last few days, Mr. Noguchi. It gives you a different perspective on things."

"It happens," Noguchi said. They tossed the empty bottles and the bag in a can and walked up the beach toward the car.

"Mrs. Cullen," Mr. Ohmori said, "where exactly is Mr. Hull?"

Mary Rose thought she'd like to know. Anybody who could carry a dead gangster through the Ramada Inn in broad daylight could probably handle whatever came up, but where *was* he? She nibbled the edge of a cookie. "He didn't precisely say."

Mr. Ohmori gave her a glance of deep suspicion. "Mrs. Cullen, I must ask you again, has there been anyone else here?"

"Not unless you want me to mention the unmentionable," Mary Rose said irritably.

"Oh, dear." Mr. Ohmori put his coffee cup down. "Mrs. Cullen, we really can't have that. You should have told me."

"*You* might have mentioned the possibility to *us*," Mary Rose said.

"You don't understand." Mr. Ohmori made a series of agitated gestures and looked around as if he expected hordes of photographers to leap from behind the curtain and photograph him associating with someone who associated with *yakuza*. "Mr. Hull assured me that the matter was settled, or I would have insisted—"

"Insisted on what?"

Mr. Ohmori turned to find a tall, muscular man with a truculent expression regarding him from the doorway.

"This is Mr. Hull," Mary Rose said helpfully.

"Insisted that you meet me at my government's official residence." Mr. Ohmori picked up his briefcase and marched to the door. "You will simply have to wait until I call you. Really, Mr. Hull, I am most distressed."

"Yeah, it's been a bad day for us all," Hull muttered. He closed the door behind Mr. Ohmori. "Do I understand that squint-eyed little bastard knew Sadao Akaishi was in this country?" he said.

"Yes, and *now* he's mad because Akaishi was here," Mary Rose said. "I shouldn't have told him, I suppose, but I was just so outdone with him."

"Don't worry about it. He's not going to be thrilled either." Hull looked at Mary Rose hesitantly.

"Philip, where's the sword?"

Hull sighed. "I sold it to Noguchi."

Mary Rose sat down on the bed.

"Well, Noguchi killed Sadao Akaishi for it and saved our tails in the process. That man was probably only slightly less dangerous than Moammar Khadafy. How could I keep it and sell it to Ohmori for a hundred and fifty grand?"

"What *did* you sell it for?" Mary Rose said after a long pause.

"Eight thousand dollars. Look, I'd feel better if you yelled at me."

"*Eight*—" Mary Rose poured a cup of cold coffee and stared at it. *Oh, damn you, Philip.* And damn Noguchi and his family honor, and damn men in general for stirring up her life with a stick. And how could she say so when Philip was the one who had nearly been killed, and hidden a body, and done a lot of other things that would probably get him thrown out of his job if anybody ever found out? A job he was now going to need. And when she knew he was right anyway? Mary Rose put the coffee cup down. "Well, I don't feel like it," she said balefully.

"Oh." He thought they were going to have a fight in a minute, but he didn't know what about since it wasn't about what he had thought it would be. "I don't think we're on the same wavelength here," he ventured.

"Probably not," Mary Rose said. They usually weren't. "I had some nice plans, is all," she said. "So what have we got now?"

"Eight thousand dollars and clean consciences?" Hull

sat down beside her on the bed. "We could go to England for a little while on it. You deserve that at least. It might even stretch to a weekend in Rio," he added hopefully.

Mary Rose looked him in the eye. She thought she might as well call a spade a spade. "You said you loved me," she said flatly, "but I don't know what that means. And I thought I wasn't going to have to worry about it for a while, because we could travel a long time on a hundred and fifty thousand dollars. But I'm not going to have much fun spending two weeks in England and knowing you're going back to California when we get home. I honestly don't think I could stand California, and anyway, you haven't asked me. And I can't see you here arresting bootleggers for Lieutenant Sawyer."

Hull's puzzled expression faded slowly. "Let me get this straight. You're upset about *me* and not the money?"

Mary Rose nodded.

Hull's face split into a grin. He put both his arms around her. "I knew a long time ago that if I messed around with you, it was going to be permanent," he told her. "I made a call to the DEA office in Washington right after we found the sword, to see if I could get on there. A hundred and fifty grand wasn't going to last forever, anyway. I know a few guys up there and it looks pretty good. I speak Spanish, which a lot of guys out here don't."

Mary Rose opened her eyes wide, looked into Hull's face for a moment, then buried her head in his shoulder.

"I probably should have said something sooner," Hull said, patting her. "Hey, now, don't cry. But I didn't know how you'd feel about it, and then after I started to have a good idea about that, things got kind of lively."

Mary Rose said something he couldn't understand and pushed her face deeper into his shoulder.

"I can't hear a word you're saying," Hull said. "I guess this isn't much of a proposal, but those are the main points. I love you."

Mary Rose lifted her head. "I said—" She wiped her eyes with the back of her hand and sniffled. "I said, I want a ring." She smiled at him mistily. "And an engagement party. And they're all going to come and look at you again. You'll hate it."

Hull chuckled. He bent his face and kissed hers slowly. "I'll bet." He kissed her again, and leaned on her until she went over backward on the bed. After a long pause he said, "Remind me later that I have to buy your buddy Shirley a chair."

"What exactly are you going to be doing here?" Louise Evans gave Hull a fascinated stare, a piece of celery stuffed with cheese dip halfway to her mouth.

"I don't exactly know yet." Hull smiled blandly. One of these days he thought he'd tell Louise a couple of stories that would curl her hair permanently, but he could see that Anne Ogilvie had her eye on him.

"Louise, be an angel and take that tray of cheese puffs away from Ettie before she drops it." Anne bustled up and pointed Louise at one of the college maids, hired for the occasion, who was trying to squeeze through the doorway from Anne's kitchen with a tray of hors d'oeuvres in one hand and an ice bucket in the other. "And shame on you for thinking wicked thoughts," she whispered in Hull's ear.

He grinned at her. He liked Anne. "Thanks for the party."

Anne looked around the room with satisfaction. "It *is* a nice party, isn't it?"

"Lovely," Mary Rose said. She kissed Anne's cheek. "And you're sweet."

"They're all curious, of course," Anne said thoughtfully. She thought Hull and Mary Rose's recent escapade—the parts they were admitting to—would give the college material to dine out on for years.

"Nonsense," Mary Rose said. "They came for your cooking."

"I'll just go see about the salmon," Anne said. She believed in having three times as much food as necessary on the table at all times. She started for the kitchen and stopped abruptly as her husband Peter passed by, a gallon jug in one hand and a devilish expression on his face.

"Peter, you aren't going to let them drink that! Where did you get it?"

"I found five of them on the front porch," Peter Ogilvie said delightedly. "I think they're an engagement present." He slipped the jug of white lightning under the table they were using for a bar and left it there, like a bomb in the path of the unwary.

Hull saw Anne bearing down on them with fire in her eye. He touched Mary Rose's shoulder. "I think we better go mingle."

"Good heavens, yes," she murmured.

They fled, arm in arm.

About the Author

Amanda Cockrell holds a master's degree in English and Creative Writing from Hollins College, and lives in Roanoke, Virginia. She is the author of a previous novel, *The Legions of the Mist*, and is at work on a third.